SeaFire

Bond did not use the lift, but went up the main staircase, two stairs at a time. The door to their suite was slightly ajar, a room service table outside.

'Did you . . . ?' he began as he entered the room, pulling the door wide open.

'Shut it, Bond.' He was looking into the circular little mouth of an automatic pistol, held left-handed by the young thug whose hand he had injured on their arrival. What had Flicka called him? Mr Archie?

Across the room, Archie's partner, Cuthbert, had one arm around Flicka's neck, the other held a small weapon Bond recognized as a little Beretta .22 mm, not exactly a stopping weapon.

'Don't do anything stupid, will you, old chap?' from Archie. 'Sir Max so wanted to be here for this. Sends his apologies and all that. Called away unexpectedly. Him and Lady Trish. Very disappointed, as were Mr Goodwin and Connie. They all wanted to be in on this.'

About the Author

John Gardner was educated in Berkshire and at St John's
College Cambridge. He has had many fascinating occupations
and was, variously, a Royal Marine officer, a stage magician,
theatre critic, reviewer and journalist. As well as his James Bond
novels, most recently *Never Send Flowers* and *Death is Forever*,
Gardner's other fiction includes the acclaimed Herbie Kruger
novels, most recently *Maestro*.

Ian Fleming's

JAMES BOND

in

John Gardner's

SeaFire

CORONET BOOKS
Hodder and Stoughton

First published in Great Britain in 1994 by Hodder and Stoughton
A division of Hodder Headline PLC

First published in paperback in 1995 by Hodder and Stoughton
A Coronet paperback

10   9   8   7   6   5   4   3   2

ISBN 0 340 62869 3

Typeset by
Letterpart Limited, Reigate, Surrey

Printed and bound in Great Britain by
Cox & Wyman Ltd, Reading, Berkshire

Hodder and Stoughton
A division of Hodder Headline PLC
338 Euston Road
London NW1 3BH

For my good friend
Richard Osterlind
As much of a Bond fan as I am a fan of
his incredible talents

Contents

1

Caribbean Prince

THE CRUISE SHIP *Caribbean Prince* had left St Thomas, in the United States' Virgin Islands, at just after six in the evening, with its passengers looking forward to two days at sea before reaching Miami.

The act of piracy took place during dinner, just after eight that evening. Later, the company, Tarn Cruise Lines, Inc., maintained that the men involved had slipped aboard at St Thomas and hidden away until the ship's very wealthy passengers had started dinner. The rest happened quickly. Two of the intruders had gone to the bridge and held the ship's Officer of the Watch, and his men at gunpoint. Two more had secured the areas where most of the crew could be found during dinner. This left six men who charged into the large dining room, their faces covered with ski masks, and their hands holding Uzis and pistols.

Two of the Uzi-toting bandits fired short bursts into the ceiling – which brought screams from the ladies and muttered protests from the men – while their leader shouted loudly, telling people that nobody would get hurt if they did exactly what they were told. This man immediately began to make his way around the tables, demanding that the diners take off all jewelry and empty their pockets and evening bags of other valuables – including wallets.

Everything was taken and dumped into a big plastic garbage bag, held by the sixth man, and there was no doubt that the intruders meant what they said. Anyone who refused, or tried to be clever, risked death.

The whole operation was carried out with the kind of calmness and planning that signaled careful, military precision.

James Bond and Fredericka von Grüsse were seated on the port side at a table for four people – the other two being a pleasant retired stockbroker and his wife from New Jersey. So, by the time the leader and his bagman reached them, Bond had already signaled to Flicka – using eyes and hands.

The stockbroker's wife was in near hysterics, but her husband stayed calm, telling her to do just as she was told. This caused a small delay, making the gunman more belligerent as he moved behind Bond, sticking his automatic pistol into the back of the agent's neck.

'If you want everything,' Bond said calmly, 'you'll have to let me stand up. I've a rather valuable fob watch attached to a chain which I can't unfasten while sitting down.'

'Well, get on with it. Do it quickly.' The leader retreated a pace, to let Bond push back his chair and get to his feet. The gunman kept his right arm stretched out, holding the pistol. Wrongly, for it is a golden rule never to leave your weapon too close to the person you are threatening.

Few were actually able to see what Bond did. It was so fast that most of the diners became more agitated, thinking that reprisals were imminent from the men with the Uzis. Bond spun around on the outside of the extended arm which he caught with both hands and jerked violently. He could feel his back pressed hard against the

2

gunman's back, but it took only a small, vicious chop with the cutting edge of his right hand to grab the pistol which he tossed, almost nonchalantly, across the table to Flicka. Then, turning again, he twisted the arm high up his victim's back, using his left hand. There was a cry, followed by an unpleasant crack as the arm broke and Bond's right forearm snapped hard around the leader's neck, giving it a lot of pressure, so that the fellow was near to lapsing into unconsciousness.

The bagman dropped the garbage sack and went for the gun that was pushed into his waistband. Bond was a fraction faster. His left hand dropped the thug's broken arm, fingers slipping into his right sleeve. On a voyage like this, he had not brought a gun, but he seldom went anywhere completely unarmed. Strapped to the inside of his right arm, high up and hidden by his sleeve was a scabbard containing an Applegate Fairbairn fighting knife. Though this knife throws better from the blade, there was no time to waste on such niceties – a split second and the knife appeared in his hand, a quarter of a second later it shot through the space between him and the bagman. Six inches of slicing tempered steel buried itself in the man's throat. He was dead long before he even began to sway.

Out of the corner of his eye, he saw one of the Uzi-carrying men turn on the balls of his feet, lifting the muzzle of the weapon, swinging in his direction.

'James!' Flicka shouted, the pistol pointed in the direction of the danger. In the double-handed grip she fired twice. As the Uzi clattered from dead fingers, Bond shouted, 'Enough. I don't want anyone else hurt, and I'll kill your leader if you don't drop those weapons.'

The remaining three men hesitated for a tense ten seconds before they realized that, while they might kill

3

some of the people in the dining room, they would all end up dead very quickly. None had the stomach for the result of what had begun as simple work for bully boy tactics. Slowly they dropped the Uzis and raised their hands, Flicka von Grüsse swinging her pistol slowly between the possible targets.

Bond pulled the leader's head close back to him, so that his lips almost touched the man's ear.

'If you want to live, friend,' he whispered, 'you'd better tell me if there are any other clowns on board.'

'On the bridge and in the crew quarters,' the man croaked, his voice constricted by Bond's forearm.

'How many?'

'Four. Two on the bridge and two below.'

'Goodnight.' Bond squeezed harder, cutting off the blood supply to his victim's brain so that he slumped heavily and unconscious to the deck, helped into a longer sleep by a swift chop to the back of the neck.

He distributed the Uzis to the stunned headwaiters and the sommelier, leaving Flicka in charge as he slipped out, carrying the bagman's pistol, making his way quickly to the bridge. The two men holding the hostages there did not really have too much fight in them. Theirs had been reckoned as an easy job, and they did not expect the fury which Bond unleashed on them – cracking the first one over the head and winging the second armed man in the leg.

The couple who were looking after the crew were taken out by the Captain of *Caribbean Prince*, and two of his officers. The dead were eventually laid out in the small mortuary next to the Sick Bay, while those left alive were locked in one of the two 'Secure Cabins' designed to take any violent or malcontented member of the crew. These two cabins had been on the list of specifications when the ship had undergone a complete refurbishment a couple of years before.

Back in the early 1980s the M/S *Caribbean Prince* had been one of the flagships of a major cruise line, ploughing its way between Miami and the islands that litter the Caribbean. With a gross tonnage of around 18,000, and a capacity for some seven hundred passengers, plus a crew of four hundred, she was an admirable proposition. But as the decade filtered into the 1990s, *Caribbean Prince* had become a liability. With the advent of the larger cruise ships – the huge floating hotels which carry over two thousand passengers – *Caribbean Prince* was not economically viable. That is, unless you had the entrepreneurial foresight of someone like Max Tarn.

Tarn had purchased *Caribbean Prince* in 1990, together with two other ships of a similar size, and begun a major overhaul, his sights set on wealthy passengers who longed to experience the kind of cruises they had either read about, or experienced, during the days when cruises were for the rich and famous only.

The refit and refurbishing of *Caribbean Prince* had cost millions, but it was done with care, turning the ship into a floating art deco palace, outfitted with the latest in comfort and luxury. The basic interior had been virtually taken apart. First, the cabins on the Main Deck, and the two decks below that, were ripped out. In their place was a mall of glittering shops, a new theater with state-of-the-art equipment, a cinema, a beautiful indoor pool and saunas – complementing the newly enlarged pool up on the Sun Deck – and four luxury lounges.

Now, *Caribbean Prince* only catered for around seventy passengers whose large and beautiful staterooms all ran along the Promenade Deck, each stateroom being a small suite, complete with bathrooms which contained both shower and Jacuzzi. In its new, sumptuous state, *Caribbean Prince* started its series of fourteen day cruises in December 1992. By late February of 1994, she was showing a healthy profit with her passengers paying up to almost three or four hundred per cent more than people who took their seven day vacations on the massive liners.

Tarn Cruise Lines – like the other small and particularly exclusive cruise lines in which individual millionaires invested – had made a huge profit out of the venture. Like everything else in big business, it had been a gamble, but the famous Max Tarn had banked on there still being people around who were prepared to pay anything for a different – even snobbish – kind of holiday.

Obviously that was why *Caribbean Prince* had been a ripe target. Passengers of that kind came on board with a lot of valuables, while some even brought small fortunes to play at being high rollers at the gaming tables.

The excitement of the attempted robbery did not die down for a long time. Those who had handed over much in the way of precious jewels, money and credit cards retrieved their property, and Bond and Flicka were soon the center of attention. In the main bar, they could have been drunk for nothing for the rest of the journey. But, in the event, there was no further journey.

6

2

Fire Down Below

THE EXPLOSION TOOK place shortly after eleven, ripping out two plates under the waterline, flooding one of the crew mess decks, and causing several injuries.

That *Caribbean Prince* did not heel over and begin to sink immediately, said much for its overall design, and the standard of building in the Italian shipyards where she had been launched in 1970.

Just before the incident, James Bond and Fredericka von Grüsse had slipped away from the bar, looking for some solitude.

They leaned close against the guard rail, aft on the Sun Deck, surrounded by a velvet night, watching the boiling plume of white water scarring the dark sea behind them.

'Well, at least that was different.' Flicka leaned her head on his shoulder. 'Old Sir Max Tarn has cleverly turned a potential loss into a big business gain, but this won't do his publicity much good.'

'The point is,' Bond said quietly, 'Tarn was, rightly, convinced that there were people out there who would still pay a lot of money to go on exclusive cruises. Others have done it, but have you noticed how the program is so carefully chosen? A new show in the theater every other night, with big name entertainers, while everywhere we've visited has been on days when no other cruise ship is in port – Jamaica, Curaçao, Venezuela, Barbados, Martinique, Puerto Rico, St Thomas. Not another cruise ship in sight. No other crowds of tourists . . .'

'James.' She held up a hand to stop him. 'James, we had enough of that kind of talk during the courses, and the fine print of economics isn't really you, darling.' Flicka turned, smiling up at him.

The courses of which she spoke had lasted for a little over a year. They included such relatively dull subjects as Accountancy (With Special Reference To Fraud); Fraudulent Conversion; Methods of Gathering Financial Intelligence from Offshore Banking; Smuggling and Laundering Money; Breaches in International Arms Control; Monitoring Illegal Arms Controls in the 1990s; The Role of Terrorist Organizations Concerning Finance and Illicit Arms Shipments, together with other such allied subjects, like large-scale drug and art smuggling.

Officers of the British Intelligence and Security Services bemoaned these subjects as a far cry from the training sessions they had undergone during the Cold War, only to be quickly reminded that the Cold War was over. Now they were engaged in what might be called a Tepid War: one in which even their allies were suspect, and their former enemies required watching like viruses under a microscope.

Of the twenty-eight men and women who took the series of courses, only twelve were considered suitable following a rigorous amount of testing. James Bond was one of these, while, to his delight, Flicka was another.

Fredericka von Grüsse, formerly of Swiss Intelligence, had worked with Bond on the case concerning the infamous Dragonpol, and both of them had run foul of the Swiss authorities. Therefore, when the last strings had been tied on the Dragonpol business, Bond had been as surprised as Flicka when M offered her a place in the British Service. He was also astounded at the warm way M had accepted the fact that they were living together. This last was definitely out of character. Perhaps, they thought, the Old Man was desperately trying to keep in step with the times. Even possibly clinging to the office which he held, though everybody knew that his days as Chief of that particular Service were numbered.

When the courses were completed, and the reorganization explained – in an exhaustive briefing – Bond and Flicka took a couple of weeks' leave with M's blessing.

'You're both going to need it,' the old Chief told them, gruffly. 'If this new Double-O Section is going to work properly, you might get no more leave for a long time.'

The new Double-O Section bore no resemblance to the old department of that name which, at one time, included a licence to kill.

The Two Zeros, as the newly organized Section came to be known and which was now under Bond's command, consisted of highly-trained men and women who could act as a troubleshooting group, dealing with cases concerning breach of international law and treaties which had a bearing on Intelligence and Security matters.

Two Zeros could be invited into a case by either the Intelligence or Security Services, or even the police. They were answerable, not to their old Chief, M, but to a Watch Committee, dubbed MicroGlobe One, which consisted of the chiefs of both the Intelligence and Security Services, their Deputies, a senior Commissioner of Police, and a new Government Minister who held the ambiguous title of Minister of Related Home and Foreign Affairs – an idiot title which had come in for much ribaldry from the Press. Nobody had missed the fact that this relatively small office was basically run by the government, for the government. The Double-O Section was not a non-partisan organization – like the Intelligence and Security Services – divorced from the center of political power.

Bond smiled sheepishly. 'You're right there, Fredericka.' He held her close, his face tilted as if to kiss her. 'You *have* enjoyed this bit of extra expensive luxury, though, haven't you?'

'Of course I have. You made a good choice, James. Wouldn't mind doing this for a honeymoon. I even quite enjoyed the little set-to this evening. Quite like the old days.' This last remark delivered with a twinkling smile.

'Talking about the old days, I think we can find more excitement in our state room.'

'Mmmmm.' She nodded enthusiastically.

Bond and Flicka were just turning away, heading for their stateroom, when the ship shuddered and lifted as the explosion ripped through the metal plates on her starboard side.

The deck beneath them tilted violently and Bond swore as his feet slid sideways, knocking him off balance, Flicka falling almost on top of him.

'Did the earth move for you too?' She half choked. 'What the hell was that?'

Bond was on his feet, one hand holding the rail. 'Lord knows. Come on.'

The ship was listing badly to starboard, and the old, well-known scent of explosives was easily recognizable. By now the ship's siren was emitting the short series of blasts signaling abandon ship, calling all passengers to their boat stations – a drill which had been carefully rehearsed as they left Miami two weeks before.

The engines had stopped, but it was not easy to adjust to the slanting deck. Flicka threw off her shoes, as they crabbed along making slow progress towards their state-room on the port side.

A disembodied voice was giving instructions through the ship's communication system, and there was a background of cries, edged with panic. As they came to the long row of state room doors and large curtained oblong windows set in the superstructure, they could see other passengers trying to keep upright on the slanting surface.

The deck was bathed in light from the emergency floods which had been turned on within seconds of the explosion. Beside the first door, an elderly man was trying to assist his wife who was sprawled on the deck, wailing in miserable alarm. Bond went to her immediately, telling the husband to get the lifejackets from his stateroom and indicating that Flicka should do the same for them.

The elderly woman had obviously damaged her arm, probably broken it, and, a moment later, two of the ship's officers appeared, banging on the stateroom doors and calling for all passengers to muster by the boat station.

Bond was called to assist one of the crew members hacking at a stateroom door where they feared the occupants were somehow trapped, frozen in terror, as well they might be, for *Caribbean Prince* was listing even more violently. As he moved to help yet another passenger, he saw a deadly flicker of fire coming from the forward companionway.

'Get to the lifeboats!' he yelled, reaching for the nearest extinguisher, banging the nozzle against one of the stanchions and directing the foam down into the fierce flames which reached upwards like terrible claws.

Another of the ship's officers joined him in a battle they were rapidly losing. He crabbed his way aft and dragged another extinguisher to the companionway, once more pouring foam down onto the flames, hearing, in the background, the sound of the lifeboats being lowered. At the same time he was aware of people shouting to him, telling him to get off the ship, but he was already throwing the empty extinguisher to one side and moving for'ard to find a third.

He had gone scarcely two steps when he heard a great whoosh, and felt the heat on his back. As he turned, he saw the officer who had been beside him attacking the fire was enveloped in flames now gushing from below decks. The man had become a screaming walking torch, fighting his way towards the ship's rails, but falling before he could get to them. Bond flung his jacket off and leaped towards the doomed man, beating at the fire with the once elegant dinner jacket, but it was too late. The flames had eaten away at the man's body and his screams had stopped.

Bond, himself, was now starting to feel the effects of the flame and smoke. His breathing was labored, and he knew that, if he stayed on board, there was a distinct possibility of the smoke and heat overcoming him.

He lunged towards the ship's listing rail, climbed over and leaped clear into the water below, immediately striking out for the nearest lifeboat.

The coxswain of one of the lifeboats spotted Bond in the water, and, in an act of great courage, turned back towards the crippled ship to help drag him from the water. Once aboard he looked for Fredericka, and to his relief, found her huddled in a corner of the boat.

The lifeboats were enclosed by tight orange colored tarpaulins stretched over a light alloy framework, with thick mica panels for the coxswain and as light sources along the side. There were some forty people – passengers and crew – in the one that had rescued Bond, and once the craft hit the water, the survivors had become aware that the sea was less friendly than it had seemed on board

Caribbean Prince. The lifeboat bounced and rolled, churning through the water with a low, almost sullen hum from its engine.

By craning to look through one of the forward windshields, he was aware of two other small boats nearby, and he caught a glimpse of the cruise ship, lit up overall but seeming to be dangerously top heavy, and sparkling with the fire that at least one man had died fighting.

To his rear, a medical orderly worked on the elderly woman who had fallen close to her stateroom door. She was still groaning with pain, so Bond worked his way aft to see if he could assist.

'Broken arm, shoulder and maybe a leg also,' the orderly said with a distinct Scandinavian accent.

'Do we know what happened, yet?'

'She fell.'

'No, the explosion? Do we know what it was?'

The orderly shrugged. 'An officer said he thought this was some mechanical problem. With the engines. An explosion with the engines. It never happened before. Could have been something those villains set to explode after making their getaway, though.'

Through one of the mica ports, he glimpsed *Caribbean Prince*, listing and wallowing, her lights and the fire blazing, throwing an eerie glow across the water.

Incongruously, an elderly female voice muttered, 'What waste. You'd think they'd have turned the lights off when we abandoned ship.'

'It never happened before,' the orderly repeated, as though he could hardly believe it had occurred now.

No, Bond thought. No, it certainly had never happened before and it certainly was not the engines. Over many years he had become sensitive to distinctive odors, and he was certain about this one. While he was fighting the fire, his nostrils had been full of the scent of explosives.

The same aroma, explosives and the stink of smoke, continued to hang around them, and was still there at five-thirty in the morning, as he stood beside Flicka von Grüsse at the rail of one of the larger cruise ships. Several ships – including two of the mammoth liners from another company – had hastened to the stricken ship. Passengers had been rescued by the two larger cruise liners, and now, in the dawn, other craft were standing off while two US Navy vessels were close by *Caribbean Prince*, having put out the fire, and were bent on taking her in tow, trying to keep her steady in the water.

'The ghost of Christmas past,' Flicka muttered, giving Bond a quizzical look.

He nodded, his mind obviously far away, though he knew what she meant: stubble on his chin, hair tousled, the pair of ill-fitting jeans and denim shirt they had found for him to replace his soaking wet clothes. 'You're not exactly a fashion plate yourself.' As he said it, Bond reflected that this was not altogether correct. Even with no make-up, and the white Bill Blass evening gown – the one with the devastating slit almost to the left thigh – in a similar state to his own clothes, Flicka von Grüsse managed to remain stunning. 'Girl of my dreams,' he often called her, and the events of the past few hours seemed to have hardly touched her. In her current, dishevelled state, she could have walked into a reception for the Royal Family and still caused heads to turn at her poise and elegance.

The afterscent of the disaster dragged his train of thought away again. There had been no shots of battle, no urgency of attack, yet he felt as though the crippling of *Caribbean Prince* had been an act of war, the most likely explanation being the one suggested by the medical orderly – that the villains who had attempted to rob the passengers had set charges to explode after they left the ship – probably in one of the lifeboats, or even in a craft arranged and factored into their plan.

Later, he was to remark that the cruise ship incident was the true beginning of the dangers which were to come in the next few months. He could still hear the Captain's voice coming through the speakers, giving the order to abandon ship, just as, in his mind, he saw the fragment of fear on the faces of officers and crew. In many ways, 'Abandon Ship' was an apt command. After years of working for his old Service, and his country, Bond felt he was abandoning ship by taking command of the Two Zeros and leaving a familiar world.

3

Fool's Errand

THE NEW HEADQUARTERS of Bond's Two Zeros Section was a beautiful Georgian house in Bedford Square. It was a deceptively quiet place, only a three-minute brisk walk to busy Oxford Street, and his office looked out on the pleasing view of what had once been the homes of the well-to-do. There was a railed-off centerpiece of trees which aped the seasons, and had seen the area go through phases ranging from family opulence, through conversion to apartments, and lastly modification to offices.

He had been ten days late in taking up the new appointment, as there were endless formalities to be gone through before their final release following the rescue. More time was eaten up with interrogations by the FBI and the US Navy CID regarding the attempted hold up, while he had also been required to give evidence at the coroner's inquiry into the young officer's – Mark Neuman's – death by fire. Ten days can be a long time in both politics and the shadowland of security matters. So, Bond's first weeks as Director of Two Zeros turned into hours and days jammed with paperwork and the kind of executive instructions and organization he most disliked – constant visits to useless meetings of MicroGlobe One.

He did, however, get a chance to look over the various confidential reports concerning the explosion on

Caribbean Prince for these were routed automatically across his desk, together with cryptic memos on Sir Max Tarn, head of Tarn Cruise Lines, Inc. and dozens of other companies in London, Paris and New York.

Bond could only presume that somebody, possibly the police, or maybe the Security Service, was taking a long look at the legendary Tarn, so the memos came and went, accompanied by the latest theories on the near sinking of *Caribbean Prince* – which ranged from plastique set by the would-be thieves, to traces of what some expert suggested could be an explosive which had not been on the market since shortly after the end of World War II.

One senior US Naval officer – an expert on damage caused by weapons – had written a pithy three-page report saying that the shape and condition of the large hole blasted in the side of *Caribbean Prince*, and the resultant fire, was consistent with the type of damage inflicted by an old, and possibly unstable, torpedo.

Nobody was likely to take this last possibility seriously. Of course they would not, thought Bond as he saw, with mounting incredulity, that the US Navy had square searched the Caribbean with Sub Hunter-Killers both on the water and in the air. Since the bombing of the World Trade Center in 1993, the American Forces had developed an almost novel fast reaction as far as probable terrorist activities were concerned.

After being a nine days' wonder, the *Caribbean Prince* incident soon appeared to be put to one side, becoming another of those strange puzzles, like events inside the Bermuda Triangle or the mystery of the *Marie Celeste*. It was still only an unpleasant, frustrating memory to both Bond and Flicka on the morning of April 8th when Bond was summoned to a sudden, and unexpected, meeting convened by MicroGlobe One, his lords and masters as far as Two Zeros was concerned.

The call came around noon, and he was warned that the meeting would probably be lengthy. It was a Friday, and this news did nothing to sweeten his temper, for he had planned a long week-end with Fredericka in Cambridge, one of their favorite places. As he left for the Home Office where the meeting was scheduled to take place, Bond reflected that at least Flicka was a professional and understood how these things worked. Many girlfriends and lovers in the past had been stubbornly put out by sudden calls to duty.

He made no secret of his dislike for committees. All his training and experience told him that committees wasted much time. They were also notoriously leaky.

The small reading room at the Home Office had the atmosphere of a private club: a long table, the scent of beeswax, comfortable chairs and ancient, almost choco-late box paintings of scenes from English country life, with the obligatory reproduction of HM The Queen at the far end.

His first impression was that this extraordinary meeting had been called at the insistence of the Police representa-tive – a short, balding Commissioner, Claude Wimsey by name – leading his friends and colleagues to call him Lord Peter. Today, however, he sensed there was something else beneath the surface in the reading room: a sensation of concern and underlying urgency, clear in the atmos-phere and the covert glances which passed between the committee members.

The Minister called the meeting to order, immediately asking Wimsey to take the floor, which he did with a clarity and brevity born of giving accurate evidence in police courts all over England.

'Sir Maxwell Tarn,' he began as though the very name

would capture attention. 'As most of you know, we have, for some time, been acting on information from within the Tarn business empire. Tarn and his wife have been under constant surveillance, and we now have reason to believe that he is behind a number of dummy corporations around the world which deal in illicit arms.'

'The first I've heard of it,' grunted Bond, almost *sotto voce*.

'We *do* still run matters on the need-to-know principle.' The Minister gave him a cold glance.

'Told 'em last week that you should've been brought in sooner,' from M who appeared to have wakened from a deep sleep.

'Please.' The Minister flushed with irritation. 'You know as well as I that Captain Bond has had his hands full since taking over Two Zeros. He was not included in the original briefings out of deference to his workload.'

'Well, at least Wimsey should tell him who got the ball rolling. You're leaving the man in the dark at the starting post.'

The Minister sighed and Wimsey fussed with his papers.

It was the calm, untroubled voice of the very matter-of-fact head of the Security Service that broke the silent deadlock. 'I think, Captain Bond, the CSIS would like you to know that *his* Service is responsible for the intelligence from within Max Tarn's vast and somewhat jumbled organization.' She spoke quietly, even dropping her voice slightly.

'Not just my *Service*,' M bristled. 'The information came to *me* from a personal friend. Well, the son of a personal friend.'

'Peter Dolmech,' Wimsey supplied.

'Quite. Knew the father for years. Old shipmate. Dolly Dolmech. Fine officer, good family. The son had no desire to follow in his father's footsteps though. Can't blame the man for that. Became a very good accountant. First Class Honors in Economics. Cut out for a political career but sidetracked by Tarn.'

'A mega-accountant,' Wimsey said dryly, glancing at his notes. 'A superlative accountant who was sucked into Tarn's business from one of the most prestigious London firms, about a year ago. He apparently set up a somewhat clandestine meeting with Admiral . . . with M . . . last month.'

Bond, now fully alert, asked if he could have this in some detail.

It was Wimsey's turn to look put out. 'Well, I suppose, if you must. We've all rather taken the thing for granted.'

'Well, *I* certainly never take things for granted,' M growled. 'Fact is, James, the thing was so hush-hush that I dealt with it personally. Peter got in touch with me at my home number, and I fixed up a meeting. All very cloak and dagger, because the man's scared to death. Had to meet him in some dreadful tea rooms in Croydon of all places.'

'And he told you what?'

'I passed it on to Wimsey. It all appears to be sound enough, and I trust Dolmech. The man's got a conscience, and what he'd discovered frightened him. Under the law it's a police matter, if they can collect evidence . . .'

'And the perfect opportunity to use Two Zeros for the first time,' added the head of the Security Service.

'That is exactly why we've called this meeting.' The Minister could not hide his irritation. 'I think the Commissioner can probably carry on now and fill in the gaps.'

There was a pause as Wimsey looked around the assembled company. He cleared his throat and began again. 'The source claims that Tarn is using at least four companies to launder money used to purchase arms illegally and pass them on to customers who pay him off to the tune of a hundred per cent profit. He says there's firm evidence that one of the container ships of Tarn Shipping Ltd carried arms and munitions on several occasions, while one of his ships from Tarn Cruise Lines, Inc. was used last year to pick up a special consignment from Odessa – the passenger list was, he says, padded with people in Tarn's employ. Also Tarn Freight Ltd has brought stuff overland. The entire network lives off the smuggling and selling of arms. That's where the really big money comes from – that and a couple of other nefarious sources: dodgy art and that kind of thing. The Tarn empire, it seems, has been built on arms deals from way back.'

'And he's buying them from where?' Bond interrupted.

'Anywhere he can get them. In the old days he spent a lot of time dodging embargoes, producing phony end-user certificates, and he bought from anyone who would sell: even British and American companies. Now, of course, the field's wide open. Under the counter from the old Eastern Bloc countries, Russia itself, intermediaries in Switzerland and Luxembourg, of course, plus all the old sources. It's big business and the larger his orders the more likely it is that no questions are asked. Accounts in the Cayman Islands, Bermuda, and Lord knows where else. Our source says it would take months to trace the various huge sums of cash without his help. As M says, Dolmech took fright when he stumbled on the full extent of Tarn's operation . . .'

'Which is?'

'Well, it's not your usual few boxes of small arms and ammunition, Semtex and semi-automatics, stuff like that. Tarn, it appears, aims a little higher. Aircraft, tanks, missiles, high-end *matériel*.' He seemed to glare around the table at his colleagues, as though daring them to dispute his statement. When he resumed, his sentences came out in short bursts, as if he were giving the bare bones of a précis. 'It's not going to be a walk in the park trying to nail Sir Max. The man probably thinks he's fireproof. After all he's one of the wealthiest men in the world. Tarn International is, as we all know, a general umbrella company for a large number of subsidiaries scattered all over the place. Dolmech is reluctant to bring documents out of the main office because he's too frightened. We'd have to pick him up as well and let him lead us through the paper trail.'

'So you're suggesting?' Bond already had an inkling of why he was being brought into the business.

'Several options.' Wimsey did not look him in the eye. 'We have kept Tarn and his wife under surveillance for the past ten days, and I do have warrants for search and seizure of documents from the offices of Tarn International. Also warrants to lift Tarn, his wife, and our asset, which seems to be the straightforward route. Tentatively we plan to do this first thing on Monday morning. But . . . Well, it's going to bring his legal department down on us like the proverbial ton of bricks, and the media will have a field day. Arrest, seizure and all that kind of thing could possibly ruin any case we might bring, because I have no doubt that the Tarn organization has a kind of self-destruct plan in the event of action by the authorities.'

'So *you* have another plan, sir?'

'Yes, there is another way to go. Problem is that it might take us some time to set up, and a delay could ruin the probability of any real success.'

'You wouldn't by chance be thinking of flushing him out by putting one of my people in?'

'It's a thought.' Wimsey left the words hanging in mid air.

'And it should remain just that. A thought.' Bond did not even try to disguise his anger. 'Have you any conception of how long it would take to put someone in? Weeks, months. It would be like the old Cold War days: putting someone into the Eastern Bloc. I've known it take years to establish bona fides and get them to bite. If Tarn's as good as you say, he has the resources of a small country anyway. It could take one hell of a time.'

'What about a walk-in?' M looked at his former agent with dead fish eyes.

'You're suggesting that one of my people calls Sir Max and lays it on the line? Says to him, "Look here, old chap. *I* know you're a decent person, but I also know that the authorities are about to lift you and go through your files like grease through a goose, if you follow me." '

'Yes, something very like that.' M was still locking eyes with him.

'Whom would you suggest?'

M gave a long sigh, a huge sucking in of breath, followed by its expulsion from his lungs. He sounded like an old steam train, though not as benign. 'I have to spell it out for you, Captain Bond?' The 'James' had gone, a sure sign that the old Chief was getting testy. 'Quite recently there was an incident concerning one of Tarn's cruise ships, *Caribbean Prince*, one of the three he operates under Tarn Cruise Lines, Inc. On the passenger list of that luxury vessel were a Mr & Mrs James Busby. Mr Busby carried a British passport which described him as a civil servant attached to the Home and Foreign Offices. You follow me, Captain Bond? JB, James Busby. JB, James Bond.'

'Ah, so, the above mentioned Mr Busby goes to Sir

Max Tarn and says he knows one or two things about the *Caribbean Prince* episode, and will spill the beans . . .'

'Not quite,' Wimsey snapped. 'The idea is that Mr James Busby has seen some confidential documents which he is willing to share with Sir Max.'

'What kind of confidential documents?'

'First, you should know that Dolmech has provided a verbal list of some recent purchases by Tarn, under the guise of artifacts for a military museum he plans to assemble on one of the Caribbean islands as a special draw for passengers swanning around on his cruise ships. One item has us worried. Last Autumn he acquired a submarine.'

'A submarine?'

'An old submarine admittedly. Possibly a very early Victor II Class Russian submarine.'

'We don't have any idea where he's hiding the damned thing,' M's voice was clipped and terse. 'But we're pretty sure that *Caribbean Prince* was, either accidentally or by design, at the receiving end of a small, and equally old, torpedo from this submarine. Damn it, Bond, you've seen all the signals: all the confidential stuff that's passed between the Americans and ourselves.'

'I've seen nothing suggesting that good old Sir Max – as the British tabloids so often call him – owns a personal submarine which goes around taking pot shots at his cruise ships.' Sir Maxwell Tarn was beloved by the British tabloids – self-made man from an indistinct background, billionaire, the giver of large charitable gifts, and good copy for the columnists. 'What are you really getting at, sir?'

'The fact that you, and your colleague Fräulein von Grüsse, have built-in bona fides. Good old Sir Max, as you put it, knows the name of just about every passenger who travels on his ships. He's a man who pays attention to that kind of detail. We know this from Peter Dolmech. Max Tarn looks out for people who can be of use to him, and I should well imagine that James Busby, civil servant working for the Home and Foreign Offices, has caught his eye. Anyone with that kind of job description can only really be one thing – Security, and/or Intelligence. In many respects I'm surprised you haven't heard from Tarn already. After all, you saved the day by putting paid to the attempted hold-up. You're tailor-made for an approach, and I am correct in assuming that you're planning to stay at the University Arms, Cambridge, this week-end, aren't you?'

'How the . . . ?' Bond began.

'Don't be a fool, Bond. The Security Service checked out *all* the bookings at this hotel for the entire week-end when they discovered that Sir Max and Lady Tarn were going to be staying there. Good old Sir Max is speaking to a convention of economists tomorrow night. He's booked into the hotel until Monday morning. Mr and Mrs James Busby are also booked in until Monday morning. I sincerely hope they were planning on leaving at the crack of dawn on Monday so that they could be in their respective offices by nine a.m.'

'They were,' Bond bit out the words. 'But how do you envisage playing out this charade?'

'I'm sure you'll think of an approach. Find the right words. Put the fix in, as we used to say. What we need is to flush the fellow out, so the tabloids can announce that Good Old Sir Max and Good Old Lady Trish have both gone missing. The idea, my boy, is to make them gallop off to some safe mansion so that we can give the ladies and gentlemen of the Press and the Tube some other reason for the Commissioner's lads and lasses to wander in to

Tarn International's ghastly building at the bottom of Fleet Street. Like Sherlock Holmes, they'll be looking for clues.'

'And I'm to tell him that you're on to him?'

'Well, you know the form. Don't worry, you won't be alone. The boys and girls from the Security Service'll be with you – unheard and unseen, but with you nevertheless, won't they, ma'am?' He flashed an almost luxuriant smile at the Director of the Security Service.

'Invisible wall.' The Director bleakly returned his smile.

'Good. Then that's settled.'

'Is this an order, sir, or are we simply floating an idea?'

'Weeeellll,' the Minister drew out the word, leaving Bond in no doubt that everything had been agreed long before he was called to the meeting. 'Weellll,' he repeated, 'we rather feel that it's in everyone's best interest.'

'Your job is simply to flush him out. Make him run.' Wimsey's body language betrayed great anxiety. 'Tip him off that things aren't quite as safe as he might think. After that, he can be followed anywhere he decides to go – which I do not think will be London. We suggest that you drop the news on him sometime late on Sunday. In turn, we'll have taps on just about every telephone within reach – including the one in his Rolls.'

'And you're sure this is a safer way than just feeling their collars first thing Monday morning?'

'Infinitely better.' The Minister looked at his watch. 'We have a slim, and incomplete dossier on Tarn which you should look at.' He slid a buff folder across the table. 'Now, you'd best be going, Captain Bond or you won't make it to Cambridge in time for dinner.'

'Thank you, Minister. I'd hate to miss dinner.' He rose.

'You *do* see that you're just about the only person we

can trust with this,' from Wimsey.

'Oh, yes. As former passengers on his torpedoed cruise ship we have all the right bona fides. I just hope we aren't all being a shade naive.'

'Oh, I think we're on the right track, Bond. Keep in touch. Usual way of course.'

'Of course.' Inwardly seething, Bond left the room. Flicka would not be as convinced as the other members of MicroGlobe One. The words "fool's errand" were uppermost in his head as he hailed a cab.

4

Prince of Darkness

'THEY WANT US to do *what*?' Flicka was half-heartedly packing a week-end case, when he returned to the Chelsea flat. 'I didn't think you'd be back in time to go to Cambridge. Now you tell me we have to burn this damned financier.'

'A little more than a damned financier, my dear.' He had given her only an encapsulated version of the facts.

Fredericka had the most distracting habit of wandering around indoors clad in only the flimsiest garments.

'Why not forget about dressing for a while, darling.' He gave her the smile that some people thought had a cruel side to it. 'Let's take a little time out.'

From the first time they had come together, in a Swiss hotel only a few hours after their initial meeting, Bond had experienced that fleeting, sudden and illogical twist of heart and mind that signaled either deep lust or something more lasting.

As they had shared danger together, living close to one another, he had come to know that this was different from lust. With the advent of Flicka von Grüsse matters had changed. What had started as a pleasant, somewhat daring, romp matured during the time they spent in circumstances where they could easily have died. Throughout that period they had grown

29

closer, and he soon realized they were, in many ways, a matched pair. Both disliked inaction and paperwork; Flicka had a well-developed sense of humor and fast wit, as well as a body to live or die for, fit, healthy and tuned for the toughest action in the field or the softest pleasures of a connubial bed. She also became very quickly jealous of any other woman who appeared to intrude into Bond's life, but their mutual fascination for the clandestine lifestyle soon put other possible dalliances out of his mind.

Now, over a year since that first meeting, they had shared their lives, each learning about the other's past, likes, dislikes and habits. Living with Flicka, Bond perceived that the relationship had begun to give him something that had never been present with any previous woman. His passion for jazz was not shared by Flicka, whose tastes ran to the more romantic classical composers. In the end they both gained new experience. She began to appreciate the varied nuances of jazz, while he warmed to what he had always considered highbrow music.

He had never been much of a theater- or movie-goer. She was passionate about both art forms, and while on the training courses for the inception of the new Double-O Section, they would sit and watch classic films on video during many of the evenings. This led to a game, often played over dinner – asking each other questions about both well-known and obscure films: quoting lines for identification, describing scenes which had to be matched to the films from which they came.

Small mental exercises like these had brought with them subtle changes, a broadening of their private horizons. Soon, it became obvious that they were slowly becoming mutually dependent.

Now, they lay, spent, naked in the dark on the big double bed.

'Do we really have to make that drive to Cambridge tonight, darling?' she asked, tracing the fingertips of her right hand along Bond's left thigh. 'All I want to do is eat and go to sleep in your arms.'

After a long silence he said that he would like nothing better. 'Unfortunately, my dearest Fredericka, we're like monks under discipline . . . Well, I'm like a monk, you're more nunnish.'

'Then we are in grave and mortal sin, Brother Bond.'

'Yes indeed, Sister Flicka. Most grave.'

He called the University Arms Hotel to say they would be late. They packed the week-end cases, went out and dined in a nearby Italian restaurant.

'I shall *have* to take a long walk in Cambridge,' she said, patting her stomach. 'All this pasta . . .'

'Not to mention the veal *and* the strawberries and cream.' He gave her a finger wagging look, and she replied with a smug grin.

Presently, as they finished their coffee, she asked, 'Why, James? Why couldn't they just stick to their first plan – pick up the Tarns on Monday morning, raid the Tarn International offices, make it look as though this accountant – what was his name?'

'Dolmech. Peter Dolmech . . .'

'. . . make it look as though Dolmech had also been arrested, and take it from there. Why couldn't they do that? It was the original plan, you said.'

'I doubt if it was really the original plan. Possibly it was one option – the last one, to be used only *in extremis*. I think it's a question of politics and money. My impression is they did not altogether trust the Dolmech end of the deal. He's promised to deliver, but they only have M's word for that. Dolmech is M's asset. There are a lot of internal jealousies and personal rivalry within MicroGlobe One. My view is that the members of The Committee don't even trust one another: that's always the problem with an organization like this – split several ways. Also, I don't really believe the Minister is his own man. You remember that old bit of doggerel:

'Big fleas have little fleas,
Upon their backs to bite 'em.
While little fleas have lesser fleas,
And so *ad infinitum*.

'I reckon that's the case with the way in which *we're* being run. We're really with the middle management – that's what MicroGlobe One is – and *they* don't want to go out on a limb – especially with someone as wealthy and powerful as Tarn. Dolmech has already said they won't be able to follow the paper trail unless they have him. So, pick 'em all up, cart off boxes of files and mainframe computer tapes from Tarn International and what have you got?'

'What?'

'Sets full of clever lawyers. An organization with the power to wipe out traces of a paper trail that goes far beyond the Tarn International offices. Our lords and masters're scared to death that Tarn would be out, at least on bail, in a matter of hours, and that Dolmech just wouldn't be able to follow through with his promises. In other words, the entire case would turn to dust and ashes and a lot of people would end up with egg on their faces.'

Flicka grunted. Then – 'And they really believe that we can put the fear of God into him and make him run for cover?'

'Yes, and we probably can. The real problem is whether they can keep a trace on him and stop him removing any hard evidence. If Tarn's the man I think he is, he's probably too clever to leave any clues, any kind of trail. In Cambridge we'll undoubtedly be hedged about with security people – watchers, vans and cars with all the latest gizmos and gadgets intent on running Tarn to earth. Whether, in the real world, they'll actually be able to do that is a moot point. What they're after is headlines on Monday which say that Sir Max and Lady Tarn have disappeared. Foul Play Suspected. Suspicious Circumstances. Enough clout to let the police go in and root around – with some of our people in tow – without a great legal chorus telling them they can't do this, or that, or the other thing. Everybody'll be forced to co-operate or look guilty as hell. They'll only be doing a public service. Looking for clues. Trying to find out if the Tarns've been kidnapped, or whether there's something even worse lurking at the heart of his organization.'

'I suppose *that* might just work.'

'They're banking on it, Fredericka, and I have to admit that it's probably a safer way than going in blind and having the Tarn legal department shouting "Unfair! Foul! Hands off!" while other people are disposing of the evidence. Nowadays you can get rid of records in a matter of hours. In fact the real records might not actually be there. Our tame Police Commissioner actually told me that Tarn imagines he's fireproof, and in some ways he probably is.'

'How're we going to get him trotting off to his favorite hiding place, then?'

'By doing what we can do best as a team. I reckon we have until late on Sunday afternoon. Perhaps a note left at the University Arms. A cryptic message which he can't ignore. That's the way I think we've got to do it.'

'Mmmm,' Flicka mused. 'Meet me at midnight, under the blasted oak. I have information that will save your life.' She mimicked a witch's cackle.

'Nothing quite as dramatic as that. I'd rather tell him to his face. After all our mentors and guides say that he'll already have my name on file – from the *Caribbean Prince*. They tell me he never misses a trick, not if he thinks it's going to be of use to him.'

'He can't be that omnipotent. You did your best to save his damned ship, tried to save one of the officer's lives. Christ, James, *you* can't believe he's got unlimited power?'

Bond shook his head. 'No, I believe that's just MicroGlobe One's paranoia, but we might as well be prepared.' He glanced at his watch. 'Time we were going. At least we'll have missed the worst traffic out of London by now.'

As it turned out most of London appeared to have decided to postpone leaving the city. Flicka drove, cursing other motorists and generally carrying on a running commentary, laced with liberal epithets concerning all drivers in general apart from herself.

Bond leaned back in the passenger seat, put on the map reading light and opened up the slim dossier on Tarn. It began with a series of photographs, the familiar fit-looking, sharp but pleasant features stared back at him, the eyes – even frozen by the camera – seemed to glitter in their usual amiable manner below the neatly trimmed iron-gray hair. Max Tarn's friendliness and approachability were traits often commented on by the Press. Though other tales persisted, hinting at a darker, brooding, more sinister side.

About three pages in, he found the usual red flag

denoting that the rest of the file – some thirty pages – was classified.

It began with a long note on Tarn's lineage:

Born: circa 1939 – possibly 20th June – and probably to the old Prussian Tarn family whose estates, ten kilometers from Wasserburg am Inn – some seventy kilometers from the Austrian border – were eventually confiscated by the Nazis. (See Note C).

His mother, Ilse Tarn, had supposedly taken him out of Germany shortly after his birth. He was certainly registered as an alien in London in 1940. The documents were extant, as were the naturalization papers which were dated 20th April 1940, but on these the Tarns – *mère et fils* – were described as Austrian Jews and classified as refugees. To this was appended a note that they were 'not lacking funds.'

The Tarns settled in a small market town in Surrey, and eventually Max was educated at a local grammar school, winning a scholarship to Oxford where he read PPE (Politics, Philosophy and Economics).

Attached to the section on Tarn's background was a short study by the Security Service which had performed a detailed scrutiny in 1968 when the Monopolies Commission was trying to rule on a takeover of one of the largest freight carrying companies in England by Tarn Freight Ltd.

The investigation turned up some odd stories, but could not gather any firm evidence. The then Director General of the Security Service had noted that, bearing in mind the circumstances of the Tarns' arrival in Britain, the stories were almost certainly true, but any release to the Press or through any other agency would in all probability bring legal action. Max Tarn and his mother – it was suggested – had all the necessary documentation to prove they were of

Jewish origin and came from Linz, Austria.

The report from the two officers who had traveled to Wasserburg (Note C in the file) was of more than passing interest. The old and proud military family with their huge estates near the unique town of Wasserburg appeared to have come to the end of its line, while the old Tarn mansion – Tarnenwerder – was, in effect, still there, a crumbling gothic ruin harboring tales of ghosts and bloody deeds. The local authorities had been attempting to have the entire estate cleared and developed for the construction of much-needed housing, but the old family lawyers – Saal, Saal u. Rollen, who still had offices in the Marienplaatz, Wasserburg am Inn, had fought every step of the way, claiming that any attempt would be met by legal action as at least one member of the family may still be alive.

In Wasserburg, however, there were elderly men and women who had worked for the Tarns. They had a different tale – especially of the last days of the great family. The old Graf von Tarn and the Gräfin, they said, had been dragged from the house, in September 1939, by members of the SS who pillaged the place, removing the entire family which consisted of the two elderly people, their son, Klaus, and one daughter, Elsa. Their fate was generally believed to have been in one of the death camps, though some said they knew for certain that the last four Tarns had been shot and buried on the estate. The house became a recovery center for SS officers, but was left to go to rack and ruin at the end of the war.

A further interesting story was turned up in interviews with two old people who were certainly members of the Tarn household during that fateful period. They claimed – but would not give a signed legal statement – that in the late 1930s the head housekeeper of Tarnenwerder was a young Austrian woman called Ilse Katz, or strictly Katzstein. Ilse, they told the investigating officers, became pregnant by Klaus von Tarn and the family kept *that* secret close. Below stairs there was talk that the old Graf von Tarn had promised to have the girl looked after and would provide for the child in return for a legal document stating that Ilse's offspring would never attempt to claim the family name, or attempt to make any financial demands on the von Tarn fortune. No legal document had ever surfaced.

Ilse Katz, the story went, had given birth to a son in the summer of 1939 and, a couple of days before the SS arrived to arrest the family and take over Tarnenwerder and its lands, she suddenly disappeared, together with a vast haul of von Tarn jewelry valued at millions of Reichsmarks.

Both the former retainers swore the story was true, though other locals claimed that the pair were in the first stages of senility. What did appear to be certain was that the vast fortune in jewelry and other valuables disappeared – though many said that senior SS officers looted it to line their own pockets.

If the supposed Tarns who arrived in England as Jewish Austrian refugees in early 1940 were in fact the housekeeper, Ilse, and her illegitimate son, it would account for the wealth they brought with them: the same wealth that had started Max Tarn in the freight haulage business in the early 1960s.

The rest, Bond thought as he read it, was history: Max Tarn of Tarn Freight Ltd had branched out; invested; acquired the stock of other companies until his freight business was the largest in the United Kingdom. To Tarn Freight he had added four major magazines, and in the boom caused by the likes of *Playboy* and *Penthouse*, in the mid-sixties he had launched *Tarn Man* and *Tarn Girl*, followed by *King of Hearts* and *King of Clubs*, the latter almost a house magazine for his famous chain of Black Shield Clubs which took off not merely in the UK but also in the United States and, then, almost world wide.

The huge amounts of money engendered by these businesses financed Tarn Shipping and, later, the relatively new Tarn Cruise Lines, Inc.

Money begets money, and the business empire stretched its tentacles into almost every lucrative field, from the business of import and export through the chains of clubs and magazines, to luxury hotels. His estimated personal wealth now ran to many billions, while he owned properties in every major world city. There was even a rumor – never traced – of a private island in the Caribbean.

The knighthood had come in the mid-seventies, for services to charity organizations. Max Tarn was full of charity, it appeared, and, after all, most of the money could be run tax free. In 1982, at the age of forty-three he had married the twenty-six year old Trish Nuzzi, arguably the most sought-after model of her time. There were those who predicted the marriage could not last more than a year or so because of Max Tarn's constant traveling in search of bigger and better moneyspinning ventures, but the Cassandras were proved wrong. Lady Trish blossomed, and wherever Max Tarn went, on business or pleasure, Lady Trish went with him, both of the Tarns trailing a small entourage of hairdressers, secretaries and bodyguards.

The multitude of Tarn companies world-wide supplied company jets, and it appeared to most people – from economic editors to the man in the street – that the Tarns lived and worked as a new world class royalty.

The final pages of the dossier dealt with the scant evidence which had sparked the recent probings. Plenty of smoke, but as yet no real fire. Enough hard evidence to warrant an investigation – which would alert Tarn – but not really enough to make arrests.

'Interesting reading?' Flicka had remained moderately silent while he had leafed through the document, and Bond snapped off the reading light, looked up and saw they had about twenty minutes before reaching Cambridge. He returned the dossier to his briefcase and sighed. 'It appears we'll be moving in a rarefied atmosphere if we get close to Sir Max and Lady Trish.' He stretched in his seat. 'I'm really quite surprised that they're actually staying in an hotel like normal human beings. Reading that thing, you'd think he owned one of the colleges as his personal home.'

'They *are* noted for parading their riches, James. Or hadn't you noticed?'

'I'm not strong on the gossip columns.'

'You're not exactly weak on the financial pages though, are you?'

'I see the names, yes. But I didn't quite realize how powerful he really was. A Field Marshal of Industry rather than a Captain. The man's like a Renaissance Prince, Fredericka.'

'The man *is* a Renaissance Prince, my dear. Jealous?'

'Never fancied being one actually. Too many courtiers waiting around to stab you in the back.'

'But Max Tarn is something else. Not just a Renaissance Prince, but a saint – contributions to every known charity, hospital wards, libraries, art collections named after him. The man's a king in his own right. That's why I wondered if he could be frightened enough to do a runner. People like that usually imagine they're above the law.'

'There are things in his background,' Bond mused. 'Dirty work in his lineage. *That* could be a nice little lever.'

'Really? Go on, James, tell me about his grubby background.'

'Well, it appears that he might or might not really be connected to the old and revered Prussian family whose name he bears.'

'Has he ever claimed to be?'

'Not in so many words.'

'There's firm evidence?'

'No. But there's enough to make him pause for a moment. Reading between the lines, his birthright may well have been stolen on his behalf, and there's no evidence that he's actually been back to the supposed site of his inheritance which, incidentally, is in need of the Tarn billions. The old estate is in ruins, and you'd have thought that he'd have dropped in to lay the ghosts of his past – that is if he really believed himself to have come from old German nobility. The place, it appears, reeks with specters from long ago.'

'You going to haunt him a bit, then?'

'Nothing like disturbing a few shades to put the mockers on the living.' Bond smiled to himself.

A light sprinkle of rain fell as Flicka threaded the car through the Cambridge one-way system into Regent Street and to the front of the University Arms Hotel, hard by the wide tract of park land known to generations of students as Parker's Piece.

It was just past ten o'clock, and in front of them a Rolls Royce was being unloaded, boxed in by two sleek black Rovers.

One of the porters motioned to them to stay back, while another came running over – 'If you'd just wait a moment, ma'am.' He bent to speak with Flicka through her rolled down window. 'We'll be with you in a second. Checking in?'

She nodded, but her eyes were on four people alighting from the Rolls. One was a tall, slender woman, one hand lifted to a mane of black hair, her head thrown back as she laughed at something the man next to her was saying.

'Trish Nuzzi, model extraordinary, as I live and go green with envy,' she muttered.

'And there's our specter,' Bond breathed, taking in the equally slim, agile-looking man following Lady Trish. He had a dark, velvet-collared coat slung over his shoulders and a wide-brimmed hat set at a jaunty angle over the famous iron-gray hair. His back was ramrod straight and he looked as fit as an athlete about to take part in some strenuous Olympic sport. As the pair walked elegantly towards the hotel doors, Bond whispered, 'They even look like Renaissance royalty. Lord, you can smell the money.'

'And they have their courtiers with them,' Flicka added. The other two men, staying a respectful couple of paces behind the famous couple, were equally well-dressed, but did not seem to have the same polish as their employers. One was tall, well-built, even burly, carrying himself like a boxer, his head turning from side to side, then back to throw careful scrutiny over Bond's Saab 9000. His companion was shorter and had his hands thrust into the pockets of a long stylish raincoat that looked like some kind of riding dust coat from the old American West.

Around the cars, more people were being off loaded, the drivers in livery, the other young men in street clothes, which looked as though they had come from the up-market designers.

41

As the Tarns reached the hotel doors, Sir Max paused, glancing back towards Bond's car. There was plenty of illumination around the hotel facade, and, for a moment, it was as though their eyes locked and Tarn recognized something of which he should be aware.

Bond quietly said—

'My worn reeds broken,
The dark tarn dry.'

'You what?' Flicka asked.

'Bit of a poem I once had to learn. Forget where it comes from, but that man will never break *my* worn reeds.'

'James, I don't know what you're talking about. It can't be a touch of the sun, because we haven't been out in any lately.'

He turned and gave her a twisted smile. 'I'm being ambiguous, Flicka. Didn't you feel anything as you watched them?'

'A pinch of jealousy over that incredible figure of hers. What did you feel?'

'Evil,' he snapped. 'You talk of him as a Renaissance Prince. He looked more like the Prince of Darkness to me.'

'Can't say I noticed that particular Gothic charm, but you're probably right.'

'Going to light him up like a bonfire.' Bond reached for the door handle only to be blocked from getting out by one of the other young men who had moved from the Rover directly in front of them. The young man held the door almost closed. 'If you'd wait for just one minute, sir . . .'

Bond flicked the cutting edge of his hand against the young man's wrist, smacking it hard against the edge of the door. There was a nasty cracking sound, an almost feminine yelp as he immediately let go of the door. 'And who are you to ask me to wait, and to prevent me from getting out of my own car, Sunny Jim?'

The young man moved closer, nursing his wrist. 'I won't ask you again, sir . . .'

'Good. Who are you?'

'Security, sir. I must ask you to get back inside your car.'

'Hotel security?'

'No, I'm . . .'

'An agent of the Security Service, then?'

'No, sir. I'm privately employed. Security for . . .'

'The people who left that Rolls? Well, don't worry about us, lad. You might tell your employer that I might be able to help him in a matter which he will find fairly pressing in a day or so.' He pushed the door wide open, and quietly told Flicka to get out. Then, turning to the young bodyguard – 'If I were you, laddie, I'd watch yourself. Also, I'd get that wrist seen to. Nasty bruise by the look of it.'

A voice called out, 'Okay, Archie. They're upstairs.'

The young man turned away and scurried in the direction of the man who had called him from beside the Rolls, and at the same moment one of the hotel porters came hurrying up—

'Now, sir. Sorry to have kept you waiting. The luggage, sir?'

Bond looked across the car towards Flicka. 'Light him up like a bonfire,' he said. 'Or even like a Christmas tree.'

'A Tarn-enbaum. Give me half a chance and I'll do some of the destroying with you,' she said softly.

5

Truth or Dare

THE NEXT DAY, Saturday, it was as though Sir Max and
Lady Trish did not even exist. Neither Bond nor Flicka
mentioned them – not at breakfast, nor during their walk
along King's Parade, past the Senate House, and on down
to Trinity and a casual stroll through St John's College.
They walked, hand in hand, through the wonderful old
courts, then across the Bridge of Sighs and through the
great stone filigree of New Court – taking them out onto
the Backs: the long grassy, tree-dotted parkland, past the
old bridges leading to the major colleges. Spring is the
best season for Cambridge. There were even a few punts
out on the river, and the banks were covered with their
springtime carpet of flowers.

Bond had always preferred Cambridge to Oxford. Here
the colleges were more visible, and apart from the somewhat brash, angular additions of the twentieth century,
colleges like King's, Trinity and John's looked much as
they had since they were first built. He even enjoyed the
nineteenth century addition of New Court at St John's
College; blasted by many as a Gothic horror, its cloisters
and carved intricacies had long since mellowed, while the
great views from the Backs gave an almost timeless
atmosphere to the old University City.

During lunch, which they took at a favorite restaurant

on King's Parade, there was still no mention of the Tarns, nor during their hike out to Grantchester, across the meadows and back again. By early evening they both felt the fresh glow of good health which came from the exercise, and the mutual pleasure of each other's company. It had just been warm enough for them to sit in the gardens at the Grantchester Arms and have tea with plates of triangular sandwiches and cream cakes before the trek back to the University Arms. Once back they rode the birdcage lift up to their room and hung out the **Do Not Disturb** sign. A couple of hours later, lying sated and happy, Bond broached the subject.

'You spot them?' he asked.

'Who?'

'Our friends the watchers. Our guardian angels and Tarn's messengers of doom.'

'Oh, them. I think I made the odd car, and they seemed to have a series of footpads walking and loitering.'

'The footpads might just belong to Tarn. I spotted our nasty little friend from last night, in street clothes. He had his hand taped up.'

'Well, you did clobber him rather hard.'

'Not hard enough, but, yes, there are around six or seven cars and vans. I shouldn't be surprised if Tarn's people've spotted them as well. The vans are pretty obvious with that reflective glass in the sides and those damned great aerials. There's also a British Telecom van across the road, which they're digging up: playing with wires and getting visits from Head Office. Did you see the couple they've got on the inside?'

'The young lovers?'

'Don't look old enough to be out on their own, and they stink to high heaven. Real lovers wouldn't spend so much time in the foyer, they'd be up in their room . . .'

'Like us, darling.'

'Exactly like us, and more of it wouldn't come amiss.'

She disregarded his last comment by disentangling herself and asking what he intended to do about Tarn.

'I'm anxious about the high-profile surveillance, but the frontal approach is really the only way. A little note, probably first thing in the morning. Then we play it by ear. If his own people have got the scent of the Security Service's highly visible look-outs, he should react favourably. On the other hand, I wouldn't put it past him to remain unruffled and just motor back to London as if nothing had happened. I've always thought that tipping him off contained the possibility of everything backfiring.'

'So, what'll The Committee do then, poor things?' All members of the Double-O Section tended to refer to MicroGlobe One as "The Committee."

'Nothing, if they're wise, though I don't set much store by their wisdom. Most likely they'll revert to their original plan and go in mob-handed, pull out the warrants and end up looking like imbeciles. In fact, I think I'll call London and test the waters. They told me to keep in touch in the usual way.'

'Whatever that means.'

'It means I call the Minister's special number and pray that I get some aide with a modicum of common sense.' He eased himself off the bed.

'You going to call from here?'

He headed towards the bathroom. 'Not on your life. The switchboard – even the automatic dialing – will be well tied up. As we speak, there's probably some damned great van full of electronics and a dozen tape machines monitoring everything in and out of the Tarns' suites and our own.'

Twenty minutes later, he headed out of the main doors

of the hotel making his way onto the scrubby meadow of Parker's Piece, where there were three public telephones, two of them already occupied by gowned undergraduates talking loudly.

Taking the spare telephone and using a calling card, he dialed the contact number for MicroGlobe One. It was answered immediately, with a 'Yes?' from a calm female voice.

'Brother James.' Bond rolled his eyes towards heaven. The Minister was responsible for the cryptos to be used in telephone contacts. They went through the ritual just for the sake of it. Even with the huge changes and reorganization, old habits died hard.

'Yes, Brother James, how's your sister?'

'As well as can be expected. I called to say that I'll be posting the letter in the morning. Probably near lunchtime. Wondered if the Reverend Father Superior had any further instructions.'

'No, everything appears to be running smoothly.'

'Good. Perhaps you'd better tell him that I believe they've located the music.'

'You mean Mr Watchman's found it?'

'Almost certainly. I think it was with the Amateur Operatic Society.'

'Oh.'

'If some of it can be toned down, it might help.'

A long silence ending with – 'Nothing else you need?'

'No, I'll report either late tomorrow or first thing on Monday.'

'I think late tomorrow would be best.'

'Whatever you think appropriate.' He closed the line and headed back to the hotel just in time to see Sir Max and Lady Tarn, dressed to kill, being shepherded into the Rolls. Max was off to make his speech, no doubt, Bond thought. He hoped the dinner was terrible and that Tarn's speech did not contain too many clichés like "The long Winter of recession is turning into a Spring which demands the courage of commitment by our financial institutions."

They went down the road to a little Indian restaurant where they gorged themselves on onion bhajjis, Lamb Korma with Bombay potatoes, chapatis and a mix of relishes ranging from mango chutney to cucumber raita, finishing with plates of sticky sweet Jalebi. 'At least we'll only taste each other,' Flicka said as they walked back to the hotel. From their room they rang down to room service where Bond ordered a large pot of coffee, specifying that he wanted it freshly brewed and piping hot, hinting that it would be sent back if it was not to his liking. Saturday nights in provincial British hotels – even in a great university city – often brought out the worst in room service. This time it worked and the coffee was excellent. They drank it together as they sat at the one small desk and worked on the note for Tarn.

It took an hour before they were both satisfied with the wording and, even then, Flicka had her doubts about the last sentence.

Dear Sir Max,
My name is James Busby, and my wife and I were travelling on your ship, Caribbean Prince, *earlier this year when the so-called incident occurred. You may well have heard of us, as we were able to come to the other passengers' assistance during the attempted hold-up. We were both exceptionally impressed at the way your captain and crew acted when we were forced to abandon ship. They were very professional, putting the passengers first, and we have nothing but*

admiration for them, and, naturally, for your organization.

I am a Civil Servant, highly placed in both the Home and Foreign Offices, and I have some rather sensitive information which concerns you and your various business enterprises.

We are spending the week-end in the hotel, and I would be grateful if you could spare me a few minutes so that I can both thank you and pass on information which should be of great interest to you.

It was signed, J. Busby, and Flicka held that the final sentence sounded like a cloaked threat of blackmail.

'That's what I intended it to sound like.' Bond did not smile.

'Put him on the defensive?'

'No. Remember, he thinks he's home and dry. We've already agreed that he imagines himself fireproof. The letter is kind of disingenuous if you read it carefully – slightly fawning, with the bit of veiled menace at the end. I want it to sound like something written by a middle management type with just a hint that he thinks he's maybe on to fairy gold.'

They spent the remainder of the evening watching an edifying TV program on the migratory habits of whales. Normally it would have been interesting to both of them, but – with the fresh air of the day and the large meal – "Mr and Mrs James Busby" were soon sound asleep in each other's arms.

The sun was shining over Cambridge the next morning, but they stayed in their room until almost eleven before going down for brunch. The hotel was two-thirds full and just about all the guests had the same idea, which led to a slight waiting time for the kipper and kedgeree. They had almost finished the meal when the Tarns came in to the main dining room, looking very much the squire and his wife relaxing on a Sunday.

The two men they had seen coming into the hotel with the Tarns on Friday evening were with their employers. The tall, burly one wore a light gray suit, the double-breasted jacket of which was so well tailored that you could hardly see the bulge under the left lapel. The shorter, stocky man was as casual as Max Tarn: gray slacks, and a matching gray rollneck.

They could see now, in the light of day, that the latter man was not simply stocky, but paunchy, around his early fifties, balding fast but with a vaguely military bearing. He also had a pair of ice blue glittering sharp eyes that took in everything at a glance. The younger man did the same thing, but with the style of a trained bodyguard, a slight turning of the head, followed by quick looks, like swift double-takes. Within seconds of entering the room, Bond guessed, this one would know exactly who was sitting where.

'I think it's time for me to deliver the glad tidings, if you'll excuse me a minute.' He stood and headed for the door as a waiter approached with more coffee.

It took only a few minutes to hand in his note at Reception. He saw that the pair of lovers, supplied courtesy of the Security Service, were still in the main lounge, sipping coffee and watching the doors, just as they had been told to do – wrongly. A Boy Scout would have marked them as suspicious, let alone any of Tarn's trained private bullet catchers.

He lingered in the dining room with Flicka for half-an-hour or so. The Tarn party appeared to be enjoying themselves, eating to the punctuation of bursts of laughter.

Back in their room, they had nothing to do but wait.

By three o'clock they were both getting edgy, but the telephone rang half-an-hour later.

'Mr Busby?' The voice had a slight growl of authority to it. The kind of voice you heard from passed-over officers in an army mess.

'Speaking.'

'Good. This is Maurice Goodwin. I'm Sir Max Tarn's Staff Manager . . .'

'Ah.'

'He's received your kind note and would like to have a word with you, if you have the time.'

'Certainly.'

'You can come up now, if that's convenient. I know Sir Max is seriously embarrassed about not getting in touch with you before this. After all, you were responsible for dealing with those clowns who tried to hold up the passengers, as well as showing great courage after the explosion.'

'Yes, I suppose we performed a small service. Tell me, where . . . ?'

'The Senate Suite. Top of the hotel. You go to the tenth floor and there's a private elevator up to the top. One of our people will be there to see you up. That alright?'

'Of course, may I bring my wife?'

There was a brief pause. 'We'd rather you didn't actually. Sir Max wanted a word with you alone. Privately. See you in a few minutes, then?'

He shrugged as he replaced the receiver. 'Sounds as though he's going to present me with a medal for bravery. Also doesn't want my wife in on the conversation.'

'Obviously not politically correct . . .'

'Flicka, I think you'd better go downstairs. Signal – as

52

gracefully and silently as you can – that I'm with him. Just a simple precaution.'

'Oh, Christ, James, this isn't going to turn out to be one of those complete security cock-ups, is it?'

'I don't know. The guy who called – Maurice Goodwin – is probably the paunchy, military type. Might just have his own reservations, or perhaps they feel I'll be more open if I see him alone. It might even be that Lady T doesn't want competition.'

'Me? Don't be an idiot, James.'

'In my book you'd be competition.'

She leaned up and kissed him on the cheek. 'Just you be careful out there,' she said in her best TV cop show voice.

It was the tall bodyguard in the gray suit who was waiting at the tenth floor. He checked Bond's name by simply asking, 'Mr Busby?'

At Bond's nod he introduced himself. 'Conrad.' He gave a wry smile. 'Sir Max calls me Connie, which is his idea of a little joke.' He raised an arm towards the small elevator cage marked *Senate Suite*. 'I handle security for Sir Max and Lady Tarn.' He carefully shepherded Bond into the lift, and before he knew what was going on, Connie frisked him with a quick expertise. 'Sorry about that, sir, but we have to be careful, you understand. Particularly with someone like yourself. We were all *very* impressed at how you and your wife handled the team who tried it on during the cruise – *Caribbean Prince*, I'm talking about.'

'Yes. Yes, of course you are.'

The elevator carried them to a large lobby which had a set of double doors with *Senate Suite* picked out in gold on a dark plate to the left. Connie opened the door and gestured for Bond to go in, following hard on his back and announcing, 'Mr Busby, Sir Max.'

Close up, Tarn looked as smooth as they came: well shaved cheeks, almost pink over a good layer of tan. He was better looking than in his photographs. Calm deep brown eyes, the nose a shade too long for symmetry, and the almost polished iron-gray hair swept back with slight wings over the small ears. His movements were controlled and his manner charming in a way guaranteed to put anyone off his guard.

'Come in, Mr Busby. Do come in. Thank you for your note. Most kind. I had planned to get in touch with you anyway. The least I could do was personally thank you for what you did during that earlier incident on *Caribbean Prince*.' His handshake was like touching a snake: dry, smooth and dangerous. The experience made the short hairs tingle on the back of Bond's neck.

'Now, how about a drink, or tea, or whatever you fancy. This, incidentally,' he moved his right hand a fraction of an inch towards the paunchy short man who stood by the window, 'this is Maurice Goodwin. He's the right side of my brain as far as travel and the staff go.'

'We spoke, Mr Busby.' Goodwin did not attempt to cross the room for a handshake. He simply nodded, a shade aloof, while his boss clasped Bond's hand in a grip as tight as a hangman's noose.

'A little tea, if that's not . . .'

'Tea it is. Excellent choice. Connie, tea for Mr Busby. You prefer what, China, Indian . . . ?'

'Just as it comes. Preferably Indian.'

'Man after my own heart. My wife adores Lapsang Souchong, but I prefer a good old dish of Darjeeling myself.' He had a tendency to draw words out. Soooochong and Darjeeeeling.

'Now, sit down. Make yourself comfortable. You were very kind about my staff and the awful *Caribbean Prince*

54

episode. Terrible business. Haven't got to the bottom of it yet, but we will.'

'I'm sure, sure you will, Sir Max.'

'Doubtless you heard about what happened to the hold-up merchants who were still alive after your bit of gunplay?'

'No.'

'Ah, thought you would have heard by now. We very carefully got them off the ship after the explosion, then handed them over to the police in Miami. Unhappily, while they were in the holding cells, mixed up with some very unsavory prisoners, someone took a dislike to them. Used a makeshift knife. All killed during a disturbance. Police cannot determine who did them, but they were certainly done.'

'I would say that was a happy ending.' Bond again felt the nape of his neck tingle.

'Yes.' He did not take his eyes from Bond's. For a second it was like being locked into a staring competition. 'Yes. Well. Yes, you have something to tell me? Your note hinted at . . . Well, I don't know what your note hinted at. Home Office. Foreign Office. Something about my affairs, which cover the entire globe, Mr Busby. What was it about?' While outwardly Tarn seemed charming, Bond got the impression that the charm was less than skin deep. Beneath the surface lay something malignant; an undertow of bleak, unbalanced evil mixed with the undeniable charisma. This was the kind of man who could bring down countries, charm the worst elements of society and make black appear to be white and vice versa. Deep down, Bond surmised that Sir Max Tarn could be a very dangerous enemy. Not only to him, but to all mankind if he chose that path. His charisma was that of a rabble rouser. If the man chose politics as a profession, he would be able to hold certain segments of society in the palm of his hand.

'I think it would be best if we talked in complete privacy, Sir Max.'

'Oh, you do?' from Goodwin still beside the window which looked out of the front of the hotel. 'You prefer privacy, eh? Those bloody British Telecom people're still working down there. Have been since we arrived. You anything to do with them, Mr Busby? Anything to do with people listening to other people's conversations on the old blower?'

Bond gave Tarn a quick quizzical look.

'It's quite safe to talk in front of Goodwin, Mr Busby. Ah, here's Connie with the tea.'

They did not speak while Conrad poured the tea, making it all a little civilized ceremony. When he had finished, Tarn pleasantly told him to wait outside, adding somewhat archly, 'Mr Busby prefers privacy. Don't be offended, Connie, I don't suppose it's personal.'

When the bodyguard had withdrawn, it was Goodwin who spoke again. 'Well, Mr B., got an answer for me?'

'I didn't quite get the question . . . Mr G.'

'We are circled about with people who watch. People who follow every movement. People who'd like to listen in to our telephone conversations – though they can't because we tend to by-pass the switchboard.'

Bond opened his mouth, but Goodwin had not finished. 'We've been quite interested in the little armies of fairy folk dogging our footsteps. You anything to do with that, Mr B?'

'I can tell you about it.'

'Ah,' from Max Tarn. 'Then please, before you tell, *why* would you tell?' The last rays of charm left his voice, and the question held within it a vestige of something deeply repulsive.

Finally, Bond replied—

'Because I wanted to do something to help. I've always admired you, sir, and doubly so since the *Caribbean Prince* business . . .'

'Admiration. That all? Nothing in it for you? Doing it out of a sense of duty – whatever *it* is?'

'Something like that, Sir Max, yes. I'm not even supposed to know about it. Just saw some things in the office that I don't think I was supposed to see.'

'So you came trotting down here to tell all.'

'No, sir. We've had this week-end booked for the past six weeks. You can check that out, here in the hotel.'

Tarn nodded, 'Yes, we already have, or I should say the old stalwart Goodwin did the checking. So tell me what it's all about. Just spit it out, James – that is your name, yes?'

'Yes, Sir Max.'

'Well, James. Tell all.'

'There's a warrant out for your arrest. You and Lady Tarn. They're going to pull you in on Monday morning; and there's another search and seizure warrant for the premises in Ludgate Circus – Tarn International – and also for your private residence. They're Security Service people watching you, and . . .'

'I told you so, Max,' from Goodwin. 'Couldn't be anyone else'd make such a ballsup.'

'Yes, you mentioned that.' Max Tarn had gone slightly pale under the ruddy and tan cheeks. 'What exactly are they arresting me for, Mr Bus . . . Oh, to hell with it, why don't we all come clean, Mr Bond? It is Bond, isn't it, not Busby? Why? How? I want the lot or you'll end up with your wife in a neat little plastic body bag. I didn't mention to you that some of Connie's people are with your wife e'en as we speak. One's the young gentleman whose wrist you almost broke on Friday night. He thinks your wife's a dish – his words not mine. I wouldn't presume. But I would presume to order your mutual demise if I don't get the right answers. So, let's have a little party, Mr Bond. Let's play Truth or Dare, just like I used to play it in my nursery with my dear old Nanny—'

6

Knight's Move

'SHE'S NOT MY wife.' Bond juggled several complex problems in his head. He had not even discussed this possible scenario with Flicka, yet from the outset Max Tarn had known his identity. Now it was up to *him* to lie. Cover every possible permutation. Lie convincingly, and pray that Flicka's story jigsawed with his own. Tarn was obviously shaken by the very idea of the arrest, search and seizure warrants. It was probably the last thing he expected, just as Bond had not foreseen the exposure of *his* name. What else did Tarn know? – he wondered in the split second between sentences.

'She's not my wife,' he repeated, pleased, and a little surprised that he sounded so casual. Deep within him, metal butterflies stirred and sent their anxiety cannoning around his guts.

'Of course she isn't, Mr Bond.' Tarn's voice silkily smooth. 'She's a former officer of Swiss Intelligence. A discredited officer at that. So, tell me exactly what this arrest business is all about, and why you, of all people, would wish to warn me in advance?'

'I haven't the slightest idea what it's about. All I can tell you is that I've seen the warrants. As for warning you, I've already told you. I've always held you in great regard. Any man who has the intelligence and flair to emerge

59

from practically nothing to become a multi-billionaire has my respect . . .'

'But I didn't come up from nothing, my friend. I came from one of the oldest, and most proud families in Germany. I don't use the "von", but I am really Sir Max *von* Tarn just as your friend is a von Grüsse, a member of another old and reputable family, originally German. Mine, however, is slightly up-market to Fräulein von Grüsse. My grandfather was a General who fought bravely in the first war, *his* father was a Field Marshal, and my great-great grandfather held one of the highest positions in the Prussian Empire, with blood ties to the Hohenzollern family. Look –' He pulled the elegant cardigan to one side, showing a small crest embroidered on his shirt. A shield, surmounted with scroll work, two crossed spears on a field of gold and below it a motto – *In Familia Vir*. *In Family Lies Strength*.

So, Max Tarn *did* claim a direct link with the old family. 'I didn't realize.' He tried to sound genuinely astounded. 'Sir Max, if you have such a respected and aristocratic background, why do you never use it?'

'Because I prefer things to look as though I came from nowhere, and in some ways I did come onto the scene out of the blue. After all, the Nazis murdered all my relatives, apart from my mother, and stole our family estates. My mother, rightly, kept very quiet about our background. Officially, I'm dead.' A friendly charming smile that caused a flash of pleasure deep in the brown eyes; the twinkling of his irises gave out a strange uncanny impression, as though they were water and a breeze came rippling across them. 'Though, of course, many of my close friends and business associates *do* know from whom I am descended. They're very good about it. Not a word has ever been leaked to the Press.' He paused, chin lifted and face set in a smile that was, at once, paradoxically condescending and welcoming.

'Well, I have even more respect for you now, Sir Max,' Bond lied. 'I came from a pretty middle class background, and I've had to drag myself up by my bootstraps. I thought I'd done quite well until almost overnight the Cold War ended. If you know my real name, then you probably know what I did to serve my Queen and country.'

'Spy. Agent provocateur. Assassin. Saboteur. Right? All those unpleasant things people do in what the Press glamorously calls "The Secret World."'

'I was a field agent with British Intelligence, yes.'

'Oh, I think something more than just a field agent, Mr Bond. Don't be modest. You were a star; a leader; decorated many times, in secret of course. A legend within your service.' A pause as he looked Bond over, from head to toe. 'I could always use a man like you. Think about it.'

'Well.' He blinked quickly, then looked away in mock modesty. 'Well, I was lucky. My problem, Sir Max, was that I thought it would go on forever. In some ways I suppose I'm well off. At least they've found me a job – at about a third of my old salary, and with a pension that drops accordingly. That's the way people like me are treated. When we are no longer needed to do the dirty work, the powers that be don't want to know. People in the armed forces are in the same boat. Entire regiments disbanded; bases closed; officers, NCOs and fighting men given a small token of gratitude and turned out into a life they neither understand nor wish to live.'

'And that's the kind of life you live nowadays, Mr Bond? Come, come, you could afford to take Fräulein von Grüsse on one of my cruises: not a cheap item. Only a hundred and twenty of your colleagues have been put on

61

the retired list – that's public knowledge. You don't appear to stint yourself. You dress well, and I understand you have a good London address.'

'Bit of a final fling, Sir Max. The cruise, I mean. The job they've given me is a dead end, it's as boring as watching sand in an egg timer. I even have a little sign on my desk that says, *Beware, the End is Nigh*. Yes, I had a little private money, as the snobs would call it, but that's been eroded over the years, and now I'm as good as being put out to grass.'

'Yes, I wanted to ask you what actually goes on in that house in Bedford Square.'

'Nothing exciting, I fear. We're a kind of repository for documents. Mainly the declassified stuff. It's a sort of research centre for old Cold Warriors who want to write their memoirs. Seems to be the coming thing, writing the story of your supposedly secret life. They're all at it.' Tarn could dig as deeply as he wanted, for Bond had just described the cover given to the new Two Zeros Section. There were even people in the Home and Foreign Offices, not to mention the Intelligence and Security Services, who thought that was exactly what was going on in Bedford Square.

'Yes,' Tarn nodded. 'I *had* heard that's what you were doing there. But tell me, Mr Bond, why did you find it necessary to use a pseudonym to cruise on my ship, and book in at this hotel?'

'I would have thought it was obvious. Fredericka – Fräulein von Grüsse – and I are having an affair.'

'Which seems to be common knowledge. You *are* living together after all.'

'There's a kind of double standard about that as far as my old outfit's concerned.' Bond gave a little shrug. 'Things have changed a little recently, but we used the Mr

& Mrs Busby names on the cruise because our relationship was frowned on at the time. It's out in the open now, but in the last few months we've stayed here on a number of occasions and used the other names. That's how the staff know us so we decided not to embarrass them by using proper names for this week-end . . .'

'Which you claim is a coincidence?'

'A coincidence?'

'That we happen to be staying here at the same time.'

'I've said so, and you can check with reservations.'

'So you've already told me.' He gave a little chuckle, 'And I've already checked.'

Bond nodded, as though Tarn was simply showing common sense. 'I might also ask you, Sir Max, how you know all about *me*? You appear to have gone out of your way to burrow into my past, and I'm sure that wasn't done just over this week-end.'

'No. No, that's fair. The truth about that is I have a staff who go through the names of all those who travel on my cruise ships. If they look interesting I authorize a little digging. *You* looked very interesting. I found the fact that you worked for both the Home *and* the Foreign Offices intriguing; particularly after hearing the details of how the pair of you dealt with those blundering miscreants on *Caribbean Prince*. I remember saying to Connie that you sounded like a couple of hired killers. So, we checked you out. Both of you. It's relatively easy, you know.'

'Of course I know, sir. I've done it myself. Even took a peep at a file on you at one time. You came up squeaky clean, incidentally, that's why the warrants concerned me so much.'

'Maybe I believe you, Mr Bond, but I really need to know something about these so-called arrest and search warrants. You come to me and tell me this because we happen to be in the same place at the same time. If it turns out to be true – which I would doubt except for the sudden odd surveillance over this week-end – I would have known nothing about this. Not that I have anything to hide; my conscience is clear. But I'd like you to think about these warrants for a moment. You say that you saw them. Where was this?'

'At the Home Office.'

'And why would you, a former big league field officer now in charge of a penny ante operation looking after files and documents, why would you be at the Home Office?'

Stick as near to the truth as you can, he thought. 'How much do you know about the reorganization of our former clandestine services, sir?'

'Only what I've read in the newspapers. Names out in the open. Addresses in the public domain. A newer, less secret, kinder and caring system.'

'Let me tell you, then. Yes, certain things are out in the open. But all those old organizations with the letters and numbers – MI5, MI6 and so forth – are now run by the bureaucrats. Run by committees and little cabals. Watch-dogs. Guardians of morality. Financial Working Parties. Junior Ministers with special duties. They've sprung up all over the place, to make life hell for those who played by the good old rules.'

'Quite right too,' Tarn almost snapped. 'What it means, Mr Bond, is that now those services are accountable. They never were before. If I were ever a power in any land, I'd make sure that you people were answerable to me, personally.'

'It also means that they can be *used* by whoever's in power.'

'What's wrong with that?'

'Under the previous system, they were always apolitical. Yes, they worked for government, but never for the particular ruling party. As soon as the political party in power has access – complete access – to those organizations, you begin to spawn corrupt organizations. You follow?'

Tarn grunted, as if not convinced. 'Well, Bond, how much of a look did you get at these warrants?'

'Pretty brief. Enough time to see your name – together with that of Lady Tarn – and the address of Tarn International's offices.'

'You say they're to be enacted on Monday. How do you know that?'

'It was there, on the papers. Monday 11th.'

'So you had time to see that also?'

'Yes.'

'Surely you know that part of the interrogator's art is to draw out things which the person being interrogated does not realize he's seen? This is standard practice with the police, and – I should imagine – your former employers, yes?'

'Yes.' Careful.

'Well, the point's already been proven. It now appears that not only did you see names and places, but also the date the warrants were to be enacted. If you had time to see those things, perhaps you also had time to pick up – even cerebrally – the reasons for these documents being issued.'

The silence stretched out, like a body on mortuary slab. At the window, Goodwin moved and muttered, 'Christ, they're using that same damned car – the Volvo. Been going round and round for the past half hour.'

Finally, Bond replied—

'No, no, I can't think of anything.' Then – 'Wait a

minute, though. I can remember something about restrictions on the sale of arms.' Out of the corner of his eye, Bond saw that he had at least got Maurice Goodwin's attention and Max Tarn's shoulders seemed to stiffen slightly.

There was a considerable pause before Tarn said that, surely, this had to be a mistake. 'Arms? Arms as in weapons?'

'Arms as in devices to kill people, yes.'

'But I've never had any dealings with armament companies.' An uncertain frown, and a slight tremor in his right hand. Then he seemed to recover. 'Ah, yes. Yes, I see what's happened. I *did* buy certain things. We're planning a small museum – a War Museum – for one of the islands the Cruise Line owns in the Caribbean. It's just a desolate strip of land, but with a pleasant beach. When my ships put in there, we fly a few people over from Nassau. They set up a couple of bars, small restaurant, a little store that sells local artifacts. The passengers like a pleasant day on the beach with some amenities laid on.'

His tone became more convincing as he continued. 'One of my people suggested the museum. You wouldn't expect to find something like that out in the middle of the sea. In fact we start building this Summer. Should be done by next year, and it'll house all kinds of things – aircraft, weapons, paintings, models, simulations. Even a submarine. Pay for itself in a couple of years we reckon. One of my companies bought quite a number of things for the museum.' He gave a sigh meant to indicate relief, but falling very short of its target. 'Well, that's it I suppose. Some idiot in one of your snooping departments has made a glorious error and taken my purchases as something dangerous and illicit.' Tarn's explanation was stilted and patently unconvincing.

'Then you'll be able to satisfy them, sir. That's good.'

Tarn turned away, his head moving in the direction of Goodwin. 'Yes, a relief. A relief indeed, eh, Maurice?'

'A relief? Oh, yes indeed.' Goodwin did not sound happy.

Tarn began to say something else to Bond when there was a knock at the door and Connie put his head into the room.

'A word, sir, please.' The bodyguard moved his head to indicate that he needed to talk with Sir Max in the relative privacy of the passage.

Tarn excused himself, leaving Bond alone with Goodwin who looked straight at him, then glanced out of the window before settling his cynical eyes back again. 'You think my boss is going to buy your story, do you?'

'It's not a story, Maurice. Just the plain, unvarnished truth. Incidentally, I was looking forward to meeting Lady Tarn.'

'You betcha.' Goodwin gave a short laugh. 'Of course you want to meet her. Everyone does. The famous beauty, Trish Nuzzi. Amazing what money'll buy for a man, isn't it?'

'Meaning that your boss bought her?'

'Now, I didn't say that, Bond. I only remarked that it's wonderful what money'll buy.'

'Yes, but . . .'

The door opened and Tarn came back into the room. 'Maurice, could you join us outside for a few moments.' Then, to Bond, 'I'm sorry about this, Mr Bond. Duty calls though. Won't be a minute.'

Bond nodded and watched as the door closed behind them. He went over to the window and looked down into the street in front of the hotel. Taking in the Security Service's surveillance teams he thought how well they were assembled. A layman would not have recognized the team as watchers. Only someone with a profound knowledge of surveillance methods could have recognized them for what they really were. So, Maurice Goodwin was well versed in these things. That was not so unlikely, for he was patently ex-military.

He was just turning away from the window when the door to the bedroom opened quietly. Lady Tarn stood just inside the room. Beautiful and even more stunning than the photographs he had seen of her, or the glimpses at the hotel.

She hesitated, her movements quick and full of nervousness. 'Mr Bond, I know your real name. I only want a quick word.' She glanced agitatedly towards the main door. 'First, I want to thank you. You tried to save the life of one of the officers on *Caribbean Prince* . . .'

'Well, I . . .'

'No, I just want to thank you. It was Mark Neuman. He was my cousin. I know you did all you could to save him.'

Her eyes glistened with tears just below the surface. 'I wanted to warn you, as well.'

'Warn me?'

'My husband. He's not what he seems. Please take great care. If you've been of use to him, he'll try to use you again and again. Max can be charming, but his goal in life is terrifying. I don't know . . .'

The main door opened, and Tarn came striding back into the room, stopping suddenly as he saw his wife. 'What're *you* doing in here?' There was a touch of merciless brutality about both his face and voice. Maurice Goodwin hovered behind him, looking a little too anxious.

'I thought you had all left.' She spoke like someone

near to pleading: as though she feared physical pain. 'I only . . .'

'Just wait in the bedroom. We haven't quite finished.' Then, as an afterthought, he added, 'My dear.'

As soon as she was gone he altered again: now all smiles obviously trying to project a conciliatory mood.

'I'm sorry to have kept you, Mr Bond. You've been most helpful. Both of you. You and Fräulein von Grüsse . . .'

'If your gorillas have hurt one hair of her head, I'll . . .'

'Mr Bond, please,' his voice oozed with an unlikely sense of serenity. 'I apologize, most profusely for any belligerence I showed when we first met. If I can do anything to put that right . . .'

'No, just let us get on with our lives,' Bond snapped. 'I came to do you a favor . . .'

'And I appreciate that. I'm quite willing to pay you back with interest. In time you'll appreciate that I had to be absolutely sure of you both. A few answers from your good friend Fräulein von Grüsse were all we needed. Just to check out the pair of you.'

'Well, you've asked your questions: presumably asked them of Flicka as well. Now, I'd like to go, sir, if that's convenient.'

'By all means, Mr Bond. You've done me a service. I'd simply like to repay . . .'

'It's not necessary. Good afternoon to you, Sir Max.' Then, over his shoulder, 'And you, Mr Goodwin.'

Outside, the burly Connie was all set to escort him down in the lift. 'Not necessary, Conrad. I'll see myself out.' He placed the palm of his right hand firmly on the bodyguard's chest and pushed him away. As the doors to the elevator closed, he saw the surprised look in the big man's eyes as he stumbled back against the opposite wall.

Flicka was standing by the window, looking down into the street below when he got back to their suite.

'You've had visitors, I hear?' Bond went up behind her and locked his arms around her shoulders.

'A pair of nicely dressed apes, yes. If they weren't so potentially dangerous, they'd be like cartoon characters.' She twisted her face up towards him. 'One of them was the oaf whose hand you mangled before we checked in. He's still not happy about that. Became definitely unpleasant about it, James, and he goes by the delightful name of Mr Archie; his friend is Mr Cuthbert. Both educated to within an inch of their lives – I detect the mark of one of the great Public Schools on both of them. They gave the impression of being related and it wouldn't surprise me if they were both second cousins of Flashman from *Tom Brown's Schooldays*. They're superior types who'd think rape was their right, and would have no bad dreams if they roasted their grandmothers and served them up as an entrée.'

'And these two little charmers asked you questions?'

'Just your usual hostile interrogation, with plenty of unveiled threats. A very nasty couple, though they seemed to believe me in the end. Sir Max Tarn's private knuckle-dragger, Connie, came down and finally checked me out. I presume we were both asked roughly the same questions.'

They talked for some twenty minutes, and discovered that Flicka had not been asked about the warrants. Tarn's inquisitors had zeroed in solely on her relationship with Bond, the reasons for their use of pseudonyms, and the kind of work going on at the Bedford Square house. They had been particularly interested in when and why Bond and Flicka had decided to spend the week-end in Cambridge.

'I gave them the answers they wanted to hear, which was basically the truth.' She shrugged. 'After that, they seemed to lose interest.'

'I wouldn't be too certain about that.' Bond pulled her close to him. Her hair smelled of hay and late summer, and he felt the familiar surge of affection which had become so much part of his life since they had met. 'I think I'd better go and make a little telephone call,' he said eventually. 'I believe the office should be kept informed.'

Outside, the bank of telephones on Parker's Piece was empty. Bond dialed the Minister's contact number. This time it was a male voice that answered.

'Brother James,' he identified himself.

'Brother James. You calling about Knight's Move?'

'No. How long . . . ?' he began. Knight's Move had been their chosen code for extreme emergency.

'Called in less than a minute ago. Move!' The disembodied voice in far away London had about it the urgency of a bomb threat.

He slammed down the receiver, turned on one heel and started to run back towards the University Arms. He was less than twenty yards away when he saw Sir Max Tarn's Rolls, accompanied by one of the Rovers, moving out from under the hotel's *porte-cochère*, nosing its way into the traffic.

He slowed to a walk, and sauntered into the foyer. 'Sir Max leaving us?' he casually asked of one of the porters standing by the door.

'Sudden call back to London. You never know with these wealthy folk. Always on the go.' The porter was looking at a five pound note – his tip from Tarn no doubt. He appeared to be considering it as paltry.

Bond did not use the lift, but went up the main

staircase, two stairs at a time. The door to their suite was slightly ajar, a room service table outside.

'Did you . . . ?' he began as he entered the room, pulling the door wide open.

'Shut it, Bond.' He was looking into the circular little mouth of an automatic pistol, held left-handed by the young thug whose hand he had injured on their arrival. What had Flicka called him? Mr Archie?

Across the room, Archie's partner, Cuthbert, had one arm around Flicka's neck, the other held a small weapon Bond recognized as a little Beretta .22 mm, not exactly a stopping weapon.

'Don't do anything stupid, will you, old chap?' from Archie. 'Sir Max so wanted to be here for this. Sends his apologies and all that. Called away unexpectedly. Him and Lady Trish. Very disappointed, as were Mr Goodwin and Connie. They all wanted to be in on this.'

7

Mr Cuthbert & Mr Archibald

BOND REMAINED ABSOLUTELY still, balancing on the balls of his feet, not moving a muscle as he tried to calculate the risk involved in any immediate action. The man who had spoken kicked the door closed, then moved in behind Bond. His breath was warm and the quiet voice full of menace. The hard cold touch of the automatic on the back of his neck banished all thoughts of any instant attempt at turning the tables.

'Now, Mr Bond, sir. We're going to take a little trip. A short journey by car. Just the four of us. Very cosy and nothing to be concerned about.' The voice was low, though there was something curious about the pitch.

'Take *me*,' Bond matched the volume of his voice to that of his captor. 'Just take me. Leave Ms von Grüsse out of it.'

'Very chivalrous.' The man holding Flicka moved slightly, pressing the muzzle of his pistol harder into her neck. 'Don't you think that's chivalrous, Mr Archibald? Something you rarely come across these days.' The timbre of his voice was almost identical to that of his partner.

'Exceptionally unselfish, Mr Cuthbert. What a pity it's not in our power to grant such a plea.'

Flicka had been very accurate in her description of these two men. As the one called Archibald moved

73

around Bond, coming into his line of vision, he saw that the pair looked like escapees from a cartoon. In spite of their immaculate turnout, they presented a bizarre couple. Each was dressed in a smart, beautifully tailored suit – one gray serge, the other in a dark material, with a very thin stripe. Their shoes were Gucci, the suits undoubtedly Armani, their white silk shirts had probably come from Turnbull & Asser, while the ties were identical, bearing the striped colours of a very famous British public school.

There all normality ended, for they spoke in that rather affected English sometimes referred to as 'Oxford,' though generally imitated by the 'Ya-Wa-Yawing' drawl of the yuppie. Both had dark hair, cut very short in a style once favoured by the Beatles, and the hair coloring seemed at odds with their pink, almost feminine, complexions. The pair were obviously related, for each had unnaturally thick pale lips, while their eyebrows were clownish – inverted thick Vs – which made them look as though they were permanently asking questions.

'I really think it's time we got moving.' Archibald moved again. 'Let me tell you what we're going to do.'

'Excellent thought, Mr Archibald. I was about to suggest the same thing.'

'We're going out of this room,' Archibald continued, 'and down the service stairs. It's five floors down and – though it sounds a shade melodramatic – if either of you makes a wrong move, both of you will die.'

'Instantaneously, wouldn't you say, Mr Archibald?'

'Couldn't have put it better myself, Mr Cuthbert.'

'And what happens then?' Bond tried to sound casual, as he desperately thought of some way of immediate escape that would pose no threat to Flicka.

'We head for the service exit, don't we, Mr Archibald?'

'Right again, Mr Cuthbert. The service exit, outside of

which there should be a car, complete with driver.'

'Then we take this cosy little journey?'

'You're very quick, Mr Bond. That's about it. Into the car and away. At this time on a Sunday evening it's unlikely we'll be seen by anyone.'

'Aren't the two of you going to miss choir practice?' Flicka asked, with no trace of fear.

'Very droll, Ms von Grüsse, but we'll have plenty of time for that later. Actually we *do* have rather fine voices. Maybe we'll get a chance to sing at your funerals.'

'Well, that's very nice for the pair of you.' Bond shifted a little to his right. 'But what if *we* don't really want to make the journey?'

'Mr Bond, you have no option.' Archibald hefted the pistol uncomfortably in his left hand, and Bond could see the bandages showing under the cuff of his right sleeve. This was certainly the young man whose wrist he had damaged against the car door on their arrival. It was clear that he was not happy using a weapon held in his left hand.

'Oh, no, Mr Bond. Please don't even think about it.' Archie moved back a couple of paces as he saw Bond's eyes take in the damaged right wrist. 'You actually broke a bone, did you know that?'

'Only one?'

'Very painful. But I'm quite good at pain. I can take it and inflict it, as you'll probably see. Now, could you move over to your lady friend.' He made a small gesture towards Flicka with his pistol. 'Oh, come on, Mr Bond, don't be tiresome. Just move.'

'Better do as he says, darling,' she smiled across the room. 'I think they've both got slightly mercurial tempers.'

Bond slowly went over to her, flashing a look which told

her that, in spite of their grotesque appearance, he had already taken in the extent of the danger they represented. When people like Cuthbert and Archie came in pairs they were usually psychotics, and he had no desire to even attempt taking them out until a foolproof moment presented itself.

Cuthbert had stepped back from Flicka, and Archie told them to hold hands. 'Pretend you're on a nice little lovers' walk to Grantchester,' he added, signalling that Tarn's people had kept them under surveillance from the moment they had arrived in Cambridge.

As their hands touched, Cuthbert stepped forward and snapped a pair of handcuffs around both their wrists. 'There,' he cooed. 'Isn't that a nice lovers' knot? Now, I suggest we move at a steady pace. Mr Archibald will lead the way, you will follow and I'll bring up the rear.'

'And please don't make us do anything we'd regret,' added Archibald.

He paused just outside the door, nodded and led them along the passage to the plain door marked *Staff Only*.

The rear staircase was bare: concrete steps and white-washed walls all the way down. Bond noted that these unlikely toughs both moved with the quick sure-footed speed of highly-trained soldiers, and the thought that they might possibly be paid mercenaries flicked through his mind. But for their appearances they could have been a couple of men from the SAS or the American Delta Force.

They were both obviously very alert during the journey down. Bond had no doubt that any attempted escape would result in fast, sudden death.

At the ground floor, Archibald made a quick gesture with his head, nodding towards a pair of doors with an interior automatic bar lock. For the few seconds it took to get to the doors the pistols disappeared, but both men hemmed in their prisoners, using their bodies to keep them close and moving in the right direction.

The doors opened onto a side street, where Tarn's other Rover sat, its engine purring, and a man at the wheel. Archibald opened the nearside door, pushing Flicka and Bond into the vehicle, while Cuthbert had the door open on the far side and slid into the rear. In seconds they were moving, crammed close in the back of the car, flanked by the two gunmen.

'Everything okay?' The driver did not move his head, concentrating on taking the car out into the main flow of traffic.

'Like a charm,' Cuthbert replied.

'Clockwork, I'd say,' Archibald added.

'Wherever we're going, you'll be stopped long before you're out of the city.' Bond felt confident about that probability. With the surveillance teams around, it should not take long for one of the units to latch onto the second Rover.

Yet nothing happened. The only moment that caused any tension in the car was when they had to pull over as, with a shriek of sirens, two fire engines, a pair of ambulances and a police car hurtled past. They reached the slip road onto the M11 without any sign of police or paramilitary roadblocks, though the driver was constantly warned by Cuthbert to check nobody was following.

Occasionally Bond glanced towards Flicka, and several times their eyes met in cold comfort, reflecting that they were both at a complete loss as to how they could evade their two weird captors.

One further worry was that neither of them had been blindfolded. Nobody seemed in the least concerned that they could follow the route with ease.

'You don't mind us seeing where we're going?' Bond finally asked.

'Do *you* mind, Mr Cuthbert?'

'Not in the least, Mr Archibald.'

The odd pair sniggered and Cuthbert added, 'I can't see the chief letting you trace the way back.'

'No return ticket,' Archibald snapped smugly.

Eventually they came off the Motorway at Exit 8, and for a few minutes Bond thought they were heading towards Stansted Airport, but they continued on through the town of Tackley, then turned off onto a minor road about a mile further on.

Now it became difficult to follow directions as they twisted and turned through a series of lanes and secondary roads with few signposts. At last the Rover made an abrupt turn through an open gateway, up a long, winding drive flanked by shrubbery which appeared to have been allowed to grow wild and out of hand. There were places where the bushes, encroaching on the drive, scraped against the car. Finally the headlights picked out what looked like a large Victorian house. In the darkness the gables and brickwork took on a sinister look: a gothic pile gone to ruin, its silhouette black against the dark sky. It could have come from the Brontës or Dickens: Wuthering Heights or Bleak House.

The driver flashed the lights of the Rover, and an answering pinpoint of light came from the doorway.

'Not here yet by the looks of things,' the driver muttered.

'Late for their own funerals,' Cuthbert said brightly.

'Never mind, we can all make ourselves comfortable.' Archibald gave Bond a prod in the ribs. 'We've arrived, Mr Bond. Everyone out.'

'All ashore who's going ashore,' Cuthbert added.

Still handcuffed together they climbed from the car into the chill night air. There was a hint of rain in the wind, and the driver was talking, low and fast, to a sixth person – a tall young woman carrying a large electric torch.

The driver turned to speak to Archibald while Cuthbert remained close to the two prisoners. 'At least Beth's got food ready for us.'

'I don't know about food, but I'm dying to use a bathroom,' Flicka spoke up.

'Well, you're the lucky one,' from Archie. 'Beth here'll make certain you won't try and run for it.'

Inside, the house appeared to be deserted with little furniture and no electricity. Candles had been set at vantage points and the three men took great care in uncuffing Bond from Flicka, crowding them both, making sure they were given no opportunity to try an escape.

In turn they were taken to a ground floor bathroom covered in mildew which was quite visible in the light from a pair of candles. The newcomer, Beth, who was careful to keep her face in shadow, guarded Flicka, and Cuthbert watched over Bond. They were then taken up the main stairs which creaked and cracked under foot. The house smelled damp, musty, full of decay and the room – two flights up – in which they were eventually locked had the paper hanging in great triangles off the wall. In one corner there was an old iron radiator to which they were handcuffed – two pairs this time – and left with a single candle burning in the center of the room.

It was a long narrow chamber with one dormer window and bare wooden boards underfoot. At one time this could easily have been a servant's bedroom, and Bond wondered what misery the place had seen in the shape of young girls sent away from home for the first time and finding themselves with this small room as their only place of privacy.

A few moments after they had been secured to the radiator, Beth returned with two cups of a nondescript soup and a couple of chunks of bread. She said nothing to either of them, even though Flicka tried to make bright conversation, and thank her. They heard a key click in a lock outside and her footsteps echoing away on the dry rotting boards as she went downstairs.

'What do you think, James?' Flicka whispered.

'I think we'd better try and get out of these damned handcuffs.'

'I've already taken a look at the pipe they've got me hooked to. Solid as a stone.'

'This one's rusty as hell, and I'm going to try.' He felt up and down the pipe with his free hand. It was obviously the conduit for hot water to flow into the radiator, but a professional plumber would have problems getting it unscrewed.

'You think they've got orders to kill us?' Flicka asked.

'Not yet, but I think it's an even bet that they're waiting for orders. If they had been told to do away with us, it would be all over by now.'

'A happy thought.'

'They're a happy little pair. Psychopaths of the kind who take a pride in their work. I guess they're Tarn's human Rottweilers.' He was twisting the cuffs against the pipe, turning his right hand over and over so the short chain tightened. Eventually he could move it no further. Now, he used his left hand to add pressure on the right handcuff, trying to see if he could get enough leverage to shatter the pipe, or even break the chain between the cuffs.

After half-an-hour he stopped, drank the soup which

had gone cold, and ate a couple of mouthfuls of bread. He did not want to raise any false hopes, but the radiator pipe was bending slightly against the steel of the cuff, causing a cutting bruise in his wrist, but certainly doing damage to the rusted metal.

He rested for a few minutes and then began again. Far away, deep below them in the house, they could hear voices as the three men and Beth talked.

'We must be well away from any other houses,' he said, panting with the exertion of working on the pipe. 'They're behaving as though they own the place.'

'Of course, we've no way of knowing if they do.' For the first time, she began to sound really concerned.

Bond told her to try and get some rest. 'Who knows, we might need all our strength before tonight's through.'

He worked on, making a little progress, and shortly heard her breathing take on the deep steady note of sleep.

Bond was not about to give up, though his wrist soon became torn and bleeding. He had no idea of what time they had left, but slowly the old radiator pipe was cracking under the tough steel of the handcuffs. Minutes turned into hours and time had absolutely no meaning, then suddenly, with a loud wrenching crack, the pipe gave way and he gently pulled his hand free of the radiator.

The candle was guttering, almost out, and from beyond the one grimy window came the first sign of dawn, the sheer black night turning into an unearthly pearly light.

There was nothing he could do about getting Flicka free as she was shackled to the main section of the old radiator. Flexing his torn, bruised and bleeding wrist, he stretched out his legs and began to try and move all his limbs which were cramped and singing with pain. He had just managed to get himself into an upright position, leaning his back against a wall when the bright light of a pair of headlamps swept across the window, and there was the sound of a car stopping behind the Rover in front of the house.

Pulling himself along the wall, Bond slowly made his way to the window, but kept to one side, not daring to let himself be seen. As he had thought, the small dormer window was set into the roof of the house, and from below came the sound of voices raised in argument. He heard Cuthbert say, quite loudly, 'But we can't just leave them here.'

Another voice, which he recognized plainly as Max Tarn, said, 'Well, that's what we're going to do. I want no more blood on anyone's hands. Not yet, anyway. We have a lot to do.'

'They'll shop us, Chief!' from Archibald.

'Get in the car, you depraved, perverted little monster and do as the chief says.' This time the voice was that of Maurice Goodwin.

'I'm not perverted. You've no right to speak to me like that. Cuthbert, help me. We can't leave that pair upstairs.'

'We have to if the chief says so.'

There was the sound of a short scuffle and a yelp of pain, from Archibald – 'That's my bloody wrist, Goodwin. Leave me alone.'

'Get in the car then. We haven't got that much time.'

Bond pulled himself right up to the window and saw both the Rovers were outside, motors running, the first one about to pull away. Then, as he strained his eyes, he clearly saw the figure of Max Tarn in the headlights, as he stomped around the front of the second car and bent to get into the rear seats. Moments later the cars moved off, their tail lights growing dim as they headed down the drive.

He waited for a good three to four minutes, crouched

by the window, listening for the sound of anyone left below them. Nothing. Not a movement nor a word.

'Flicka,' he called gently. 'Flicka. I'm free and . . .'

'And they've gone. I heard. What the hell's happening?'

'Well, we're alive, so I'm going to see if they've left anyone behind.' He went over to the door, tried the handle, felt slight movement against the flimsy lock then stepped back and kicked. Once. Twice. On the third kick the woodwork around the lock splintered and the door swung back.

A slight glimmer from the dawn was starting to filter into windows below. The candles had been extinguished, so he waited until his eyes adjusted to the darkness before making his way along the passage to the stairs, then down to the second floor landing, with its long balustrade leading to the main staircase and the hall.

In the hallway the front door had been left open, blowing a chilling wind into the shell that was the house. Some debris, papers or leaves, flicked through the door, making a scratchy sound on the quarry tiled entrance.

In the hall, by the foot of the stairs, he saw something small, hunched and black, which, at first, he thought was a cat or, worse still, a large rat. He kicked out in a reflex and to his surprise the object skittered along the floor, hitting the skirting board with a dull thud and the sound of a bell. It was an old telephone, still attached to the wall.

He lifted the receiver, expecting nothing and almost jumped with fright as he heard the dialing tone. Automatically he dialed the contact number. It was a female back at the distant end.

'Brother James,' he said, hearing the rasp of his dry throat and realizing that he was out of breath.

'Give me the answer to question three, Brother James.'

Obviously nobody back in London was taking any chances. Before leaving for Cambridge they had been through the usual list of word codes and what they liked to call telephone security. Bond viewed all this with a certain amount of cynicism, but he dragged the correct word out of his memory.

'Just hold one moment, sir.'

'James?' It was the voice of Bill Tanner, M's former Chief of Staff who was now officially the Secretary of MicroGlobe One. 'James, where the hell are you?'

'I haven't got a clue. You'll have to do a trace. It's somewhere the other side of Stansted Airport. Not certain of the exact location. Old Victorian property falling to pieces. I think it probably belongs to the Tarns because they've just left here.'

'They can't have done.' Tanner sounded almost shocked.

'Well, put a trace on this damned telephone.'

'Yes, we're doing that.'

'And why can't the Tarns have just left here?'

'Because,' Bill Tanner said slowly, 'they were killed in a car accident just outside Cambridge last night. I've seen the bodies myself. Sir Max, Lady Trish and their driver.'

'You've *seen* the bodies?'

'What's left of them. Burned out of recognition, but it couldn't have been anyone else.'

Behind him, Bond could hear Flicka calling out from upstairs. In the creaking darkness of the old building her voice echoed shrill, leaving behind it the wail of a banshee.

8

Boxwood

'SO, NOBODY ACTUALLY saw the accident?' Bond looked up from the pile of grisly photographs which lay on the table before him. Weak late afternoon sunshine slanted through the window and across the highly polished table, around which the members of MicroGlobe One were seated. They were back where things had started, in the reading room at the Home Office, with the events of the previous day lingering uncomfortably in everyone's mind.

Two police cars and a further three vehicles used by the Security Service had arrived at the house within fifteen minutes of Bond's conversation with Bill Tanner. Only later did they discover that the property – Hall's Manor – was a crumbling relic of better days, five miles south of the village of Hope End.

Originally built by a mid-Victorian businessman, Sir Brent Hall known for Hall's Peerless Pills – a useless placebo which made him a fortune by shrewd advertising and a society that would take anything for minor ailments – the rambling house was locally thought of not only as a 'Folly' but also a place of hauntings. People in nearby villages usually steered well clear and recently there had been stories of lights in the night, and other forms of ghostly activity.

The Hall family had followed in the path of so many

similar self-made Victorian clans who had struck it rich with a good-selling contrivance. The Halls, they said, had gone from rags to genteel poverty in three generations, leaving the dilapidated Manor as a huge, quite useless blot on the landscape. Any sale of the land was now blocked by a mad old relative who lived in a home for ladies in reduced circumstances while she clung to the dream that Hall's Manor would one day be great again.

Flicka – usually unshakable – was almost in a state of nervous exhaustion when the rescuers arrived, and was taken to the nearest hospital for a couple of hours to wait while Bond had his wrist dressed and attended to.

Bill Tanner arranged for the Saab to be driven to the hospital and they continued their journey back to London where they lunched well, returning to the flat off the King's Road to rest and recover.

By the evening, they were restored enough to take a short walk to one of their favorite restaurants, after which they retired to bed and slept, holding each other close, for almost twelve hours. Eventually they were woken by the telephone call which summoned both of them to a full meeting and briefing on the situation.

Over a late breakfast, they went through the papers. Sir Max had certainly made the headlines – **Tycoon and Wife Killed in Horror Car Crash! Accident Claims Lives of Philanthropist and Wife**. Prominence was also given to the fact that, within hours of his death, Tarn's headquarters near Ludgate Circus, and his Chelsea home, had been raided by police officers – including members of the anti-terrorist and bomb squads, as well as officers from the fraud squad and security experts.

Bond was almost immediately on the telephone to his Bedford Square office, knowing that the 'security experts' would be members of his own Two Zeros Section.

Before they left for their assignation with The Committee, he made certain that his four best people, two men and two women, had been assigned to the project.

The Minister opened the proceedings – 'Now that the warrants have been acted upon and we seem to be in a paper maze, it would be best that the Double-O Section takes over the entire investigation.' So Bond was able to tell him that he had personally appointed members of his group to liaise with the other agencies.

The complete membership of The Committee was present, including Bill Tanner who, as Secretary, was rarely required, for his job with MicroGlobe One was really a behind-the-scenes position, as organizer and head of liaison. It was to Tanner that Bond was speaking now, for his old friend had been in charge of co-ordination with the Security Service's surveillance teams in Cambridge.

'As I said, nobody actually saw the accident. So, will you go over events again, Bill, just to humor me?'

Tanner smiled bleakly. Things, he said, had not gone well from the start. The surveillance teams had been unable to tap into both incoming and outgoing telephone calls. 'Tarn seemed to be using some very sophisticated electronics,' he told Bond who recalled Maurice Goodwin's boast about 'People who'd like to listen in to our telephone conversations – though they can't because we tend to by-pass the switchboard.'

'It was only after the sudden departure last night that we managed to steal a peep from them,' Tanner admitted. 'Even then it was some chatter between two of the cars. They were heading for Duxford airfield, we thought that was probable, but they were staying off the Motorway, taking side roads, going by the villages. As you know, some of those minor roads are dangerously narrow.'

The surveillance teams had Sir Max's party well boxed

in. The Rolls was being led by one of the Rovers, and Bill Tanner's people were able to drive well in front, with another party staying back about a mile.

'We were checking out Duxford. Wondering if Tarn's corporate jet had landed there, which was unlikely, and, in the event, it hadn't. Our people who were following got the first hint that something was wrong. When the accident occurred, there was a trail of flame and smoke which could be seen from the Motorway itself.'

The police, by this time on the Tuesday afternoon, had put things together, and their findings lay next to the photographs. The Rover, ahead of the Tarns' Rolls, had disappeared, but the Rolls itself had been in a head-on collision with a heavy tanker which had no business being on that particular secondary road anyway. The driver of the tanker, together with the Tarns and their driver, had probably died instantly, their bodies consumed by the flames which followed the impact.

'As I told you before, James, the damned tanker was carrying highly flammable jet fuel. It was the tanker that exploded. Probably engulfed the Rolls in a matter of seconds.'

Bond turned back to the photographs which showed the Rolls as a skeleton of twisted, burned metal, concertina'd into the cab of the tanker which had been reduced to a similar skeletal wreck. The road, they said, had been closed for almost six hours.

In the next set of photographs what was left of the four victims had been laid out in the mortuary at Addenbrooke's Hospital, Cambridge: unrecognizable charred remains, each in the grotesque boxer's position that is assumed by the human body after death by burning. The only real evidence was that three of these terrible black mounds had once unmistakably been males, the fourth was a female.

'What about identification?' Bond asked.

'James, you know as well as I that the old dental records are really for the thriller writers. You can seldom get hold of them, but we're running DNAs on all four bodies, using traces of hair and the like, taken from the Tarns' home as comparisons. A week, maybe ten days for solid proof. The only things we have to go on are the remains of a necklace identified as having been worn by Trish Tarn, and what's left of a Rolex that could have belonged to Sir Max.'

'But *we* know that the bodies can't belong to them – at least Sir Max's can't.' Bond looked straight into Tanner's eyes and saw his old friend look away. 'So,' he continued, 'none of you are going to take us seriously. You have bodies removed from the Rolls and the tanker. *I* have my own eyes and ears. At least Max Tarn was still alive early yesterday morning and was there at Hall's Manor. Now, let's go through the possibilities. You maintain that only the Tarns and their driver occupied the Rolls, so how many people were crammed into the Rover?'

Tanner repeated his earlier statement that, when it left the University Arms, the Rover contained a driver by the name of Hawkins; Maurice Goodwin; the man they called Connie – in fact identified as Conrad Anthony Spicer – Lady Tarn's maid, a girl called Susan Fawkes; and Tarn's valet, George Drum.

Bond went through the information they had on these five members of the entourage.

As far as they could see, Maurice Goodwin was employed as Tarn's fixer. He had overall control of the security, and also dealt with mundane matters like travel arrangements, hotels – when they were used – and the general running of Sir Max and Lady Tarn's lives outside business.

'I've a shrewd suspicion that he was deeply into the daily running of Tarn International as well,' Bond had told them when they first went through the list. 'He seems to be on pretty close terms with Tarn. While I was with them he talked to Sir Max as an equal. A partner even.'

The Police Commissioner, Wimsey, told them that there was 'Nothing known' – as the police computers showed – regarding either Goodwin or the driver, Hawkins, while the maid and valet were also simply ciphers. Conrad Spicer was another matter entirely: personal bodyguard, probably with control over other 'muscle' employed by Tarn International. Connie Spicer had a record which included one short prison sentence for GBH – Grievous Bodily Harm – and another charge concerning firearms of which he had been acquitted. His past, however, included a military background with several years spent with the Special Air Service. He had even received a citation for bravery during the Falklands campaign.

'Alright.' Bond leaned back in his chair. 'I'll tell you again. Flicka and I were placed in the dangerous position of being prisoners of some of Tarn's other bodyguards. A precious pair who called each other Mr Cuthbert and Mr Archibald. Anything known there?' His question was directed at Wimsey who shook his head and deflected the query towards Tanner.

'They are fully described by the surveillance teams. We even have photographs, but there's absolutely no other information, and I have to ask you, James, if this could have been a personal matter. You *did* have a run in with Archibald when you arrived at the University Arms. We've even got that on tape. A slight case of overkill we thought.'

'Not from where I was standing. The little twerp was being officious, trying to stop me going about my business. If you have a soundtrack on the video, you'll also know that he threatened me and even presented himself as official security – which he was not.'

'So you would deny what happened on Sunday afternoon and early evening being in any way a personal thing?'

'Absolutely, and I suggest you question Flicka to back me up. They left us in no doubt that they were acting on Tarn's instructions. Personally, I think those two jokers – and they *are* very weird people – believed that they were going to be ordered to kill us and dispose of the bodies at Hall's Manor. Now, by the end of Sunday, and in the early hours of Monday morning, *I* saw or heard the following people: Cuthbert and Archibald, one driver whose name was never mentioned, a tall, long-haired girl called Beth, Maurice Goodwin, and Max Tarn. I am simply presuming that Lady Tarn was also in the Rover which arrived at the Manor in the early hours. Cuthbert, in particular, was very annoyed that they were just going to leave us there. I was not drugged, I had managed to get free, damaging myself as I did so.' He lifted his right wrist. 'But I *do* know what I saw and heard. You, on the other hand, received no reports on either of the two Rovers.'

Tanner shrugged, giving a slightly grudging, 'No.'

'Yet police and the other surveillance people were on the look-out for both cars?'

'Yes.'

'Which leaves us with one possibility.' He leafed through the papers in front of him. 'It would seem that Lady Tarn's maid, the Fawkes woman, and Sir Max's valet were of a similar build and stature to their employers.'

'We'd have to agree with that, yes.' Tanner's face showed that he did not like the direction Bond was taking. 'I can tell what you're going to suggest, James, but can you really believe that someone like Tarn could be so ruthless?'

'Yes. Out of the blue he's suddenly in deep trouble. If M's informant, what was his name? Peter Dolmech . . . ?'

M nodded, but contributed nothing to the conversation.

'If Peter Dolmech is correct, friend Tarn, captain of industry, pillar of the community, philanthropist extraordinary, was about to have the rug pulled out from under him. If Dolmech is right, the man's conscience hasn't stopped him from dealing in death – smuggling arms and explosives. When I dropped the news on him, Tarn was incredibly calm: really extraordinarily cool under fire, though Goodwin appeared to be more shaken. I don't see a man like Tarn thinking twice about doing what I'm going to suggest . . .'

'And you're suggesting that he's faked his own death, together with the death of his wife.'

'In fact, he's murdered four people – Lady Tarn's maid, his valet and two drivers.' This from Wimsey.

'Exactly. Anything known about the tanker driver?'

There was a long, tense silence at the end of which Claude Wimsey shook his head. 'Tell you the truth, Bond, we don't even know where the tanker was coming from, or even if it belongs to some local firm operating out of Duxford airfield.'

'So doesn't this convince you?' Bond was appealing to the entire committee. 'I followed your instructions; tipped him off that he was about to be arrested on illicit arms dealing, and that the headquarters of Tarn International was about to be searched. Object – your idea – was to flush him out; con the Press and pick him off as he tried to get rid of evidence. Instead, he puts together a very quick plan to turn up dead and unidentifiable. Doesn't any of that make sense to you?'

'Far too much sense.' The Minister glanced towards M who nodded and turned to Bond.

'James, the fact is that I suppose we really didn't want to hear any of this. I know you well enough to believe everything you say. You've outlined a distinct possibility. Now, what's your gut instinct about Tarn's movements after he picked up the three people from Hall's Manor?'

'They were very close to Stansted, sir. I heard one of them, Goodwin I think, say they didn't have much time. An educated guess would be that they flew out of Stansted within an hour of leaving Flicka and myself.'

Commissioner Wimsey rose from the table. 'I'll get my people to go through private departures from Stansted yesterday morning. We're looking at what? Eight passengers?'

'Nine, I fear.' M looked grave and miserable. 'I've kept in touch with your squads at Tarn International HQ and at his private house. Nobody's seen hide nor hair of Peter Dolmech. It's very much on the cards that he's been spirited away. Or worse.'

The Police Commissioner left the room, and there was a short silence before the Minister spoke. 'Captain Bond, it would seem that you are basically in overall charge now. I'll see to it that the police work closely with the Doùble-O Section. Our only hope is that you can sort your way through the paper chase. If Wimsey comes up with further firm evidence that Tarn may be alive, we'll naturally alert everyone, from Interpol to agents of the Secret Intelligence Service, to go on an offensive look-out for him. Now, is there anything else you need?'

'I'd like to know a little more about the two clowns,

Cuthbert and Archie, and try to pin down the identity of the girl they called Beth. It wouldn't be a bad idea to find out if one of Tarn's companies has acquired Hall's Manor as well. Someone mentioned that the locals have kept clear because of lights and activity in recent weeks. If Tarn has some right to use the building, he certainly wouldn't simply bring it into play for his plan to turn up dead. The place is too close to Stansted for my liking.'

He was about to continue when Wimsey returned, his face a mask of anger. 'Bad news, I fear. A corporate jet, belonging to a company called *Rendrag Associates*. There's no such company, of course, and the aircraft livery looked as though it had just been done. Also the descriptions fit and they had filed a flightplan to Paris, Charles de Gaulle, but there are indications that this was not their final destination. I have people working on it.' He sat down, took a deep breath and tried to control his anger. Eventually – 'I'm sorry. This should not have happened. My people've slipped up badly.'

The Minister opened his mouth to speak, but the one telephone, which sat in front of him, purred softly. He picked up the instrument and spoke into it quietly – barely a whisper. Almost immediately his eyes lifted, glancing across towards M.

'He's here. One moment.' A hand covered the phone as he told M it was for him. 'Urgent,' he added, holding out the handset.

M grunted into the telephone, then became suddenly alert. 'You're absolutely certain it was Boxwood? . . . And the voice print is a match? . . . Good . . . Yes . . . Yes, have it sent over immediately, with an armed guard . . . No, No, I am *not* joking. When I say an armed guard I mean it. The Chief of Staff will be outside to pick it up from you. Yes. Now.' He replaced the handset and, before saying anything else, looked at Tanner. 'Get downstairs, Chief of Staff. The DO's sending a small packet over. We need it here, and we need it now.'

Without a word, Tanner rose and left the room.

'I presume we have such a thing as an audio cassette player in this building?' He addressed nobody in particular, but the Minister nodded. 'What . . . ?' he began, but M was already addressing the entire committee.

'It seems that my man Peter Dolmech has surfaced. We have a secure line with voice analysis and a number of other technical wonders built in. Dolmech left a message on the tape about half-an-hour ago. My duty officer has had it unscrambled and it's undoubtedly Dolmech. His code name is Boxwood and the DO says the message is ultra urgent.'

The Minister excused himself from the room while he personally went in search of an audio player. Nobody spoke, even after he returned with a sophisticated piece of electronics. After that, the conversation remained at a minimum until Bill Tanner came back carrying a small cassette box encased in metal.

M slipped the tape into the machine, adjusted the controls and asked that nobody speak until the tape had been played at least once.

The voice was controlled, pitched low, but its owner spoke with confidence:

'This is Boxwood,' he began. 'I don't think I have long, but what I have for you is of the utmost importance. You may be under the impression that our mutual friend Morgan is dead. He's not, neither is his lady. We're at a villa he owns in the hills above Seville. We flew into Paris and then on to Spain early yesterday morning, and I'm obviously under a certain amount of control. Two of the party are watching me quite closely, though they're not difficult to evade. I have all the papers you'll need to get at the heart of the evidence. I can get away with ease tomorrow, and will be in the Jardines del Alcázar at midday precisely. I shall be wearing jeans, a denim shirt and jacket, and will carry a satchel over my right shoulder if the coast is clear. If things are difficult, it'll be over my left shoulder. I'd suggest that you pick me up, by car or motorcycle, from the street known as San Fernando. I'll expect somebody carrying a copy of tomorrow's *Financial Times* using the same signals as myself: right hand okay; left hand uncertain. If you can pick me up, all well and good. If anything goes wrong, get the satchel at all costs. From what I've overheard we are only going to be here for two days so we have only one shot. I'm not going to pinpoint the villa for you because any assault would be very dangerous. Also you need what I have in order to unlock the doors to Morgan's secrets. Tomorrow. Midday.' There was an audible click on the tape as Dolmech hung up somewhere near Seville.

'Admiral?' The Minister was giving the floor to M.

'As I said, Boxwood is Peter Dolmech, and he knows more than anyone about Tarn's dealings. Morgan is Tarn. We thought an old pirate's name was acceptable. Now, there's only one answer to this.' M's eyes scanned each member of the committee, settling finally on Bond and Flicka von Grüsse. 'As much as we want Max Tarn behind bars, our first loyalty must be to Peter Dolmech. Without him we might have months of work ahead. I'll see to it that a team of my best people fly out to Seville tonight.'

'Sir,' sharp and uncompromising from Bond.

'Forget about it, Captain Bond.' M's face became granite hard and his eyes appeared to change to the color of pewter. 'They know who you are. You and Ms von Grüsse both.'

'With luck, Tarn and his people'll never see us, sir. I'm simply requesting that we pick up Dolmech for you. I'll make a plea for going after Tarn later. I think he's our due. He's mine to hunt and kill if necessary. This is a sideshow that Fräulein von Grüsse and I can do standing on our heads.'

The long pause was finally broken by M. 'Be it on your own heads, then. If you fail, Bond, I'll see you out of the service for good. Understand?'

9

Cradle of History

THE GIRLS FROM the Seville Flamenco School presented a unique splash of color, their long skirts lifting and whirling as they danced on top of the *tablao* – the slightly raised platform – which had been set up some fifty yards into the Alcázar Gardens. There were two guitarists, and the four girls who danced gave a counter rhythm with castanets and stamping of feet, while one of the guitarists broke into an occasional *jaleos*, those guttural shouts of encouragement which are always a part of a *juerga* – a carousal or spree of singing and dancing.

Juergas are held regularly in the open air during the Spring and Summer in Seville. The distinctive melodies and chords, the almost aggressive beat of the dancers' feet with the counterpoint of clapping, together with the traditional movements, some stylized, others spontaneous, made an essentially Spanish scene come alive for locals and tourists alike, who crowded the gardens.

The whole was a mix of music handed down, rendered, borrowed, and developed from traditions which had their sources in Greek, Carthaginian, Roman and Byzantine musical systems to form the throbbing, colorful and exciting art of flamenco.

Looking out to the back of the palace that was the Alcázar, and the huge Cathedral, just visible behind it, eyes and ears were stunned by the music, the sensual beauty of the movement, and the almost overpowering backdrop of massive architecture which was a blend of Moorish and the distinctive conventions of Iberia. The mixture was enough to seduce anyone into a love of this part of Spain.

Men and women, like those engaged in the *juerga*, had been performing like this for centuries, for Seville and its surrounding area are the cradle of many civilizations. Carved on the famous Jerez Gate, close by the Alcázar Palace, are the words *Hercules built me, Caesar surrounded me with walls and towers; the King Saint took me*. Earlier that morning, Flicka and Bond had looked up at the Gate, walked through both the Cathedral and the Alcázar Palace and drunk in the sense of history which shows in both architecture, setting, and even in the faces of the people of this melting pot of Europe.

Though the sky was a light, cloudless blue, the sun was still thin and there was a chill in the air. In a month or two the heat would be strong and unrelenting, but now – at around ten minutes to noon – Bond was glad of the motorcycle leathers he wore as he sat at an outside table in front of a small bar looking out across the Alcázar Gardens, a glass of rough Spanish brandy in front of him.

They had come in via Gibraltar, courtesy of a Royal Air Force jet from Northolt, on the previous evening. Two dark-skinned men, who spoke Spanish with the accents of Andalucia, and an English so faultless that it was difficult to determine their true origin, had driven them across the frontier. Then they headed up the coast to Seville, depositing Bond and Flicka at a small apartment where a third man, together with a silent suspicious-looking woman, waited to make sure they had all they needed: food, drink and the other essential items for the pick-up due to take place at noon on this, the following day.

On the aircraft they had both studied detailed street maps of Seville, and marked out the route Bond would take once Dolmech had been lifted. Now, they would have time to organize the final stages of that journey: a route which would bring Bond and the rescued Dolmech back to the apartment.

The man and woman at what was so obviously a safe house, checked that the motorcycle leathers and helmet were right for Bond, showed him where the big Triumph Daytona was hidden, in a small lock-up three minutes' walk from the apartment, and did not leave until they were satisfied that the plan for the following day was timed to the second. M had insisted that some of his other people were around to act as back-up. Bond did not recognize any of them from his past long experience in the service, but he *did* recognize the type: people bound by the silence of secrecy, and dedicated to seeing that a dangerous job was carried out with no hitches. If anything were to go wrong, the fault would not lie on the consciences of those who planned the operation.

For the first time in months, Bond had been given his 9 mm Browning ASP and six magazines of ammunition, while Flicka was armed with a smaller, though equally deadly, Beretta automatic – her weapon of choice for the mission. In the early hours of the morning, they sat in the small apartment, stripped the weapons, checked and re-checked them, then, holding each other, drifted off into shallow sleep.

The silent woman had returned at five-thirty in the morning, gently wakening them, preparing coffee, newly-baked rolls with butter. They hardly spoke to one another as they ate, or later as they walked through the town, taking in the main vantage points around the Alcázar

Gardens, and the streets that twisted around the area.

Now, as the hands of his watch moved nearer to midday, Bond tossed some currency onto the table and walked away, turning left into the street around the corner from the café. He had timed it earlier: exactly two minutes to get from the café to the Daytona, draw on his gloves and settle the helmet and visor on his head. He swung into the saddle, kicked the engine into life, and felt the immense power begin to rumble under him, his hand on the throttle, twisting and running the engine in short, noisy bursts. No wonder people who rode these beasts all the time became addicted, he considered. Finally he checked that the automatic pistol was in place and could be reached easily if necessary before knocking away the bike's stand and slowly pulling up to the street that led into the San Fernando. Across the road he caught a glimpse of Flicka moving purposefully towards his left, her shoulderbag held in her right hand, together with a copy of the *Financial Times*. Dolmech had arrived.

He swung the bike out onto the street, filtering into the traffic going right. There was a large roundabout some twenty yards down, and this allowed him to turn full circle, bringing him back into San Fernando, so that he could stop on the right hand side, within feet of Flicka. He negotiated the roundabout, and thirty yards away, he saw Dolmech break from the crowded Gardens walking casually towards her. He was dressed exactly as promised: blue jeans, denim shirt and jacket, the heavy leather satchel hanging almost carelessly over his right shoulder.

Bond pulled over, glancing in his mirror to the right, then left. It was as his eyes flicked over to the left that he saw the other bike. It was a Harley Davidson, but with a pillion passenger. He cursed as there was no way he could cut it off as it came roaring up behind him, swinging and passing close enough for him to feel a slipstream that had him momentarily fighting for balance.

Everything, from that moment, seemed to happen in slow motion. Bond had been alerted by the second bike, but did not completely take in the danger. As he straightened his motorcycle, he was aware of the Harley picking up a burst of speed, cutting in front of him, slewing to the right, causing him to brake violently.

He saw the back of the second bike and watched helplessly as it shot ahead, pulling over to slow slightly right in front of Flicka and Dolmech. Then the pillion passenger reached out, a small black shape in his gloved hand. Later Bond could have sworn he heard the three loud pops. He certainly saw the driver flick his hand out and grab at the satchel as Peter Dolmech was whipped backwards by three bullets, his head disappearing in a fine mist of scarlet as the bullets caught him in the face. He saw Flicka's eyes and mouth, a dreadful carving of horror. The mouth frozen open in a scream of anger, her eyes wide, flaring; he saw her reach for the gun in her shoulderbag and turn sideways as though she expected to feel bullets penetrating her own flesh.

He was powerless, and thought that she had also been hit as the crimson cloud appeared to float over her, producing great red blotches of blood and matter across her face; but, by the time she had the weapon half out of her shoulderbag, the motorcycle was roaring away, weaving through the traffic.

The Daytona under him leaped forward as his hand opened the throttle: at least, he knew that this bike was more agile than the Harley. Whatever else had happened, the only thought now filling his mind was the recovery of the satchel.

In the heavy traffic which clogged the streets of inner

Seville, he only managed an occasional glimpse of the bike carrying the two men. To keep up speed and follow them demanded all the concentration he could muster. The Daytona handled perfectly, and he was able to weave and dodge through the thick, slow-moving crush of cars and trucks which seemed to stretch in an endless snake. Bond leaned to left and right, slaloming through narrow gaps, behind vehicles which seemed to be bumper to bumper. His one concern was to get as near to the other motorcycle as possible. If he had been running their operation, the passenger would already have left the bike and spirited the satchel away on foot, but as he managed to get closer, he was relieved to see that both men were still on the machine. They were also heading away from the city center, out towards the perimeter of the ancient walls. Within fifteen minutes they were almost free of the city streets, bearing out into the open countryside where the flow of motor vehicles was steadier.

He was now about half-a-mile behind his quarry, and thought that far away behind him he heard the wail of a police siren. By this time he was touching speeds of just under a hundred miles an hour, which meant that the bike he was chasing was reaching a speed well in excess of the ton. It flashed through his mind that, with a passenger up, the torque on the machine must at times reach a dangerous level.

As it was, Bond could feel the forces of gravity on his own bike and upon himself. While it was exhilarating, there were moments when the wheels hit small indentations which caused the bike to lift and bounce. Even with the helmet and visor, his body was, at times, pressed back in the saddle, and he found his brain making decisions well in advance of reaching other traffic.

They hit a long incline. He could hear and feel the first

strain on the engine, so changed down quickly, opening up the throttle again to maintain speed. Slowly, he realized, he was beginning to gain on his opponent.

They were on a three lane highway now with no oncoming traffic, the main hazard being cars and trucks that did not bother to signal when changing lanes. The speed and power were exhilarating, and he had to focus his concentration, constantly dragging his mind back to the Harley now only a couple of hundred yards in front of him.

Without warning, he saw the bike suddenly veer off to the right, rider and passenger leaning over as the machine took a forty-five degree angle, then righted itself and shot across the oncoming traffic, disappearing down a sliproad.

Bond signalled and saw a large heavy van moving to the left behind him. He opened the throttle wide, leaned with the tilt as the Daytona began to angle over, heard the rasping horn of the van as it braked when he crossed directly in front of it to get into the far right lane. The exit came up very fast and he felt the rear wheel begin to lose traction swinging outwards. He changed down, tapped the brake and hauled the bike back to the straight and level as he shot into the exit.

Now he knew where they were heading, for he caught a glimpse of the green and white sign which said **Itálica**. They were going into the very womb of the Roman Empire, the remains of the large Roman town where both the Emperors Hadrian and Trajan had been born. Ahead was a ticket point with a large notice in four languages saying the ruins were closed. He also saw the brake lights of the Harley as it whipped through the entrance, dipped and headed up the path leading to the sprawl of skeleton buildings rising up the hillside. A great view to his right, and, slightly ahead, the steep slope which, like a bowl in the earth, contained the remains of Itálica's amphitheatre. He was chasing a pair of modern murderers into one of Europe's examples of the cradle of history.

Once more Bond opened the throttle in an attempt to get even closer, but this was no place for speed. He saw the bike slew to the left, down what had once been a narrow cobbled street, but when he reached the turn there was no sign of his prey. He throttled back so that the bike was just ticking over, straining in the saddle to try and catch the sound of their engine, but the world had suddenly gone silent and his mind sprang forward, latching on to the worst possibility – that the couple on the Harley had a prearranged meeting here in the shadow of what had once been a thriving Roman community. If that was the case, he had lost, so might just as well get out now and save what was left.

He reminded himself that he had never given up on an assignment yet, reaching inside the leather jacket to slowly remove the ASP and one spare magazine. He switched off the Daytona's engine, then, with his back against the old dry and crumbling wall of what remained of the buildings, he inched forward, instinctively feeling that he was being watched.

It was some twenty yards to the end of the street. The first shot came as he reached the point where the cobbles ended and the remains of the buildings ran into what was virtually a T-junction. He heard the crack as the bullet hit the stone just to the left of his head, gouging a small crater, splaying dust which fell across his visor.

He ducked to the right, flicking the visor up and jumping into the ruined street that formed the crosspiece of the T, fanning his hands in a wide circle, gripping the butt of the pistol a shade too tightly.

There was movement to his left and he reacted,

swinging his body in that direction without moving his feet, squeezing off the standard two shots. The figure was too quick for him, ducking back down an alley before the first bullet struck the wall where, a split second earlier, the man had been standing.

He turned again, knowing that the two men were trying to circle him, coming in a pincer movement. Sweeping his hands from left to right, back hard against the stone, he whirled in the direction of the target he had just missed. As he wheeled to his left a second time, something moved in the periphery of his vision. This time he was faster; hands coming up to a firing position, and centering the guttersnipe sight of the ASP on the black-clad figure's chest.

The two rounds he fired both slammed into the target, ripping at the leather, sending a sickening gout of blood and viscous matter into the wall behind him. Now the odds had evened.

He turned left again, reached the junction where a line of uneven ruins made another rough street, parallel to the one in which he had left the Daytona. For a second his mind drifted and he felt that he was among ghosts, the men, women and children who had once peopled this place; laughing, arguing, loving and dying. Taking a deep breath he moved, stepping out cleanly, in a firing position, ready to take out anything that lay in his path.

The street was empty, but he could see that the man he stalked might easily be crouched within one of the undulating, fragmented buildings. The ground under his feet began to angle down. For a second he looked past the end of this row of bleached masonry and saw the beginning of the fantastic view which looked out right across the Guadalquivir Plain. This one lapse of attention almost cost him his life for this time two bullets came from the left, shattering the stillness and hitting the old stonework to ricochet with a deadly whine within inches of his face.

He returned the fire, shooting only in the general direction from which it had come. In the quiet that followed he could hear the thudding of boots moving away from the clumps of stone.

He took off down what was left of the street, changing magazines as he did so, feeling a terrible draught of frustration as a motorcycle engine burst into life from nearby. The second killer had got to his – Bond's – machine, and he hurtled down the slight hill, pistol still in both hands as he came out on the edge of the ruins. He saw the motorbike moving slowly to his left, disappearing from view, towards the plain which stretched below.

As he reached the open he saw it again, rushing down a grassy slope, heading straight for the remains of the town's amphitheater, now an irregular oval of stone benches, with the big acting area far below. The Daytona was bumping almost casually down what had once been an aisle leading through the seating, the rider trying desperately to put on speed, but braking constantly to keep balance on the sheer angle of the hillside.

It was a long shot for a pistol, but his hands were steady as he brought the sights to bear. Later he realized that he must have fired off practically a whole magazine of ammunition. He felt the weapon jumping in his hands and saw the little explosions of dust around the motorbike, then the two shots which caught its rider in the back, lifting him into the air and returning him to the saddle, his body slumping over the handlebars. As the Daytona slewed to one side, now out of control, Bond reflexed, putting two more shots in the vicinity of the target.

The rider was still actually on the bike as it toppled over, the leather strap of the satchel slung across him over the right shoulder so that the pouch rested against his left hip as the bike and body slid in a long jarring skid down into the acting area of the amphitheater.

It was Bond's last shot that hit the petrol tank.

He saw the flame dance from the bike, before he heard the roar of the explosion. The fire seemed to flicker and then rise, enveloping machine, rider and the satchel he carried, in what looked like an unquenchable blossom of flame.

Bond leaped forward, running at full tilt, down through one of the aisles towards the disaster – here, where hundreds of people had laughed and cried at the crude translations of the Greek classical theater, and the more robust and ribald offerings of the Roman plays, he imagined that he could hear cries urging him on. By the time he got to the furnace bursting around the motorcycle, devouring its last rider, he realized that the cries were real, but they came from Spanish police officers, ringing the edge of the bowl above him.

The smell of burning flesh wrapped around his nostrils as he plunged a gloved hand into the fire and pulled at the blackened satchel which was just about to be eaten by the flames.

10

Cathy and Anna

IN SPITE OF the arrangements that had been made between MicroGlobe One and the Spanish authorities, there were a lot of questions to be answered. There were no less than six police cars, several motorcycle officers, and two ambulances parked in the area that usually contained the cars of visitors.

The police showed little respect, and immediately treated Bond as though he were a renegade villain, despite him telling them that they should get in touch with certain senior Spanish intelligence officers whose names he carried in his head. Even though he argued, they removed the blackened satchel saying that this could be used as evidence. As for the ASP automatic pistol, it was wrested from him and treated as if it were Jack the Ripper's original knife.

Back in Seville, they took him to the main police station, where he found Flicka, sitting, silent, in an interrogation room, and, for the next hour, they were both subjected to hostile questions from two plainclothes men who smoked filthy Spanish cigarettes throughout.

Finally the inquisitors left the pair of them alone – almost too obviously in the hope that they would incriminate each other in a conversation which was being recorded – sound and video – for posterity.

During the interrogation, Bond had asked Flicka – on several occasions – if she had told them to call in the officers in command of their security and intelligence services. She said she had, but did not know what had been done about it. Apart from that, their answers had been of the name, rank and number style.

Flicka seemed to be in deep despair, and the usual glint in her eye, and her sense of humor had been severely blunted. She was concerned about what had happened, so, because of the listening devices, Bond told her just enough to make her at least smile and nod with relief that he had retrieved the satchel.

'Mind you, I don't know what condition it's in,' he said. 'The outside's burned pretty badly, but I think I got to it before the papers were damaged. I just hope these people aren't fiddling with it.'

She went through the trauma of Dolmech's death again, slowly repeating her description of what had happened, as though trying to come to terms with it. He leaned across the bare table and took her hand in both of his. 'He was set up, poor devil.' He looked into her eyes, saw the pain and anger, so added, 'We were all set up.'

'Easy to say after the event.'

'I know, but we'll get the bastard.'

Half-an-hour later things changed. First, a smiling policeman came in with coffee and sandwiches. He was followed by a senior officer who made what just stopped short of being a formal apology. Within the hour, two senior officers in plain clothes arrived. They spoke to Bond and Flicka in helpful, pleasant tones, returned Bond's ASP and Flicka's Beretta. Then, finally, they gave back the satchel, encased in a plastic bag, and said they were free to leave.

Outside, the two men who had picked them up on the

previous night, were waiting with a car. They drove back
to Gibraltar, pausing for a mirthless and silent meal on the
way. There were no customs or immigration formalities at
La Linea and they drove straight to the airport. An RAF
transport took them to Lynham, where a car waited to
shuttle them up to London.

They drove first to the office, where two of the Two
Zeroes staff had been instructed to take the satchel
directly to a member of MicroGlobe One. By one in the
morning they were back in the flat. Immediately, Bond
stretched out on the bed.

'What a damned tiring and frustrating day.' He let out a
deep sigh, and Flicka, who was fast recovering from her
depression, came towards him, kissed him gently then
gave him a little loving bite on the lip.

'Not all that tiring, James darling. I hope not *that*
tiring.'

'Ah,' he smiled. 'No, never *that* tiring.'

During the following week, they suddenly appeared to be
in business at the office in Bedford Square. Memos and
instructions began to filter down from on high. Documents, obviously from the contents of Dolmech's satchel,
were being brought over by special messenger, and the
Double-O staff began to follow paper trails from the many
boxes of files, computer disks and tapes which had been
taken from the main offices of Tarn International.

Flicka spent every waking hour poring over the computers, which were her specialty, and slowly they started to
make sense out of Tarn's many business dealings. Most of
it was old-time arms dealing, but with the help given to
them by Peter Dolmech, who had been brought back to
England for burial – which Bond was strictly forbidden to
attend – they started to see exactly to what lengths the

multi-millionaire was prepared to go in supplying buyers with the latest in arms and military matériel. This was not a small business, running little loads of Semtex, or M16s to the IRA, but an operation on a huge scale. Aircraft to Libya, tanks and missiles to Iran and Iraq, a plethora of shady deals throughout the Middle East, specialist equipment to just about every known terrorist group in the world. Tarn had been, literally, the Quartermaster to countries on which there was an embargo, and to major terrorist groups. Some of the items were more than worrying – plutonium, unaccounted for, to North Korea and China; surface to air missiles to terrorists who had long claimed that they would soon be capable of bringing down commercial airliners at the major airports of the world, including Kennedy and Heathrow.

The evidence built very quickly once members of the Section were provided with the leads from Dolmech, but, in spite of the urgency, Bond found himself getting fidgety and irritated. It was nothing new, for this feeling of being trapped within the four walls of an office had been a problem he had borne, with a certain amount of stoicism, throughout the years whenever he had been forced to work out of the service office. He was a man of action, happy only when he was out there in the midst of danger, almost like a person with a death wish.

As the days went by, he wanted nothing more than to be allowed to leave the country and hunt down Tarn, kill him or put him where he could do no more harm. With Tarn still at large, the deals would continue to go down, and he felt strongly that he was shackled to a desk in London instead of being active in the field. There were times when he even contemplated putting himself out to grass and resigning.

Towards the end of the week, Bond took a call from the

Minister's political secretary. 'Sorry to tell you this, sir. But your old Chief has been taken ill. He's at home, and there's a nurse in residence. He has been asking for you, and the Minister would be grateful if you could get away to see him as soon as possible.'

It was noon when he took the call, and Bond immediately made plans to get out of the office. He instructed his new secretary, who rejoiced in the name of Chastity Vain and sported a figure that would give pause to the saintliest of men, telling her that he would be away for the rest of the day. He gave her M's private number in case of any major panic, then left the building, taking the Saab and heading out towards the M4, turning off at the Windsor exit, making for M's home *Quarterdeck* – the beautiful Regency manor house on the edge of Windsor Forest. He stopped off for a pub lunch, and finally arrived at the house just before two-thirty.

His ring – on the famous ship's bell which hung outside the main door – was answered by a nubile nurse who introduced herself somewhat formally as Nurse Frobisher. 'Thank heaven.' She breathed a sigh of relief when he told her his name. 'He's not the best of patients. Should rest all the time but is always working on papers, or making telephone calls. I tried removing the phone yesterday, but had to let him have it back. He works himself up into such states. Come on up. Perhaps you can persuade him to relax. If he doesn't, then I fear he'll not be long for this world.' This last said with a hint of sadness which worried and depressed Bond.

'I have my doubts about that.' He followed her up the stairs to M's bedroom.

His old Chief lay back, propped up by pillows, the bed covered with papers and note pads.

'James, my boy. Thank heaven you've come. I am being

115

driven half mad by interfering women.'

Nurse Frobisher raised her eyebrows and quietly left as M beckoned him over, telling him to sit by the bed.

'I'm swinging the lead a bit, my boy. Doing a bit of poodle-faking, if you want the truth.' Though his speech was bright and strong, the look on his face told a different story. The clear sparkle of his gray eyes had turned dull, and his weatherbeaten face showed signs of strain. Under the tan, which the old man cultivated, there was a paleness that Bond had never seen before, while the skin of his face had started to stretch tightly against his cheekbones.

'Now listen to me.' He hardly paused for breath, 'I know you have no leave due, but I'm wondering if you can persuade that damned Committee to let you take a long week-end. Something's come up that I would entrust to nobody but you – well, maybe you and that nice Swiss girl.'

'I can always creep away without the Committee knowing.'

M frowned, then gave a thin-lipped smile. 'Wouldn't be the first time, eh?'

'I suppose not, sir.'

'Right, let me put you in the picture, then. You already know that we drew a blank in Spain?'

Bond nodded. He had carefully read the eight page memo that dealt with the follow-up to the incident in Seville. With the assistance of the Spanish authorities, they had pinpointed Max Tarn's villa in the hills above the town, but, by the time arrangements had been made to raid the place, the cupboard was bare, and there were signs of an unexpectedly hasty departure.

'Well,' M leaned back against the pillows and the tired look came back into his eyes. 'In the satchel poor Peter

116

Dolmech was carrying there was a short letter addressed to me personally. There's been a delay in it being passed on to me, unhappily. Nowadays things get snarled up. I don't have the same, unquestioned power any more.'

'So I understand, sir. The letter?' He wanted to get to the meat without tiring the old man.

'Mmm,' M stretched out to the night table and took a neatly folded single sheet of paper. 'Read it for yourself.' He handed the paper across the bed.

It was short and to the point—

Dear Admiral,
Just in case I don't make it, a small piece of information has just reached me. It appears that Lady Tarn is not conversant with Sir Max's business, as we know it. I am unaware of her status of enlightenment, but she has left this morning for Jerusalem. I have no details of where she will be staying, but you may recall that, as Trish Nuzzi, she has made frequent visits to Israel, so it is just possible that she may have an apartment in Tel Aviv or Jerusalem. It might be worth while following up on her. I have a vague notion that she sometimes uses an Israeli doctor, though cannot swear to it.

Hope to see you soon.

It was signed, in a neat hand, *Peter*.

Bond handed back the letter. 'You want me to go and take a look-see, sir?'

'I have no real authority to send you, James. By rights I should hand this straight over to the Committee, but . . . Well, as it was a personal letter, I thought I should handle it personally. I've been in touch with our old friend Steve Natkowitz, from Mossad. Trish Nuzzi is booked into the King David. You might just care to drop in on her. It's

117

possible, of course, that she is looking for somewhere safe. I can't see *that* lady taking to her husband's dealings too kindly. If she would like safety . . . Well, why don't you bring her back to London?'

'I'll do all I can, sir.'

'Yes,' M nodded gravely. 'When there's talk of peace, that little country becomes a shade heated, but you've been there before.'

'I'll slip off on Friday night.'

'Tomorrow? You can't manage it tonight, or in the morning?'

'Don't think that would be wise, sir. Don't worry, though, I'll report back to you personally before I bring anyone else into the charmed circle.'

'Good, and in return I'll make certain you're covered at this end. Get on to the usual number if you need back-up. You know how to get hold of Natkowitz?'

'No problem, sir. Now, don't you think you should get some rest?'

'I'll have plenty of time to rest in the hereafter, James. Stay and talk with me for a while. That dratted nurse has a good old naval name, but she has no heart.'

As if on cue, Nurse Frobisher appeared with a tray on which she had set tea, three cups, and a plate of biscuits. 'It's time for the Admiral's medicine anyway.' She gave them a bright smile. 'I thought tea wouldn't come amiss.'

It soon became obvious to Bond that he was also part of M's medicine, for Nurse Frobisher began dropping broad hints that he should stay and talk. At one point she said quietly that it would be a good idea to tire her patient so that he would be forced to rest. In the end it was after five before he left, heading back to London.

As soon as he opened the door to the flat, he knew that Flicka was not in the best of moods.

'You didn't even have time to let me know you were going to be out?' she asked, a tincture of acid in her tone.

'It was very secure, I'm afraid, but . . .'

'Yes, I got that impression from Lady Muck in your office. I suppose you *do* know that she treats everyone as if she's the boss when the boss is away?'

'No, I . . .'

'Oh, yes. Acts like a wife, and has that stupid name – Chastity – which certainly doesn't go with her figure. Her skirts have been getting shorter by the day since she took over, but I don't suppose you would notice anything like that?'

'Will you shut up!' Bond shouted at her. 'This is important and it concerns you.'

There was a long pause, during which they seemed to smolder at each other across the room. Then—

'What concerns me?'

'Going to Jerusalem tomorrow. There's a lot to arrange.'

Flicka remained silent during his explanation of the visit to M, except at the point when he mentioned Nurse Frobisher. Under her breath she muttered something about nurses' uniforms and she supposed this one was a hundred and eight.

'No, mid-twenties and very attractive, but I was there to talk with M.' He cut her down.

'So we tell nobody?' she asked when he had finished relating the entire story.

'Not a soul, so you keep your pretty little mouth closed.'

'Now?' she asked, sidling up to him and lifting her face to be kissed.

Whenever he arrived at Ben Gurion International, Bond

felt the same paradoxical sensation. Around him couples greeted each other with kisses, hugs and, even tears. These were people returning to the homeland, and they emanated a huge sense of joy. Yet mixed with the joy there was always a feeling of danger. Every time he flew into this part of the world he felt it like a dark cloud around him, and saw it in the faces of the soldiers and police on duty at the airport. It epitomized the way this tiny country had clung like a lion to the small strip of land it called its own, the homeland, the hope, Israel.

'James.' The familiar figure of Steve Natkowitz – that most un-Israeli looking of men – came striding from the crowd waiting for passengers on the El Al flight from London's Heathrow. 'James, it's good to see you.' He embraced Bond, like a long lost brother, then turned to Flicka.

'And you must be the famous "Fearless Flicka."' Natkowitz gave her a beaming, all embracing and infectious grin.

'Who in heaven calls me "Fearless Flicka?"' She looked genuinely baffled.

'James' old boss. Called you that over the telephone to me. Mind you, it was a secure line.'

He led them outside where a car waited to take them into Jerusalem.

'I hope the King David's okay for you, James.' Natkowitz had an unfortunate habit of driving as though the traffic would take care of itself, for he constantly took his eyes off the road, even turned right around in his seat while travelling at speed.

'Still as noisy as ever, I presume?'

'Terrible, but if you build an hotel in the middle of Jerusalem what can you expect. You've stayed at the King David, Flicka?'

'I haven't had that pleasure.'

'Oh, then you're in for a treat. It's faded Victorian England at its best. Well, perhaps not at its best because it's a sort of mixture – Victorian elegance with a blend of the Orient. And don't think about the noise, because it's well insulated. The pool and Oriental gardens make me forget I'm in the middle of a city as old as Jerusalem. Nothing fazes them, either. I sometimes think the staff all imagine they're still living under the British mandate.' He launched into the old story, perfectly true, that while the war of independence was at its height a telephoned bomb threat to the King David was taken with typical British *sang froid* – with disastrous results. They simply did not see it fitting to warn guests or take any precautions, but simply waited for the blast which, when it came, did a great deal of damage and killed dozens of people.

Steve waited in the lobby as they were taken up to their room, which Flicka pronounced to be absolutely wonderful. Together they went into the famous Regency Grill where they could have been eating in the heart of London – the menu was more British than most of the hotel restaurants in the capital of the UK, but by the same token it also included the best of Jewish food.

They talked like any old friends meeting for the first time in a couple of years, and Steve Natkowitz made certain that Flicka was not left out. It was not until they were about to leave that Steve said quietly, 'She's in suite 510. I can provide any help you might need, if she wants to go back to London with you. A very beautiful lady, and her companions are equally exciting.'

'Companions?' Bond queried.

'Couple of girls she's traveling with. They seem to be very close, but they're a pair of stunners.'

Natkowitz gave Flicka his charming smile, and a

promise to call them in the morning.

'I think we should try her straight away.' Bond explained that, with the limited time they had available, it might be best to see what Lady Tarn could add to the information they already had in their possession. 'If she feels under any threat from Max, she might like to know that she has our support.'

Flicka simply grunted as they got into the lift, and Bond stood back to let two young women – a blonde and a brunette – into the cage. As the doors closed, he took a quick look in the direction of the two girls, there was something inexplicably familiar about them. They were dressed in a similar manner in stylishly designed pant suits, one in gray, the other scarlet and both with white silk shirts. It was only when they all walked out of the lift on the fifth floor that he saw the bandaged hand on the blonde.

At the same moment, the brunette spoke in a low, husky voice. 'How nice to see you, Mr Bond. We thought we'd never meet again.'

'But we have,' the blonde added, 'And with the lovely Flicka as well.'

Flicka's mouth dropped open as the truth hit her.

'It's really us,' said Cuthbert.

'In the flesh and in our *true* personas. You didn't even guess that we were girls, did you? I'm Anna – my proper name as well – and this is Cathy. We presume you've come to visit our boss, Trish Nuzzi. Well, just step this way, she's going to be so excited.'

'Almost as excited as us,' chimed Cathy. 'We've all been absolutely dying to see you again, haven't we, Anna?'

'Going out of our minds.' Anna gave a tinkling little giggle.

11

Trish Nuzzi

'JUST WAIT WHILE I open the door.' Cathy, in her new
role, slid the oblong plastic security key into its slot,
waited until the light changed from red to green, then
opened the door to 510, walked in and called, 'Trish,
we're back, and we've brought some nice old playmates to
see you.'

Anna came in behind them, closing the door, calling,
'Trish, where are you? We've got a lovely surprise.'

She came out of the bathroom, and even the usually
sanguine Flicka gave an audible gasp. They had both seen
many photographs of Trish Nuzzi's dazzling face and
figure – indeed who had not? – from the days when she
was a top model before her marriage to Sir Max Tarn. To
see this gorgeous creature in the flesh was a different
matter altogether: as both Bond and Flicka could affirm
from Cambridge.

She wore a silver evening mini-dress with a diamond
choker, but at first sight all they took in were the famous
legs, long and incredible, reaching up forever and a day,
for she was around six feet tall. Though enviously slim,
she was beautifully proportioned, with a nut brown tan,
and that other great attribute, the thick long black hair
which had been her trademark in the old days.

Then they saw her face.

What had once been called both elfin and gamin by a hundred fashion journalists must still have been there under the livid bruises, and the obviously broken nose, for it was as though someone had used her features as a punch bag. When she spoke, there were traces of nasality, and a slight tremor.

'So?' glancing from Anna to Cathy and back again, not even trying to meet Bond's or Flicka's eyes.

'This is *the* Mr Bond, and Fredericka von Grüsse. We told you about them. They're friends. In fact, I think Mr Bond's probably a knight in shining armour.'

Trish gave a kind of lop-sided smile. 'Mr Bond I have already met and talked with. Ms von Grüsse I've only seen from a distance. It's nice to see you again, Mr Bond, and good to meet you . . .' She nodded in Flicka's direction. 'Forgive my state of physical dishabille, and please call me Trish.'

'You've talked to . . . ?' Anna began, then lapsed into silence.

'Just a minute.' Bond had stepped over to Anna, his hand taking her undamaged wrist, gripping like a steel trap. 'The last time I saw you – dressed as a very unpleasant thug – you were arguing with this lady's husband outside an almost ruined house called Hall's Manor. You wanted to come up to the room in which you'd left Ms von Grüsse and myself. You were very clear about your intentions. You wanted to come up to finish us off. You made bizarre men, the pair of you, and I do prefer you as women – if that's what you are . . . ?'

'Of course we're women,' Cathy almost spat at him. 'We did the other thing for Trish here.'

'Including trying to kill us?'

Under his tight hold, with her arm strained behind her back, Anna let out a little groan. 'We were trying to let

124

you go,' she said, her voice dropping to a whisper. 'Cathy was coming back to tell you what was really going on. We had the handcuff keys. Tarn would only have let us come up to you if we said it was to kill you. You've no . . .'

'She's telling the truth.' Trish Nuzzi nodded, and he saw that it even hurt her to speak. There was some wiring on her jaw on the inside of her mouth. 'She's being honest with you. It was all done for *me*. They persuaded Max that it would be a good idea to get you both out of the way. He was reluctant, but finally allowed them to stay behind in Cambridge. Please, they're telling the truth.'

Unwillingly, Bond let go of the wrist. 'Why should I trust you? Any of you?'

'Sit down. Please.' Trish Nuzzi gestured to the chairs and a long sofa. 'Cath, get a bottle of champagne and we'll have a drink. I'm in need of it, the painkillers are wearing off, and I can't take any more for a couple of hours.' The grimace on her face was evidence enough that she was not acting.

'Who did this to you?' he asked, one hand rising to indicate her face.

'Who do you think?' She gave a cynical little laugh and patted the place next to her on the sofa. Flicka gave a long sound, as though clearing her throat, and indicated one of the comfortable easy chairs. Bond raised one eyebrow at her as she cut in front of him and seated herself next to Trish.

As he sat down, his eyes caught Anna's, who had been glowering at him. Now she gave a little knowledgeable smile, then glowered again, touching her hair – 'Wigs,' she snapped. 'Wigs for us both until our hair grows again.'

'I prefer you with real eyebrows as well,' Bond said, straight faced.

125

'And you.' Anna made an obscene gesture as Cathy came back into the room with an ice bucket in which rested a bottle of Dom Perignon, and glasses.

'Who?' He turned to Trish again.

'I asked who do you think?'

'Your husband?'

'Part of it. Max likes to inflict pain, but he leaves the real bone breaking to that bastard Connie Spicer.'

'Then this isn't something new? Sir Max has a penchant for battering you?'

'It's one of the reasons I brought Cathy and Anna into the marriage.'

'You brought . . . ?'

'I am right in saying you are with the British authorities, and that you want to put Max Tarn into a high security prison for a thousand years, aren't I?'

'A thousand and one actually.'

'Make that two thousand,' said Flicka.

'Good.' Trish accepted a glass of the Dom Perignon from Cathy who had waved away Bond's offer of help. She took a long sip. 'I need this. If I have to talk for a while, I need help at the moment.'

'Take your time.' Flicka patted her arm.

'You said that you brought Cathy and Anna into the marriage?'

'Look, Mr Bond. I know I've been an idiot. I had the pick of the field. I could have married anyone. Max could be amusing, and he had other things to offer – like money. I married him for his money, that's plain and simple. I knew he got some of his kicks through hurting women, but, before we married, I thought it wasn't all that dangerous. Games. You know the kind of thing. Then, well, he suggested that, once we were married, I should have a couple of bodyguards. He said he'd arrange it. I said that *I* would arrange it. That's where Cathy and Anna come in.'

'We offered a service for lots of people in the business,' Cathy joined in. 'We're trained in the martial arts, and we know how to shoot.' She pirouetted and a small automatic pistol appeared from under her jacket. As Bond moved, she gave a small laugh and returned the weapon to its hiding place. 'We can be a right pair of dangerous bitches when we want. Also, we got on well with Trish. She came to us with a proposition, and we ran with it.'

'Max wouldn't have taken them seriously as women . . .' Trish began.

'Max is still your average male chauvinist.' Cathy shook her head, as though male chauvinists were an endangered species.

'It meant disguising them,' Trish continued, 'and they looked bizarre enough for Max to take them seriously as men. He has some odd tastes in bodyguards.'

'You knew he could be violent. Did you also know anything about his business affairs?' Flicka again.

'Not until much later. The girls knew before I did, because Max gave them a couple of jobs to do. They weren't that happy about it, but they did try and shield me from the worst.'

'Until it was too late.' Anna sat, in a good upright posture on one of the easy chairs.

'What *is* the worst? The scope of his illegal arms dealing, or the contempt he shows by constantly abusing you physically?'

'Oh,' she frowned and looked a little bewildered. 'Then you don't really know Max at all. I can normally put up with his bouts of sadism, but, about five years ago I discovered the end product of his deals and intrigues.' She took another sip of her drink. 'At first I couldn't understand why he became angry every time I visited Israel – I make a couple of trips here each year.' She explained that some ten years before she had undergone treatment for a slight eye problem. 'My doctor – Julius Hartman – did the procedure and follow-ups in Harley street. Then, being a good Jew, he finally decided to leave London and live here, in Israel. So I had my six-monthly check-ups with him. Here in Jerusalem. Anna and Cathy always came with me.'

'Funny.' Bond looked first at Anna and then at Cathy. 'I thought I chased you two all over Seville on motorcycles. I thought I had killed the pair of you.'

'You did what?' Anna sat up even straighter.

'If you left with Trish, you missed a little unpleasantness. I killed two of his toughs, and a man called Peter Dolmech got murdered.'

'Oh, no.' Trish Tarn put her hands to her face. 'Peter? He was one of the nicest men around Max.'

'He was also providing us with information and his luck ran out, I'm afraid.'

'You probably did in Pixie and Dixie,' Cathy supplied.

'Pixie and . . . ?'

'That what we called them. It was what everyone called them. They had been stunt drivers at one time. Stunts with cars and motorbikes. Very nasty gentlemen. Did a lot of unpleasant jobs for Max. Their real names were never mentioned, and I got the impression they were wanted by the police in about seven different countries.' Trish held out her glass for more champagne, and took a deep breath. 'But to get back to Max, I really laid into him when we got to Seville. I knew a lot more by then, but I was out of my mind with anger and grief. It would've been more prudent to keep quiet, but I told him the truth and this is the result. He was so furious that he did most of it. Connie Spicer broke my nose and jaw. Max, as you must know, suffers from a kind of *folie de grandeur*. He's done nothing but spread death and destruction for most of his adult life, but he thinks he can, in some way, make amends. When he does, he reckons that everyone's going to forget about the weapons and people – because he also deals in people, mercenaries mostly – and hail him as a hero. As the true hero. I shouldn't have told him on that last day in Seville.'

'What was this horrific thing you told him, Trish?'

'You can't guess?' She gave a bitter little laugh. 'I told him the truth, knowing that it would explode his mind. The truth. You see, I'm a quarter Jewish, on my mother's side, and me a good Catholic girl. My father was Italian, and my mother English. When I was coming up to my first communion they told me. It was a big family secret. A quarter Jewish, and that was enough to spark off my dear husband when I threw it in his face.'

'He just beat you up and then let you walk away?' Bond still only had an inkling of what she really meant.

'Not quite.' Again the bitter laugh. 'He lost control. Said he would have to bathe four times a day for the rest of his life, to get the Jewish filth from his body. He shouted at me. Said nobody must ever know; said he loathed himself. Did some damage to my face and ribs. I said I was going, so he put Connie in. I think the idea was to disable me so that I couldn't leave, but Connie hadn't banked on the girls.'

'You took Connie out?' Bond's tone was one of admiration.

'We kind of incapacitated him.' Cathy did her roguish smile.

'Let's say he won't be satisfying any ladies for a while,

yet, knowing Connie, he has amazing stamina. Probably be able to hobble around by now.'

'Trish, I'm sorry,' Bond was searching for the right words, not quite certain that he understood the complete subtext of what she had told him. 'Are you saying that Max has Fascist tendencies?'

This time her laugh was not bitter, but one of genuine amusement, and it was echoed by chuckles from Anna and Cathy.

'James,' she said finally. 'No, Max does not have Fascist tendencies. I thought you'd already know. In fact, I really believed that was why you're after him. Max Tarn is not just another Fascist. Max Tarn thinks of himself as the Nazi Messiah. He's the reincarnation of Hitler, Himmler, Goebbels – you name them, he is it. The whole arms dealing thing has been a means to an end. Stage one in his comeback. Weapons poured into the wrong hands over the past couple of decades have been for one reason: the complete destabilization of Europe – if not the world. He danced – really danced – with joy when the Berlin Wall came down. When the news came through he actually said, "My time is now near. The destruction of the Wall will bring all true Nazis into the open. By the time I am ready, they'll respond to me just as those in the 1930s responded to the Führer." '

Bond tried to disguise his horror and fascination. 'And he let you walk away when you told him about your Jewish blood?'

There was a pause before Trish said – 'It's not quite as easy as that, James. Like the Nazi leaders of old, he has that uncanny knack of being able to doublethink. After the first few years of our marriage I realized that he really regarded me as a showpiece. He just may be able to ignore the tiny bit of Jewish blood in my veins. Max has a

terribly long reach. He can probably find me and have me
hauled back, though I think his hands're pretty full at the
moment.'

'Like the Nazis who turned a blind eye to those Jews
they needed in order to function?'

'Exactly. Do you know that Hitler was always aware
that the gravediggers within the Nazi kingdom were Jews?
They didn't touch them because they were necessary.
Certain people are necessary to Max, and I might be one
of them.' She gave her head a little shake, as though trying
to get rid of some nightmare. 'Let me give you another
instance. He owns – that's the right word, *owns* – an
African-American girl who happens to be a junkie. He
talks to her using the most appallingly racist language.
That is when he's forced to go anywhere near her. But he
tolerates her because she is an assassin who takes a pride
in her work. Orders are given to her by either Connie or
Goodwin, because, while they're loyal to Max, they do
not really have the same scruples about being near her.
When he's around, he makes certain she keeps to her own
quarters. If she has to be in the entourage, he makes sure
she travels in a different car.'

'What's her name?'

'Beth. I don't know any other name for her. Everyone
calls her Beth. That's it.'

'But, Trish, I gather he claims lineage with the von Tarn
family . . .'

'I don't think he needs to just claim lineage. I think it's
genuine. But . . .'

'But the Nazis are supposed to have murdered his
family.'

'A family that, over the years, he's come to despise.'

'I see.' The shock of these latest revelations was just
starting to bite home.

'Max *is* powerful, James. Don't ever doubt that. He *is* a very dangerous beast.'

'You wouldn't happen to know where he is now?' Bond made it sound so casual that it almost went unnoticed, but he saw Anna stir and flash a look towards Cathy.

'He could be checking in downstairs for all I know.' Trish's hand went up to her hair for the first time since they had been in the room, fingers splayed, raking deeply into the thick soft forest. 'But I don't think so. What you're really asking me is where you can go and pick him up, yes?'

Bond leaned forward. 'I can offer you safety, Trish.'

'Oh, please.' She laughed. 'You cannot offer me safety until you have him six feet under. He has an army out there.'

'Trish,' Flicka took over, 'we *can* give you some safety. We can get you out of Jerusalem first thing in the morning. Once we have you in England we're one hundred per cent sure we can keep you safe. You, and the girls.'

'The girls can always look after themselves, but, yes, I'd like them around for a while.'

'Then you'll come with us?'

'I've nowhere else to go, and Max will know I'm here. Even Connie will have it figured out. Yes. Okay, take me to London and squirrel me away where none of Max's idiots can get their hands on me. What's in it for you?'

'Your safety, Trish,' from Bond. 'Your safety, and co-operation.'

'You have my co-operation in any case. You want to know where Max is? Okay, I can tell you where I think he'll be, if he's not on the way here to take me back by force.'

'Is that a possibility?'

'Always, but I don't think he has much time to come chasing me at the moment.'

'So, if he's not on his way here . . . ?'

'Well, maybe not yet, but eventually, he'll end up in the Caribbean.'

'Playing with his toy cruise ships?'

She gave a tired smile, and the pain showed through again. 'He has two main operating bases, both of them really sewn up. Seville is one. Being an inland port it's useful. He paid a lot of people not to ask too many awkward questions. The other port he uses is San Juan in Puerto Rico.'

'And he has that one closed up as well?'

'Pretty much. He also owns some property there. We have a suspicion that he stashes cargo away in Puerto Rico and that is where he plans to become a world hero.' The "we" included the girls, for she waved her arm in their direction, and both Cathy and Anna nodded in agreement. 'We think he owns warehouses, and other little bits of real estate, and he's spread money around the place as though cash is going out of fashion.'

'So, he runs a complex operation from two distinct bases. One in Europe, the other in the Caribbean, where he has some kind of ace up his sleeve?'

'That's about the size of it. His merchant bank launders the money, I should imagine.'

'You imagine correctly. We're getting that sorted out. There's a great deal of evidence and we're putting the financial side together now.'

'He said *that* part could never be broken.' Cathy had gone back into one of the other rooms and brought another bottle of Dom Perignon. 'In Seville, I heard him say that his banks were a hundred per cent foolproof.'

133

'It would've taken until doomsday if it hadn't been for Peter Dolmech.'

Anna stirred. 'You said he was dead.'

'He left us a little legacy. A map of the laundry so to speak.'

There was a short pause, during which Trish and the girls did not look at each other. Then Trish broke the silence. 'Poor Peter. At least he did something worthwhile before he died. Max trusted him absolutely and I would never have thought he was the spy in the camp.'

'You suspected a spy?'

'No, but Max did. He was paranoid about it. Always changing procedures, and playing games to trap people. Though he never did – trap anyone, that is.'

'Well, he did more than trap Dolmech, and he almost destroyed the information.' He went on to describe what had happened in Seville, leaving out the most gory of the details.

Again there was a silence. A pause which went on a shade too long. Trish Nuzzi once more put a hand to her hair, then quietly said that she was sorry but she really had to lie down. 'Doctor Hartman saw to it that my nose and jaw were fixed,' she added as a kind of afterthought.

'So, Max'll eventually end up in the Caribbean. Where else might he be?'

'He could be in Germany. Wasserburg. He's quietly restoring Tarnenwerder – the old family seat – to its former glory.'

'He is?' Bond asked of nobody in particular.

'Then, tomorrow we'll take you back to London and some safety?' Flicka asked.

'Yes. Yes, of course. It's all I want now: to be out of it all and in some normal kind of life.'

'What time?' Cathy asked, sounding businesslike.

'We'll give you a call first thing.' Bond had already decided to book seats on the first possible flight back to Heathrow. 'I think there's a flight at around noon. Now are you going to be alright tonight?'

'If we're not, we'll give *you* a call.' Anna sounded smug and, if anything, over-confident.

'So, what do you think?' Bond asked when they were back in their own suite.

'You mean the amazing sex change, the distraught Lady Tarn, or the reincarnation of Adolf Hitler?' Flicka had started to undress.

'All three, I suppose. You happy with them, Flick? Trust them?'

'The dedicated crazy Nazi thing shook me, but I can see it's probably true enough, and the time is ripe in Germany. There are so many dedicated Nazi organizations coming out of the woodwork now. The skinhead groups, the toughs we call neo-Nazis, but that's the wrong name for them. They're not neo anything. They are Nazis plain and simple: Germany for the Germans, and then only the pure bred Germans. Out with any foreigners. Even people who, up to a couple of years ago, said it could never happen twice, are now having doubts. As for the rest, right up until we mentioned Dolmech, I trusted them. Then things came apart slightly.'

'Could be that Lady T was having a ride around the park with Dolmech.'

'The thought had crossed my mind. Either her or . . . No, they wouldn't have let their guard down – the girls, I mean.'

'To be perfectly honest with you,' Bond raised his voice as she passed through into the bathroom. 'To be perfectly honest, I wouldn't trust those two with anyone – except La Nuzzi, of course. They're obviously devoted to her.'

'And I'll be perfectly honest with you, my darling, I wouldn't trust any of them with you. Even with the bashed up face, Trish was drooling, and the two terrors would have kept you happy for hours.'

'I didn't notice anything unusual. I think you're exaggerating, Flicka.'

She did not reply, so he smiled to himself and went over to the telephone to call both El Al and BA. There was an El Al flight from Ben Gurion International to Heathrow at noon, and they had seats. He booked five, giving their names and saying that he would get back to them with the information on the other three passengers first thing in the morning. As ever, El Al were tight-lipped.

They both slept well, spooned close together in the big double bed. The telephone dragged them up through a few layers of unconsciousness. Bond looked at his watch and saw that this was not his wake-up call requested for seven, as the time showed ten minutes past six. Groggily, he croaked into the phone and Steve Natkowitz came on strong and clear at the other end, telling him that this was a secure line.

'I think you might have a small problem.' The Mossad man dived straight in.

Bond was immediately wide awake. 'What kind of problem?'

'I don't know how you got on last night, but I've just had a call from BG International. It appears that Trish Nuzzi and her entourage left on the six o'clock to Paris.'

Bond replied with a single oath. 'Shit!' he said.

12

A Horrible Way To Die

IT TOOK THEM less than ten minutes to decide that it
would serve no purpose for them to stay on in Jerusalem,
and that there was no point in chasing Trish Nuzzi and the
girls to Paris.

It was raining, there had been a shooting in Jerusalem,
some kind of tear gas and stone-throwing clash in Tel
Aviv, and another bit of violence on the road between the
two, which eventually made them nearly late for the flight
– El Al suggesting around three hours before check-in,
instead of the former two. It was all part of the constantly
shifting dangers of the Middle East, but there were other
passengers who arrived almost at the last minute which
made for a very late departure and an unhappy flight
crew.

They were back in the London flat at around seven in
the evening to find twelve messages waiting on the secure
telephone, and one showing on the private line. The
twelve on the secure telephone were quick and to the
point – would he call the Minister as soon as possible;
would he call Bill Tanner as soon as possible. They had
started coming in late on the previous evening, and the
last had been left only an hour before their return.

He called M's Chief of Staff first, for at least he knew
where he stood with Bill Tanner. There was panic in the

streets, according to Tanner, and the Minister had been searching for him to attend a meeting with relevant members of The Committee as soon as possible. It appeared that there had been a break in the Tarn case.

He immediately telephoned the Minister's private number, to be told the same thing. 'We've been away for a couple of days,' Bond said lamely.

'In future I'd appreciate it if you left a contact number with your office when you're going to be out of London over a week-end.' The Minister gave him short shrift. 'I can get people together within the hour, so would like you at the Home Office by eight o'clock sharp.'

'Bang goes a quiet evening in front of the television.' Flicka tried to sound piqued.

'Since when have we ever had quiet evenings in front of the television?' He looked up, saw her grin and shrugged.

He was tempted to leave the message on the private phone, but he ran it back and pressed *Play* almost automatically. The husky female voice was immediately recognizable—

'This is Cathy, James. We're sorry that Trish decided to run out on you at the last minute, but, as you can imagine, she really doesn't trust anyone at the moment – anyone except us, of course. Don't worry, we'll see that she comes to no harm, and we'll keep in touch.'

While the tape was still playing, he touched the button on the *Caller ID* unit next to the telephone. 'Well, they're not in Paris,' he frowned. 'That was made from an 071 London number. The girls've brought her here, and how in the blazes did they get this telephone number?'

Flicka said that she would get the number traced to an address and call him at the Home Office. 'We don't want you to upset the Minister by being late,' she soothed. 'That would never do.'

'Wouldn't have happened in the old days. At least we weren't run by damned committees. By the time they've stopped arguing with one another, it's usually too late to do anything about anything.' He was at the door. 'Oh, Fredericka, could you contact M's nurse – Frobisher – and see how the Old Man's getting on?'

'Of course, but how are you going to handle The Committee?'

'In what way?'

'You going to lay the news on them about the Nazi thing? This is for real, James. Every other night, here in Europe, we're warned on television about the far right wing in Germany. The marches, drum beats, acts of violence against foreigners: the whole grotesque display of the neo-Nazi movement.'

'The *Nazi* movement, Flicka. There's nothing neo about those fanatics. As for The Committee, I'll use my own judgment. It's possible that we should keep that piece of information in reserve. They might already know, of course. That could be the break in the Tarn business.'

He left with a black cloud hanging over him, and anger too near the surface of his emotions.

At the Home Office only the core members of The Committee were present, plus Bill Tanner. Wimsey had a Chief Superintendent with him, while the Director General of the Security Service was represented by three people: a trio about whom Bond had deep reservations. The first of these was a rake-thin man with lank blond hair whose name, Thickness, was at odds with his appearance. With him were two female officers, Judy Jameson and Jane Smith, both known to have great influence with the Director General. Everyone looked edgy and concerned.

Bond reflected that he had crossed swords with them on

relatively minor matters before this. Their presence only
suggested a clash of wills over Tarn.

'At last.' The Minister sounded more than a shade
sarcastic. 'The prodigal returns.'

'Where in blazes have you been, Bond?' from Thickness.

'Trying to find Tarn if you really want to know. I'd
forgotten that The Committee owned me.'

'In many ways we *do* own you, Bond. Things have
changed. As for Tarn, that's the latest break. The man's
back in this country. We have proof positive.' The Minister signaled to Bill Tanner who went over to a large screen
television with a built-in VCR and slipped a cassette into
the machine.

'The soft route, via Dublin, late yesterday afternoon,'
Jane Smith said by way of introduction. The tone of her
voice suggested that Bond should actually have been
present.

The screen cleared to show the long corridor up to the
baggage collection area in Terminal One at Heathrow.
Some seventy people straggled past the immigration
officer and the one man from the Security Service who
always manned the desk at the entrance to the baggage
carousels.

No chances are taken with flights coming in from
Dublin. Normally a bus picks up the passengers and brings
them straight into the terminal where they are herded
through a one-way door. Like sheep – which is what
airline personnel call passengers anyway – they are forced
to pass this checkpoint. It is rare for anyone to be stopped.
Security cameras double check the passengers, and arrests
sometimes take place as they go through customs. In other
cases, a 'face' – which is Security Service language for a
suspected criminal or terrorist – is quietly followed. The

system is reckoned to be foolproof, though sometimes it is just proof of fools.

There, large as life and twice as natural, walking calmly into the baggage collection area came Max Tarn. In the distance the camera picked up Maurice Goodwin and Connie Spicer, followed by a muscular, fit-looking black girl in jeans, white shirt and a fashionable waistcoat. Without knowing exactly why, Bond suddenly realized that this was Beth, the girl who had met them in the dark at Hall's Manor – the girl whom Trish had called an assassin.

'Thinks he's bloody omnipotent.' There was a growl in Jane Smith's voice. Bond could only think of Trish Nuzzi's remark about Tarn being a victim of *folie de grandeur*.

'So we've got them boxed in?' he asked.

There was a slight shuffling of feet and the odd cough.

'Unhappily, our people lost them.' Thickness did not even look distressed. 'They were picked up again, in London.' The Security Service officer seemed to imagine they were all involved in some game.

Wimsey cleared his throat. 'My officers, together with members of the Security Service, moved in, but I fear the whole bunch got away again.'

'Whereabouts in London?'

'A flat behind Harrods. It's owned by Tarn, nothing but the best for him.'

'And have you ID'd the black girl yet?'

'What black girl?' Judy Jameson from Security asked sharply.

He made them re-run the tape and pointed out the girl following Goodwin and Connie Spicer.

'We didn't even make her. Who do you think she is?' from Thickness, who seemed to have lost his casual attitude towards the situation.

'The one called Beth who was at Hall's Manor.'

'Ah. Better put her on the list then.'

'Talking of Hall's Manor, not everything's lost . . .' The Minister tried to sound cheerful. 'We have one other piece of interesting information. As you know, Bond, we were running a check on the Manor.'

Bond nodded. His gut reaction to all this was not good. Something was badly wrong.

The Minister continued, 'It appears that the last remaining member of the Hall family finally relented. The whole estate – a thousand acres and the house – was sold off in January: bought by a firm that calls itself Bulwark Real Estate.'

'Don't tell me.' Bond leaned back in his chair. 'Bulwark is a subsidiary of Tarn International.'

'Got it in one.' The Minister sounded very pleased.

'So, you're all banking on Tarn going up to that ruin?'

'I think it's a natural assumption.'

'You do, sir? The place is falling down. It's also right out in the open. You had no idea that Tarn owned a flat in Knightsbridge, so, for all we know, he could have a dozen bolt holes here in London.'

'I think not.' Jane Smith sounded smug. 'One of Commissioner Wimsey's units came back to us – a little late, I admit – with the information that a car traced to Tarn had been spotted on the M11.'

'What exactly do you mean by "a little late"?'

'It was a borderline speeding case. They took the reg, then recognized it when my people sent out the details,' Wimsey blustered. 'Called in straightaway.'

'So, let me rephrase my former question. You all *know* Tarn is going up to that ruin?

'Indeed.' The Minister spoke in the kind of voice used by schoolmasters who will brook no argument. The

Pontius Pilate voice, as Bond called it – "what I have written, I have written."

'Well, I presume you have people surrounding Hall's Manor at the moment?'

'No. We have *one* man. Security brought him in from the SAS. He's very good, and they got him in and hidden by late last night. If Tarn shows up there, we'll know within seconds.'

The Minister smiled benevolently, as though he had already trapped Max Tarn single-handed.

'Why would a man like Tarn risk coming back into the country, with half his entourage, sir?' Bond asked quietly, knowing there could be no clear answer. 'He came in clean, no attempt at hiding his identity. Now, I believe that he's got something going which he reckons will be a boon to society and he'll risk anything to see it through. I haven't a clue as to what it is. But I do know that politically he's slightly to the right of Adolf Hitler and Genghis Khan. People like that often truly think they're invincible. Only a fool or a zealot would walk into the country so brazenly. The question is why did he come back?'

'Must be something important.' The Minister coughed, then frowned when he realized that he had made an obvious statement.

'And you believe he's at Hall's Manor?'

'What else can I believe? The man can't run far.'

'Can't he? I think he can probably run us all off our feet. To come into Heathrow as he did means that he knows the score: knows how we operate with suspects. He came in to lead us on some merry dance, sir. I'd put money on it.'

'Nobody's asking you to put money on it.'

'No, but I would. He's here either to get something, or

deal with unfinished business, and he wants us to know about it. You think you lost him by chance? No, sir. This man's obsessive. He's been arming renegade armies, selling death to terrorists, providing arms and means to countries and organizations who will use the weapons – and not in any good cause either. He's a world-class political loose cannon, sir. He's also a man who rarely takes chances. I repeat, he wanted you to know he was here, so he'll also probably let you know when he's left.'

'So, you don't think he'll be heading for Hall's Manor?' It was a rhetorical question.

'He could well be going straight there, sir. But I don't think it wise to have only one man waiting for him . . .'

'That was a conscious decision, Captain Bond. One that wasn't made lightly. We agreed that one trained member of the SAS would be able to give us radio information very quickly and without being detected.'

'And you've got a whole troop of SAS people sitting a few miles away so that they can go in and get him?'

'We have armed police and security officers on standby. They can be there in a matter of thirty minutes.'

'*If* that's where he's heading.'

'Every policeman in the country, every security officer, every airport and seaport is on the alert for him. He's in, and it's up to us to be sure that he doesn't get out.'

'Again, sir, why here? Why take this risk?'

The Minister was about to speak when the telephone purred on the table. He answered and, sounding very irritated, told Bond that it was Flicka wishing to speak with him – 'And I trust that it's business, Bond. Something concerning this case.'

'I've no doubt that it's business.' He took the instrument and spoke into it quietly. Everyone in the room realized there was something wrong by the way his back stiffened, and his eyes traversed every face in the room. 'Wait there. I'll be back soon, and thank you.'

He replaced the handset and looked straight at the Minister as he repeated the address just passed on to him by Flicka. It was a flat situated in an area just behind Harrods in Knightsbridge. 'Is that where you thought you had him cornered, with his people?'

'Yes. How do you know? Nobody else but The Committee, a selected number of trustworthy police and security officers, have that address.'

'Because there was a telephone message on my private phone when I got back to my flat, sir. The *Caller ID* gave the number of the place behind Harrods. Fräulein von Grüsse has been checking it out for me.'

'A telephone call?'

'That's what I just said, sir. I think Tarn's intent on leaving a message at Hall's Manor for us. A very unpleasant message.'

'Bond, you're not talking sense.'

'I'm talking a lot of sense, sir, and I want The Committee's permission for me to go up to Hall's Manor with Fräulein von Grüsse, immediately.'

'I need to know why. Have to get in touch with our man on the ground there.'

Quietly, and quickly, Bond explained some of the facts of life – particularly those appertaining to Lady Tarn, and the control Sir Max had over Seville and San Juan in Puerto Rico. 'I gather that, eventually, he's going to provide some spectacular event in Puerto Rico, and that's going to be sooner rather than later.' He left out the fact that Max Tarn – and presumably many others – regarded himself as the Nazi Messiah. 'My fear is that your SAS man could be in serious trouble.'

'Why just you and Ms von Grüsse? Why not send police and SAS in now?'

'You want a pitched battle in which we might be seen to have acted a little prematurely? I need your authority to get up to Hall's Manor, and I need it now.'

'I don't think I can . . .'

'You can, sir. If you don't, then you get my resignation from the Two Zeros here and now. I'm privy to quite a lot of information about Tarn. I don't think you can really get him without my help. I'll wait outside until you've made up your minds.' He rose and stalked out of the room.

Ten minutes later, Bill Tanner joined him. 'They're not very happy.' He did not look too jovial himself. 'But they've agreed to your request with certain limits.'

'Which are?'

'That, if they've heard nothing by one in the morning, they'll issue their own orders, one of which will probably be your arrest, for precipitating matters.'

Behind Tanner the door opened and a worried-looking Minister stood just inside the room. 'It appears that we've already got another problem.' His eyes showed uncertainty. 'We can't raise the SAS man at the Manor. The line's open but he's not answering any signals.'

'Voice signals?' Bond asked.

'No, we've got a code with a series of clicks, so that Tarn's people can't pick him up on any scanners they might be carrying.'

'So, we can go?'

'Tanner's told you about the deadline?'

'Yes, sir. That's okay by me. If you don't hear anything from us by one a.m., we'll need you to take over, because we won't be operative if you don't get a report.'

They wore black. Black jeans, black rollnecks, black

leather gloves and black sneakers, while their heads were covered with black Balaclava helmets. They carried weapons and equipment on broad black belts: Bond with the ASP, a radio which would allow him to signal London, a standard field compass and a high-powered torch. Flicka with her Beretta, and a couple of flash-bang grenades. They had left the maps and other gear in the car, parked in a side road a mile away from Hall's Manor.

Now, they approached the old house from the West, through a wood and scrub land, occasionally taking bearings with the compass. It was in the wood that they found the SAS sergeant's body, and there was no need to switch on the torch to know that the man was dead. The black stain running from his neck told of a severed throat.

It made Bond even more apprehensive, for if a man trained to the perfection of this sergeant had been taken by surprise, he and Flicka would be easy game.

They crouched on the edge of the scrub, the ground uneven, the silhouette of the big house stark against the sky. There were no sounds, except for predatory night animals. No lights. No sign of life, but they both knew this was no guarantee that Tarn and his crew were not out there, waiting and watching in the dark.

The luminous dial of Bond's watch showed it to be sixteen minutes past midnight. They had, in fact, made incredibly good time, and now he wondered if they should just go charging in, or take it stealthily all the way. The deadline was running out.

'Gently,' he whispered to Flicka, and together, crouching low, they moved forward. 'Shoot first and then ask the questions,' he breathed again as they reached the house. He saw her nod, then put a hand out to touch the stone.

They circled the entire building, pausing close to

windows, their eyes fully adjusted to the darkness and the now slanted moon.

The front door was open, almost as they had left it on their last visit, but they knew others had already been there before them that night; might still be there, silent and unmoving in the shadows. Taking a deep breath, he nodded to Flicka and took a step inside the door into the hall, switching on the torch, held next to the automatic pistol, firm in his hand. The smell of must and decay hit them like an invisible wall, but mixed with it were other scents: the smell of women's perfume and other luxurious lotions. If the house were truly empty, it had only recently been vacated.

Together they began moving from room to room on the ground floor, sweeping each room and passageway as they made slow progress, jumping at shadows, hearing the creaking of the old place, and standing, listening, waiting for another of Tarn's horrors to come leaping out at them.

The ground floor and the below stairs area were clean, so, at last they began to make a steady progress up the stairs which gave out loud cracks and little squeals under their feet.

The next floor was also clean, and they both felt the fringes of fear as they began to go on upwards, towards the little room in which they had been held prisoner. As they moved along the short passage which led to the door, half open, there was a distinct noise from within the room: the sound of something straining followed by a subtle hint of movement.

Bond raised the torch, his finger tightening on the trigger of his pistol as he edged inside the room. Flicka gave a little scream as she saw it, then began to hyperventilate. The torch beam traversed the room quickly and then went back to the thing that hung, swinging from a crossbeam in the ceiling, centering on the face.

The bruising was still visible, though in death the face seemed to have swollen into a caricature of itself, the mouth open and tongue half out. He thought immediately that Trish Nuzzi had probably been strangled before they had hoisted her up on the rope, her lovely long black hair falling to her shoulders on either side of the grotesque face. The feet were together, but her arms seemed to be spread away from her body, making her look like a huge terrible doll, hung up by some evil child.

Then, from directly behind them, came the husky voice. 'A horrible way for her to die, wasn't it?' said Cathy.

13

Hell of an Engagement Party

FLICKA SCREAMED, BACKING against the wall, as though
trying to push her body through the lath, plaster and
stone, while Bond swung around, his torch beam illumi-
nating the empty doorway. Later, he realized that, at that
moment, he expected death to come hurtling in from
either Cathy or Anna, but there was no one there, and the
only sound was the macabre creaking of the rope around
Trish Tarn's neck.

He allowed the torch to sweep completely around the
room, the beam finally falling on a long black box in the
corner. He went over to examine it, and found it was a
stereo tape machine which clicked off as he reached it.
From the back of the machine, a wire had been stretched
to another small gray square box screwed to the floor just
inside the door. He recognized it immediately as an
electronic eye, cheap but serviceable. The kind of thing
you could buy at any electronics store to help fit a
do-it-yourself security system. The eye had sent a signal to
the tape machine as Bond and Flicka had crossed into the
room, switching on a prepared tape.

'Meant to scare the pants off us.' He played the torch on
Flicka, and saw her relax.

'I know of better ways,' she breathed, summoning a
weak smile.

Neither of them could keep their eyes from the obscene corpse which swayed slightly on the rope, so he took her by the shoulders and gently led her from the room. In the passageway outside, he unhooked the radio from his belt and pressed the *Send* button. Within seconds a static-laden voice came faintly from the speaker—

'Micro One. Over.'

'Brother James. Your SAS man is dead, and Lady Tarn is now really deceased. She's hanging in the attic at Hall's Manor. Over.'

'Roger that Brother James. Police and Security will be with you shortly. Over.'

'Has The Committee broken up? Over.'

'Roger that also, Brother James. You are to brief all interested parties at nine ack emma.' He knew the voice at the distant end was Bill Tanner.

'Roger. Wilco and out.'

Together, they went downstairs to await the arrival of the authorities, Bond restless, moving from room to room, peeping into bare, moldy cupboards and examining doors and windows.

In what had once been a huge dining room he came across burned paper in the grate of an elaborate fireplace, so he stirred the black mess around, soiling his fingers, but revealing a couple of small pieces of paper which had not been wholly consumed. One was the edge of a large sheet, and some numbers were still clearly visible. The other charred piece looked as though it had come from a memo pad – the kind of thing that executives carry around: little oblong pages which fit into a leather holder. The writing on this was only partly readable. He could make out – *Call,* followed by the British Telecom get-out code and the German get-in code and a series of digits. There was a tick against this telephone number and a scrawl which said, *Book for four nights from* and the day's date.

He went back into the hall and called the main headquarters which overlooked Regent's Park. His work name was still registered there and he would at least find a duty officer and a couple of secretaries *in situ*. Identifying himself as *Predator* he asked if someone could take a back bearing on the number.

It took only forty seconds with the magic of the mainframe computers. The number was that of the *Vier Jahreszeiten* – Munich's best address. *The* Hotel for the rich and famous.

Munich, he thought. Munich tonight; Munich, the old capital of Bavaria and within easy reach of Tarnenwerder and Wasserburg am Inn. At least he knew where they were heading, and this time they had not wanted him to know.

Fifteen minutes later, three cars pulled up in front of the house, and both Bond and Flicka gave short statements before getting a ride to their car, stashed a mile away.

'So, you think Cathy and Anna have sold out?' Flicka was restless, and did not seem to be getting comfortable in the passenger seat. Usually she had that wonderful gift of being able to remain still and unmoving in any situation. Now, she was all muscular tics, arranging and rearranging her body as though she could not find a restful position.

'That's certainly what we're meant to believe.' He was driving fast, just within the limits, streaking up the M11 towards London. 'With these people it's difficult to know what's the truth and what's just laid on for our benefit.'

Presently he said that his gut reaction told him Cathy and Anna had belonged to Tarn almost from the word go. 'Money, as they say, talks. It's possible they were originally hired by Trish, who admitted marrying the man for

153

his money. Max Tarn appears to have a way to circumvent loyalty, and that way is almost certainly through his cheque book and ideology. Yes, I believe both of them are part of the Tarn organization, and have been for some time. Lord knows who else has been bribed.'

They drove back to the flat, took showers and stretched out on the bed for a much-needed sleep, for, by now, it was almost five in the morning. Bond could not sleep. His mind would not carry him off into the healing dreamless dark, while Flicka still seemed restless.

He had his back to her when she whispered, 'You still awake, love?'

'Too much on my mind, Flick. Are you too tired to talk?'

'No, I'm haunted by that body. Unusual for me, I know, but I thought Trish was a nice person. In a way I looked forward to seeing her after all this was over. Women need friends of their own sex, James, and I've precious few of those left now I've cut adrift from Switzerland.'

'Give it time. Look, I've got to talk to you. Serious stuff.'

'Work serious, or personal serious?'

'Work. I think we should leave the personal until all this is over.'

'Well, we could keep it a secret.'

He seemed lost in thought for a full two minutes. 'My dear girl, I haven't felt like this about someone for a very long time. In fact I don't think I've ever really felt what I feel for you. Never in my life. So, when all this is over, will you marry me?'

Her lips brushed against his as he turned to face her. 'James, you already know the answer. I've hoped for this ever since we first met. Yes, of course I'll marry you and

I'd like to shout it from the rooftops.'

They kissed. They moved close. For an hour they celebrated their betrothal.

'Pity it has to remain a secret,' she said at last.

'I know, but I think we're probably going to need each other professionally in the next week or so. If we announce it formally, they'd take you off the active list, quicker than hell would scorch a feather.'

'Quicker than . . . ? I've never heard that.'

'Something my sainted old grandmother used to say.'

'Then she had a fine turn of phrase.'

'She was fine about most things. Just like you, my dear Flick.' He paused. 'Now, I *have* to talk about work, and you're not going to like what I have to say.'

'Try me.'

'I'm going to ask permission to go out in the field on my own.'

'Over my dead body.'

'Seriously, Fredericka. This is a one man job, and it has to be done quickly.'

'You mean I'd hold you up?' A tiny touch of irritation.

'No, but I don't think it would be wise for us to go together. Let me explain.' He told her about the fragment of paper and what he had discovered. 'If they're off to Munich today it probably means that Max is going to see his German lawyers in Wasserburg, and is also possibly taking a look around his ancestral home. I'd like to see exactly how things stand. You recall what Trish told us? That Max is quietly restoring Tarnenwerder; and there's the whole matter of his family claim to the place. We've even got the name of his lawyers, remember the dossier? Saal, Saal u. Rollen, who still have offices in the Marien-platz, Wasserburg am Inn. If I'm to do a swift search of their office, it's best that I do it on my own.'

155

'Oh, James. Two's company.'

'Two's also what they'll be looking for. Tarn and his buddies regard us as a team, and it's a mighty small team if he's already becoming the accepted leader of a resurrected Nazi Party. That's exactly why I'm going on my own. One against many works better than two.'

'Let me think about it, James. It's bad enough not being able to sing, shout and tell the world about our private lives . . .'

'You've been in this game long enough to know . . .'

'Oh course I have, you idiot. I know you're *right* about that. I just don't want to let you out of my sight.'

'My love, it would be most unsafe for you to come with me.'

'I bet The Committee will hum-and-ha about it for so long that Max'll be in the Caribbean by the time you get the okay.'

'We'll see about that.'

'Just let me think.' She wrapped her arms around him and in less than five minutes was asleep.

The ghosts of past loves began to float in and out of Bond's mind. Only once in his life had he been truly and intensely in love with a woman: Tracy di Vincenzo, murdered only a few hours after their marriage. With Fredericka the emotion was different, perhaps because of the love he had felt for Tracy. His feelings for Flicka seemed to him to be an entirely novel experience. She was also responsible for a deeper commitment from him – a mature understanding of what a man and woman could share: something that had little to do with sex, and much more concerned with their entire lives. Two people blending together as one.

Yet, in the early hours of that morning, the specters of other women seemed to gather in the room, as though telling him to rid himself of all the emotions he had once felt for them, and make a new start with Fredericka von Grüsse.

Over the years many of his former lovers had remained more than simply fond memories from the past. He still regularly visited the cemetery at Royale-les-Eaux where Vesper Lynd lay at peace – the peace she had sought for so long. There were times when old dreams caught him unawares, sending pictures of once-loved girls and women skittering through his brain – the wild, almost tomboy Honeychile Ryder with her broken nose and firm body; Domino Vitali, she of the slight limp and sensual mouth. More often than not the picture was faint, though the sensual memory strong – a beloved Asian face swimming above him, and the voice, soft and tender, of Kissy Suzuki. Now all these past loves seemed to smile upon him in his happy, half conscious, state of a true obligation to Fredericka. Man and woman joined by the invisible but inescapable bond of love and duty, one to the other.

They arrived at the Home Office, refreshed in a new warmth to one another, happy, but somber, at exactly nine o'clock. The Committee was assembled in its entirety but for M who – Bill Tanner said – was as well as could be expected.

Bond sensed some hostility from the likes of Thickness, Ms Smith and Ms Jameson, not to mention Commissioner Wimsey, but the other members seemed pleased enough to see him again. The Minister appeared neutral, though as ever he remained stiff and a shade cold.

Both Bond and Flicka made statements, which resulted in a general clamoring regarding the whereabouts of Tarn and his cohorts. There was little doubt that this final act of brutality had put fire under the bulk of The Committee members, and it was Wimsey who provided the possible clues.

Once more, right under everyone's noses, it seemed that the entire gang had flown out of Stansted.

'I was under the impression that all ports and airports were under a red alert for the man.' The Minister was more than chilly towards Wimsey, who countered that this time they had almost certainly left, in disguise, under new – probably forged – passports. Two of the men, presumably Tarn and Goodwin, had boarded a flight bound for Berlin, while the two women and several other men had almost certainly left as members of a tour group heading for Corfu. This last had only just emerged, and the tour company – WellRun Tours Ltd – had been questioned.

'This particular company,' Wimsey reported with a trace of sheepishness, 'has admitted they were five places short of the full complement on their reasonably priced nine day trip around the Greek islands. Late yesterday afternoon, they apparently jumped with joy when they received an inquiry about availability on *any* tour leaving Stansted last night. It was a night flight and the man who telephoned them had given a valid credit card number for all five free places. They've been in touch with their guide in Corfu. Only one of the last minute bookings reported to her at Corfu airport. A man – undoubtedly Spicer – told her they had been forced to return home immediately because of a family crisis. As yet we have not been able to check out what other flights they boarded, though two are thought to have gone on to Athens.' He paused as if for applause. 'My private theory is that they're heading to a prearranged meeting place in Europe.'

Bond interrupted. As yet he had not mentioned the charred paper discovered at Hall's Manor. 'I can tell you exactly where they are, for the next four nights at any rate.'

This remark got everyone's attention very quickly, so he took them through the entire story.

'Then we get the German authorities to pick up the lot of them in Munich,' the Minister snapped.

'I doubt if that would work, Minister,' Bond told him quietly.

'Why in heaven not?'

'Well, Minister, to be fully truthful you'd probably get them arrested, though Germany isn't exactly co-operating with us at all levels at the moment. Arrested, they're of no further use to us. Arrest Tarn and those close to him and you charge him with murder, the others with being accomplices . . .'

'Then we can slap the other serious charges on them when your department's fully sorted out the papers and provided hard evidence. Nothing more simple. We'll have taken a Grade A, 22 carat villain out of circulation.'

'Maybe, Minister, but there're still loose ends to be tied up. I would like The Committee to grant me one more request.'

'We've already given you one hell of a lot of leeway, Bond . . .' Wimsey began.

'With respect, Commissioner, I think that if you grant my new request, it'll save a lot of time in the long run.'

'Get on with it, then, Captain Bond. What're you suggesting? That we allow you to go charging off to Munich and dash in with guns blazing?'

Bond paused, looking around the long table, taking in the reactions of every member of The Committee, capturing each person's eyes briefly with his own, almost accusatory stare. 'Please correct me if I'm wrong,' he began, his eyes still roving around the various members noting that, while M and the Director General of the Security Service were absent, it was the latter organization which was represented by three people. His own old service had only Bill Tanner as its delegate, and he was wearing the Secretary's hat as well as being M's deputy.

'Correct me if I'm wrong,' he repeated. 'My understanding of the rules and regulations of MicroGlobe One, the Watchdog Committee over my Department, state that the Minister and one other member can recommend a course of action being taken over short range activities. If the Minister rubber-stamps some action, he is not required to give an entire quorum of The Committee the details of that action.'

'But *must* do so after four days of the recommendation,' the Minister barked.

'After four days, yes,' Bond agreed. 'Therefore, I would like a meeting, *in camera*, with the Minister and the representative from the Intelligence Service – now.' He knew that he was well within his rights and, as he left the room with Tanner and the Minister, he tried to avoid the pleading eyes of Flicka von Grüsse, who had more than a glimmer of an idea regarding what he was going to ask.

They went straight to the Minister's office, a bare, uncluttered room, one floor above The Committee's reading room.

'Well, what is it you want to request in such secrecy, Captain Bond?' The Minister showed signs of frustration and not a little irritation before they were seated.

'Simple, sir. I want four days' leave, with nobody asking awkward questions as to where I am, or what I'm doing.'

'And where will you be?'

'I'll be in Germany. Bavaria. Looking over the old Tarn estate, Tarnenwerder, and probably talking with Maximilian Tarn's lawyers in Wasserburg.'

'You know The Committee wouldn't sanction that, Bond. You know they wouldn't even discuss it. So why should I recommend it to them?'

'Because somebody close to this Committee – probably a member – has a link to Tarn that goes back a very long way.'

'That's outrageous!' The Minister's complexion went from shock white to purple anger. 'Can you support these unconscionable accusations?'

'I think I can. Tell me, what time did Sir Max and his crew arrive at Heathrow the day they came back in?'

'On the Dublin flight that gets in at around five.'

'And when were you alerted?'

The Minister's jaw dropped. 'Not until seven. After we lost them the first time. Or I should say after the police and Security Service lost them.'

'Who else knew about the place behind Harrods?'

'Nobody. The Committee and a few officers in the field: and then only after the Security Service discovered that he owned the place.'

'Yet Tarn and his group were long gone before anyone moved in to take them. I must say that Max Tarn is either a psychic or he's very well informed.'

'This seems ludicrous.' The Minister sounded like a man who did not really believe what he was hearing.

'I don't see how he can be operating without help from the inside. I mean the blatant arrival at Heathrow and the way he was lost. Doesn't happen like that, Minister, and *you* know it. There are other things as well. The only way it makes sense is if somebody is feeding him information.'

'Can you point a finger?'

'Not really. If I were asked to bet on it I'd say one of the Security Service people – Thickness, Smith or

Jameson. They'd be our most obvious targets.'

'So, you really believe that someone on The Committee has been taking back-handers from Tarn? Passing him information?'

'I think it's a matter of common sense. From the beginning Tarn's been tipped off. Just tell me whose idea it was for Fräulein von Grüsse and I to feed him that story in Cambridge? You must know as well as I do that there was absolutely no way that Tarn could've planned that phony car accident without previous knowledge. He's been playing us for fools right down the line. He even knew exactly when I was to pick up Dolmech. He had a getaway planned for last night. He's not psychic. It *has* to be someone in that reading room. Tarn's too well informed. Think about it, sir.'

'Oh, my God.' The Minister had gone white again. 'You may well be right. I really have no other option but to recommend that you take a look around Germany. They won't learn anything from me. Go to it, Bond, and good luck.'

He asked Bill Tanner to send Flicka out to him, and Tanner nodded, muttering a quick, 'Take care, James.'

He saw the sadness in Flicka's eyes as she came in to join him. 'I presume you've convinced him? You're really going on your own?'

'I told you, Flick. It's the only way to work this.'

'I love you, James.'

'And I you, dear Flicka. Come and help me get organized.'

'You *will* come back?'

'I always come back, my dear. I'm like the Mounties, I always get my man.'

'So do I.'

'Hell of an engagement party.' She almost smiled.

14

Legal Nightmare

BACK IN THE flat, Bond spent half-an-hour hunched over the telephone calling Lufthansa, and booking a return flight to Munich leaving late that afternoon; reserving a single room at Munich's Splendid, where he would be well out of the way, particularly hidden from the Tarn party staying at Vier Jahreszeiten. The Splendid had long been the Munich resting place for those who wished to keep a low profile. Actors and artists had often called it home, and the hotel had been the late Federico Fellini's favourite hideaway. Bond gave a little smile as he put the phone down. There was some irony in it, for the Splendid was situated in Maximilianstrasse – a street that could easily have been named after Tarn.

Another call assured him of a hire car that he could pick up at Munich airport, and lastly he dialled a final German number – the Hotel Paulanerstuben, in Wasserburg am Inn. This place was listed as average good, in the Michelin Guide, but its main draw was the address, Marienplatz 9 – the same square in which the Tarn lawyers, Saal, Saal u. Rollen, had their offices.

When all these arrangements had been made, he packed a light garment bag, and then dragged his special briefcase from its hiding place in a disguised part of the wainscot. The automatic pistol, ammunition, together with the Applegate Fairbairn combat knife and scabbard, all went into the compartment at the bottom of the case, where they would not be detected by electronic security scanning devices. The latest in miniature cameras – which would take clear photographs of documents under most conditions – gloves, a set of lock picks disguised as a Swiss Army knife, and other items, including maps and documents, went into the main open, top section of the case. He also retrieved everything he needed for his Boldman identity, the one he used often when travelling abroad – passport, wallet complete with credit cards, and several letters addressed to J. Boldman Esq. at a fictional business address which was really a front for the Intelligence Service's overseas mail.

He then showered, changed into slacks, a light cotton rollneck, blazer and a pair of his favorite soft, comfortable moccasins.

Throughout all these preparations, Flicka had remained seated quietly in the bedroom, and it was only when she saw he was ready that she spoke.

'James, we need to talk.' She patted the edge of the bed.

'Of cabbages and kings?' he asked with a smile.

'Of what you're going to do; where you're going to be; your entire schedule.'

He opened the briefcase and pulled out a detailed map of the Wasserburg am Inn area, similar to a British Ordnance Survey map. 'I'll be playing a lot of this by ear, Flick, but here's the general plan.' He went through his intended movements, giving rough times and where he expected to be during the next couple of days, after which Flicka spoke again, her tone serious and commanding attention—

'Believe me, James, I understand the reason you have

to do this on your own. I understand it, but I don't like it, nor do I condone it. I've left a note with Bill Tanner to that effect. I'm not being difficult, but I think you should have back-up close by you. Naturally, I believe that back-up should be me. Now, please let's work out a telephone code so that you can at least keep in touch.'

It took them only about twenty minutes to cobble together a simple system, for they had used techniques such as this before.

When it was time for him to leave, Flicka hugged him tightly, but shed no tears. Nor did she use any feminine wiles to make him feel in the least bit guilty for leaving her out of this small and essential operation. Again, it was one of the plusses of their relationship: Flicka had been an intelligence agent for too long to make any silly fuss over such things.

'Take care of yourself,' she said in a matter-of-fact voice, then, softly, 'I love you, James.'

In the cab on the way out to Heathrow, her very low-key farewell did more to make him feel guilty than all the tears and histrionics that she could have produced. By the time he had checked in at the Lufthansa desk, Bond had already started to wonder about the wisdom of leaving Flicka behind.

The flight to Munich was, as usual, boring and the German efficiency at passport control and the car hire desk left nothing to be desired. He collected a cream colored VW Corrado, driving straight to the *Splendid*, where the car was parked for him by the staff of the hotel, the façade of which managed to draw anyone's attention away from the place. It is one of the delights of the *Splendid* that it looks like nothing and yet, for comfort, security and service, was everything which an incognito traveler would wish.

He ate a dinner so light and frugal that the head waiter raised his eyebrows and frowned, and by eleven was back in his room. He called Flicka to let her know that he was in Munich with no signs of Tarn watchers on his back, and she was so loving on the telephone that he went to bed decidedly frustrated. It did not stop him from sleeping though, for, during his many years as an agent in the field, Bond had perfected the art of putting the world, and professional or personal problems, out of his mind. His head had scarcely touched the pillow before he dropped into a deep sleep from which he woke, totally refreshed, when the telephone rang with his wake-up call at five in the morning.

He was on the road by just after six-thirty, and, by seven had left the outskirts of Munich far behind, heading out on the B-304. Before eight o'clock he came into Wasserburg, which seemed to rise from the light morning mists, like a great, faded ancient galleon.

With its untouched, medieval atmosphere, the town appeared to be surrounded by water from the River Inn, for Wasserburg was built within a few yards of a tight lazy curve in the river which nuzzles the southern limits of the town's center and enfolds its eastern boundary with great crags of rock, plunging straight down to the gentle flowing water below.

He drove the Corrado into the large parking lot on the northern bank of the river and set off on foot for the traffic-free town center, his garment bag over his shoulder. He walked quickly through the narrow lanes until they spilled out into the Marienplatz, the very center of the town, with its Gothic brick town hall and the 14th century Frauenkirche.

He stopped, on the edge of the square, listening to the soft flush of the river less than a hundred yards away, while taking in the extraordinary timelessness of the view. He even caught sight of what remains of the castle, to the south, from which Wasserburg – Water Castle – takes its name.

The town was already bustling: a cassocked priest walked from the Frauenkirche, with its old watchtower, while the few old shops were open and local people could be seen hurrying to them, or leaving with baskets of fresh bread and other produce.

At the *Paulanerstuben* they showed no surprise at this guest arriving at eight in the morning, but welcomed him in, showed him his pleasant room overlooking the square and offered him a second breakfast, which he accepted, ruminating on the many four star hotels throughout the world where he had been treated as a pariah when arriving this early in the day.

Assenting to a second breakfast was not a matter of greed, but a way to engage the one elderly waiter in conversation, so the meal passed with skirmishes of dialogue. Bond's German was excellent enough for him to pass as a native, and the exchanges yielded several useful pieces of information. The local people were slightly reserved when it came to foreigners, and he soon learned that this conservative trait had reached a high level during the week.

'It's the new owner of the Tarnenwerder estate,' the waiter told him, shuffling around, constantly fiddling with slightly shaky hands. 'It's said he's the last living relative of the old von Tarn family, and already he has over one hundred men and women restoring the house. There's no room for these people here in the town. How can there be? Anyway, the ancient boundaries of the estate stop a couple of kilometers from Wasserburg. We can't compete with these workmen, as we have none with their skills, so we won't prosper from anything just yet.'

'Surely, when things settle down . . . ?' Bond began to say, but the elderly man cut him off.

'Something funny's going on.' He shook his head in marked disapproval. 'Nobody knows how this claimant to the von Tarn name has survived. There's even a story that he's been living in places all over the world under the name Tarn, and this Tarn was supposed to have died, only recently, in a road accident in England. Can you believe any rumors these days?'

He went off to bring a plate of ham and eggs which he set in front of his customer, carrying on his monologue as though uninterrupted. 'Yet here he is. Large as life. Yesterday I saw him. He visited the lawyer Saal, over there,' pointing to an old half-timbered building across the square, beside the door of which was a brass plate. 'The Saals have managed the Tarn estate for six generations. Old Helmut Saal has blocked any purchase of the place since the end of Hitler's war. I'm not saying he's a liar or a cheat, but I think he would do anything to keep his hands on that estate. It's kept the Saal family in style for a very long time. This new von Tarn could be Saal's man for all we know. Put there to keep the Saals in the style to which they have become accustomed over the years.'

Bond told him that he wanted to see a lawyer with regard to purchasing property nearby, but was brushed aside with a, 'You should go to Fritz Saal, Helmut's brother. He deals with the purchase of property, but there are other things the town's not happy with.'

'Such as?'

'Such as this new von Tarn allowing dubious young people to camp in the grounds of the estate. Some of them look to us like the skinheads who do terrible things in the cities – you know what I mean: attacking foreigners, burning buildings, parading in the streets. Let me tell you, I heard stories of people like that from my father. I can even remember some of them myself. Hitler's people, that's who these young ruffians behave like.'

'How long has this been going on?'

'The skinheads? Only a couple of days, but some have come into the town to buy food, and they haven't always been too pleasant to the shopkeepers. We've turned them away from here. Anyway, they'll be gone tomorrow or the day after, I understand. They're here for some rally the master of Tarnenwerder's allowed them to have in his grounds. Don't hold with it myself.' The old boy went off chuntering to himself – as all old men do – about how it wasn't like this in his day.

No, Bond thought, you're of an age when it was, first, the survival of the fittest, and utter obedience to the Nazi Party; then, an age when the German people were trying to live down the excesses of Hitler's régime, which had brought your country to its knees. The old man, he thought, had also seen the upsurge of West Germany as *the* thriving industrial centre of Europe, and now the toil and turmoil of a country restored and not split in two. The restoration of a single Germany had brought with it problems and a desperate search for a new identity – or, worse, a return to the old way of the Nazis. He could not blame the waiter for being edgy about foreigners, and these German skinheads were, particularly, foreigners here in Wasserburg am Inn, a town that had survived, almost unchanged, centuries of *Sturm und Drang*.

After breakfast he returned upstairs, surprised that such an old and beautiful building from former days actually provided telephones in the few available rooms. The local directory was not large and he found the number for Saal, Saal u. Rollen. Within seconds of dialing, he was speaking to Herr Fritz Saal, explaining that he was a British businessman, looking for perhaps a large property in the area. An investment, you understand. For a consortium, you will follow. Naturally Herr Boldman.

Saal was bright and friendly on the telephone, but gloomy about the prospects, though, eventually, he remembered that there were a couple of estates on his books. Perhaps Herr Boldman could call on him at the office, say in half-an-hour. Herr Boldman was pleased to accept the invitation.

Bond then rang Flicka in London, stressing that he was fine, had arrived and discovered some interesting facts already. He also said that he would call again after his meeting with what he called a property lawyer in the town.

The building from which the Saal brothers and Herr Rollen carried out their business, while obviously very old, had been constantly renovated over several centuries. Initially, the building had probably been a small townhouse for some local worthy. From the half-timbered exterior, and the visible leaded windows, he reckoned that it probably had a largish entrance hall, with rooms to left and right; while upstairs it possibly maintained what had originally been three bedrooms.

On reaching the door he found that it was a solid oak panel, with metal bindings and hinges, into which had been set a large Yale-type lock – much bigger than the kind of thing you saw on houses in the rest of the world, but still small enough to slip with a thick piece of celluloid or a credit card.

He took a good look at the door surround, and all the windows, and sought out any tell-tale wiring or electronic boxes signaling a sophisticated alarm system. There were none, and the telephone wiring came in high, from an overhead pole on the right hand corner at the front of the building. Bond knew by the size of the telephone input box it was unlikely to contain any extra surprises.

He pressed the bell, and some seconds later the door was opened. He found himself staring into a pair of large gray eyes, topped by amazingly long lashes. Below the eyes was a pert little nose and below that a wide mouth, obviously designed by the Almighty to set a completely new standard of temptation for men. The woman wore her thick blonde hair in what at one time would have been called a French Pleat. Nowadays he had no idea what they called the style, but the hair was so perfect and thick that he had an immediate desire to plunge a hand into it and see if there were gold coins hidden under the smooth glossy surface.

The vision looked to be in her mid-twenties and was dressed modestly, in a manner at variance with her looks – and also the twinkle in her eyes. A second later, he saw a black-haired young woman, identically dressed, in a kind of long black nylon coverall which certainly hid whatever street clothes either of the girls wore. This signified that the young women wore these rather ugly uniforms as a protection against damaging or marking their own clothes while laboring in Saal, Saal u. Rollen's vineyard.

By the time he could draw his eyes away from the blonde's charms she had asked if he was Herr Boldman. He, somewhat haltingly, said yes and he was here to see Herr Fritz Saal.

The smile remained warm, embracing even, as she asked him to follow her upstairs – something she said in a slightly arch fashion which made it into a more personal invitation.

He pulled himself out of his reverie and looked around, realizing that he would have to examine the lower interior

171

of the building more thoroughly on the way out. His casual glance revealed nothing in the shape of electronic code pads for alarm activation. In fact all the electronics appeared to be two computers and a large laser printer. The dark girl, he had glimpsed briefly, was now seated behind one of the computers, rattling away at the keyboard as though her life depended on it, which, he thought, bearing in mind the association of the Saals with Max Tarn, it probably did.

As he had thought, there were three doors which led from a small landing at the top of the stairs, plus a short corridor which slid off to the right and ended in another door which, he concluded, was a bathroom.

The three doors were individually marked with the names of Herr H Saal, Herr F Saal and Herr K Rollen. The blonde vision tapped at Herr F Saal's door, opening it immediately and announcing 'Herr Boldman.'

Fritz Saal appeared to be sitting behind a huge desk, angled into one corner of the room, but it was only when Bond gave him a smiling bow that he realized Herr Saal was standing, prior to coming around the desk.

It was impossible to put an age on the man, and his appearance immediately brought to mind the Tenniel drawings of either Tweedledum or Tweedledee from *Through the Looking Glass*. The head was slightly out of proportion to his stature which was, to be politically correct, impaired. In plain language he was a dwarf of around four feet two inches, including the obvious lifts built into his shoes. Like others in his predicament, Saal made up for his lack of inches by a cheerful, even ebullient, manner. He greeted Bond with a firm handshake, and very quickly it became obvious that his height in no way affected his voice, charm or business acumen. Returning to his desk, Saal pushed two folders towards him. They were both of moderately sized estates – though one was a working farm – and, for the next half-hour or so, they discussed the possibilities.

Eventually, Bond said that what his consortium was really looking for was a place the size of – he went through a show of looking up the name in a notebook – Tarnenwerder, which he was under the impression had been left to rack and ruin.

Saal shook his head sagely. 'Tarnenwerder,' he said, without the hint of a smile, 'is something else altogether. To be truthful, Mr Boldman, I'd rather not discuss it.'

'I understood that you had dealings with *that* particular property.'

'No. No, I personally have no dealings with it. My brother, and our father before us, deals with Tarnenwerder. In fact, the place has been on our books for many generations. If I had my way, we would have passed it to another firm decades ago, but I fear that I rarely get my way in this company. You see, it's the only thing my brother Helmut deals with, and we have not spoken for twenty years on account of it.' He gave a sad little laugh. 'I would have left this firm years ago if it hadn't been for our strange legal position. No male of the Saal or Rollen family is allowed by our company articles to leave the firm, except, of course, in the event of death.'

'That's a strange legal point.'

'Very strange, and drawn up a number of centuries ago. The firm is tied to Tarnenwerder and the von Tarn family as if by an unbreakable umbilical cord. Unhappily, the very anomaly of the company articles makes it more binding. Originally, the Saals and Rollens were the stewards of the von Tarns. They moved up in the world to become lawyers, but the von Tarns saw to it that we remained, for all time, joined hip and thigh.'

'And all this has caused a split in your family?'

'As I say, I have not spoken to my brother in twenty years – and he's seven years older than I. His wife does not speak to my wife. To the end of their days, my mother was on good terms with me and my father did not even acknowledge me in the street. It's a strange world, and has nothing to do with my shortness of stature. Every fourth male Saal is born a dwarf.' He made a small waving motion with his hand. 'Yes, we're supposed to talk about ourselves in a different way these days, but I have never been politically correct – and the politics of my country are slowly descending into the pit of the 1930s again. Did you know that?'

'I have heard about it, and have seen some of it.'

'If you want concrete proof, just go over to Tarnenwerder at nine o'clock tonight and you'll see what our ancestors saw in the 1930s. History, particularly when it is the history of politics, is a circular thing. As the Americans say, what goes around comes around. The scourge of the 'thirties and 'forties is coming around yet again.'

They talked for another fifteen minutes, with Fritz Saal making notes regarding the mythical consortium and its requirements. Bond gave him the London address and he said he would be in touch.

Saal walked with him to the door and out onto the landing. They were just shaking hands once more in farewell when the door to K Rollen's office opened. Bond stepped back a pace, for the man who looked out from this office was a giant. He stood around six foot four, had hands like bunches of steel bananas, a large shaven head and a face that reminded him of a gargoyle.

'It's alright, Kurt,' Saal said gently. 'Nothing for you to worry about.'

'Ah, so, good.' The voice was as slow and lumbering as

that of an imbecile. The grin did not reach his vacant eyes, and he withdrew into his office as though that simple action was a feat of great skill.

Saal looked up at Bond. 'Every sixth male child of the Rollen family is born with a defect also. Yet he is a partner who does nothing. He's incapable of anything but the simplest task, and he can be a shade intimidating. Also, he has an uncanny memory. He remembers things and people from twenty years ago. I once heard him describe, completely, his own baptism. Unhappily, when roused, poor Kurt can be violent. Rather dangerously violent unless you know how to deal with him.' He gestured towards the bottom of the stairs, 'Now, our lovely Heidi will see you out.'

"Lovely Heidi" was the blonde eighth temptation of man.

'I think I once read a book about you, Heidi,' Bond said with a smile as she held the street door open for him.

'Oh, no, Mr Boldman. She was my Swiss cousin. Also, she was a good little girl.'

Out in the Marienplatz again, he allowed Flicka to come flaring into his mind and, quickly, she banished all thoughts of what could be done with Heidi, given the right time and place.

He then pondered on the near nightmare quality of the law firm of Saal, Saal u. Rollen, realizing that, in all probability, the throwbacks in both the Saal and Rollen families came from some incestuous relationships, when Wasserburg had been truly a Bavarian backwater some hundreds of years ago.

He strolled slowly to the edge of the square and turned into an alley which took him to the rear of the buildings. It needed only a casual glance at the back entrance of the lawyers' office to be certain that there was no overt security or alarms on the place. Also, he noted that the back door appeared to have only a normal lock. As long as they did not secure that lock with its retaining catch, the rear door would be his easiest way in.

Turning, he headed to the car park where he had left the car. Given what he intended to do that night, he thought it would be as well to look over the landscape – in particular the escape routes.

He opened the car and rummaged around in the front for a few minutes, glancing into the mirrors to make certain that he was not being observed. He could see nobody, and that sixth sense which had so often saved him before, told him he was clear.

Outside again, he walked back to the parking lot exit, strolling along the road that would take him onto the B-304. A few steps along this side road he saw a lane turning off to the right. On the wall, beside the lane, there was a notice warning of danger. This narrow road led out onto a smooth plateau which ended abruptly in rocky outcrops and a line of white warning poles. He could hear the river from practically anywhere around the Marien-platz, but now the roar was very close and, on reaching the wooden poles, he saw that he stood at the edge of a huge craggy cliff face. Two hundred feet below him, the waters of the river Inn snarled over more rocks.

The local Lovers' Leap, he thought, retracing his steps and making his way back to the hotel where the first person he saw was the elderly waiter who told him they had excellent Gänsebraten mit Kartoffelknodeln for dinner. 'People come from a long way to sample our roast goose with potato dumplings,' he added. 'I should be quick into the dining room or you will miss this delight.'

Indeed, the goose was a delight, and the potato dumplings were probably the best he had ever tasted, but he left the table a little concerned, for Bavarian food, while tasty, could lie heavily on the stomach. His mind, however, dwelt on the strangers he had seen in the square on his way back to the hotel. Thugs, toughs, young men and women, many of the men with their heads shaved, all of them in various kinds of disreputable dress. The kind of louts, he thought, who over the past couple of years had made the German cities unsafe: attacking foreigners, firebombing synagogues, and marching in anti-government protests.

Back in his room he called Flicka, who sounded brighter, particularly when he said that he hoped to be back either tomorrow or the day after. Then he used code words to let her know his intentions for that night.

'Should I tell the vicar?' she asked innocently. The vicar was their password for the Minister.

'I don't see why not if it makes him happy. He is like Dad, keeping Mum?'

'Like the grave, but I think he fancies his chances. He came into the office this afternoon and sat a little too close for comfort. Held my hand with a squeeze when he was leaving.'

'Never marry into Whitehall, my dear. The Junior Minister of today is not always the Prime Minister of tomorrow. You can get your name in the papers as well, consorting with members of HM Government.'

'I know it.' There was laughter in her voice as she used a particularly ribald code word. One that she had thought up, signifying certain desires.

It was eight-thirty by the time he had changed into black jeans, rollneck and denim jacket. The holster for his automatic was firmly in place on his right hip and hidden by the jacket, while spare ammunition magazines were distributed about his body, and the knife was strapped on his left forearm. He also carried the disguised Swiss Army knife and a small, powerful torch in his pocket. Earlier he had sat on the bed and memorized the route from the detailed map of Tarnenwerder, provided by Bill Tanner.

It was almost a ten mile drive, mainly on small country side roads, but it took him to a point on a boundary road of the Tarnenwerder estate where he could safely leave the car, backed in among a thick cave of shrubbery by the roadside.

Quietly he left the vehicle, standing, as usual, for several minutes to let his eyes adjust to the darkness. He knew that the ground sloped upwards from the road, and at the crest of the rise he would be able to look down onto the old house less than three hundred yards away.

He now saw that the way up was lighted by the reflection of what seemed to be flickering fire from the other side of the rise. He could also hear the voice, electronically amplified, of Max Tarn and he shivered for already it sounded like the rabble rousing oratory of someone from the historic past.

15

Tarnenwerder

WHEN HE REACHED the crest, the sight that struck him, almost like a blow to the mind, was even more reminiscent of some replay of an old 1930s movie.

The house itself was huge and bathed in light – a great tall oblong edifice in gray stone. In front a long raised terrace with central steps and an ornate stone balustrade stretched the entire length of the building. In the center at the top of the steps, a solid wooden lectern had been set up and Maximilian Tarn, in a brown uniform which also owed much to another era, stood – flanked by men in similar dress – haranguing a crowd of two or three hundred – a sea of people, men and women, girls and boys – ranged in well-ordered lines across a vast lawn. Each of these people held a blazing torch which threw disconcerting and moving shadows against the trees and the façade of Tarnenwerder. Tarn's shadow was, by some pre-arranged trick of lighting, huge and glowering against the house itself.

'It is with these thoughts in our minds that we must go forward. Fight. Keep faith. Stand firm, shoulder to shoulder. Remember the glorious dead who were betrayed.' Tarn raised both his hands, in little jerking movements, as he held the audience entranced. 'Only if we stay true to the message of our great forefathers . . .' One hand swept

179

upwards, clawing the air. 'Only if we stay true to the oaths of those who went before, will we rebuild what the glorious Adolf Hitler succeeded in building before he was betrayed – One Empire . . . One People . . . One Leader.'

Bond felt a cold sweat clouding his forehead. Tarn's voice, gestures and manner were almost exact replicas of those which had belonged to Adolf Hitler sixty odd years before. Even the last words – '*Ein Reich . . . Ein Volk . . . Ein Führer!*' were Hitler's words, and they were a signal to the crowd which bellowed back in a great series of waves, like crashing surf – '*Sieg Heil . . . Sieg Heil . . . Sieg Heil*!' Hail Victory.

Then came the moment that made Bond's stomach turn over and the cold sweat envelop his entire body. The sudden launching into song – one that he knew from old films and recordings and that conjured up the whole Nazi horror:

Die Fahnen hoch, die Reihe dicht geschlossen!
The flags held high! The ranks stand tight together.

It was the Nazi hymn, its marching song, its anthem, the *Horst Wessel Song*.

The very tune brought images, culled from books, news film, documentaries, and photographs, sharply to his mind: the young men shot to pieces on the ground, the sea and in the air; he almost heard the jackboots stamping, his mind seeing the flamboyant uniforms of the SS, and the sinister faces of the Gestapo. Europe a ruin, and the thousands who had disappeared to the camps. The six million Jews who had gone to the gas chambers. It was as though an entire montage of terror had filled his head: the walking dead of Auschwitz, Belsen, Dachau and the other death camps; the piles of skin and bone; the smoke from the dread chimneys. The horror of those past years early in this century when the whole of the continent shrank under the Nazi yoke. Was it all returning again?

There was no doubt now that Sir Max Tarn had already captured the leadership of the new Nazi Party, resurrected from its brutal past, fed by the indecision of the present German leadership, and watered by the requirements of a new age ripe for the taking.

Max Tarn, he knew, had banked on some spectacular act that would bring him forgiveness for former dealings in death, and set him up as a figure to be reckoned with on a global scale. It was, the unhappy Trish Nuzzi had told him, going to happen in the Caribbean. So this obscenity he now watched was but a prelude of what would come if by any chance the obsessive man could pull off some incredible coup that might make him untouchable in the eyes of the world.

Through all the flashing pictures in Bond's head, the words of the infamous *Horst Wessel Song* seemed even more prophetic—

Kam'raden, die Rotfront und Reaktion erschossen,
Marschieren im Geist in unsern Reihen mit.
Comrades who, though shot by Red Front or Reaction,
Still march with us, their spirits in our ranks.

Indeed, old Nazi ghosts would revel and caper among this crowd, while the once defeated leadership – from Hitler to Himmler – would stand close to this would-be Führer, smiling and nodding at what he was intent on bringing back, plunging the world into yet another dark age, and dragging the old abominations from their very graves.

Bond was so wrapped up in revulsion, that he failed to catch any sign of danger to himself. He had been oblivious to the security patrols which were obviously circling the perimeter of the Tarnenwerder estate. His first glimpse of an emergency came as a sudden flash of movement from within the grounds and to his left.

He turned to see two, brown-uniformed men about fifty yards away, unleashing a pair of German Shepherd attack dogs. The trained animals had sensed him as an intruder, and now they flew towards him with low growls.

He was on his feet and blundering down through the shrubbery heading back to the car, as the two beasts came bounding over the rise. He pulled his knife with his left hand and unholstered the automatic pistol with his right, running for his life and aware of the dogs closing like a pair of express trains.

He did not quite make the car before the first animal attacked, snarling and leaping for his right arm, its weight carrying him against the car, knocking the breath from his body. He felt a sharp pain as the dog's teeth sank into his forearm and pulled. For a second, the heavy Shepherd made a mistake, snapping at his arm again, but putting itself between Bond's body and the pistol. He put a bullet into the beast which seemed to stop dead before being thrown backwards with a long yelp of agony.

The other Shepherd, hearing its partner yelp and seeing it fall, hesitated for a fraction of a second, but it gave him enough time to slide into the car and close the door.

The dog landed heavily on the bonnet, barking and clawing against the windshield, saliva running from its jaws, the sharp teeth clearly visible. Bond started the engine, slammed the vehicle into gear and shot from the cave of overgrown shrubbery, wrenching hard at the wheel and throwing the dog to the ground, as he accelerated onto the road.

Two bullets struck the rear of the Corrado. He felt the heavy thumps, but could not detect damage. Hunched over the wheel and driving as though the hounds of hell were after him, he screeched around a long bend, and headed back towards Wasserburg. If his mission were to be truly successful, he had one more important thing to do, and he knew only too well that he had jeopardized the whole business by making the trip out to Tarnenwerder.

After ten minutes he was sure that nobody had followed, but he considered that would only be a matter of time. The dog handlers had got a good look at the car, so it would not take them long to report the matter. When that was done, Tarn's orders could only take one form – Bond's death warrant.

It was almost ten-thirty as he steered the car into the parking lot, where he chose a space close to the exit. For a few moments he sat in the driving seat, examining the damage to his forearm. There was blood, but the dog's fangs had not gone deep. He counted four long lacerations which he covered with a handkerchief tied tightly and soaking up the blood immediately.

Time was now at a premium, so he rolled down his sleeve over the makeshift bandage, removed the miniature camera from the glove compartment and left the car, jogging away towards the rear of the buildings on the side of the Marienplatz in which Saal, Saal u. Rollen was situated.

It took less than five minutes to reach the back of the lawyers' offices, and only thirty seconds to slide a credit card between the curved bolt and its housing. Nobody, it seemed, had bothered to clip down the retainer which would have posed difficulties.

He stood for a moment in the darkness inside the office, switching on the torch and shielding it with his hand, then making his way along the passage which led to the large entrance hall. All was silence and he could see the computers under their protective hoods. Again he stood listening. Not a sound, so he began to move silently up the stairs, across the landing and to the door with its little notice which read H. Saal.

He had expected to need his lock picks to get into Helmut's office, but the door was open and he was able to swing the torch beam around the room. The huge desk was similar to the one in Fritz's office, but the wall opposite was lined with a tall bank of gray filing cabinets.

Listening again for a few seconds, he went over to the one window and pulled down the blind, then made for the cabinets which were neatly lettered by alphabet. The letter T took up half of the wall, so it took little brain to realize that Helmut kept a large number of documents on Tarn, and Tarnenwerder, there, in his office.

The latest legal work for Tarn, Bond decided, would be in the last drawer labeled T. Slowly he removed his lock picks, in their Swiss Army knife disguise, and got down to the business in hand.

The cabinets were normal commercial pieces of equipment, about as easy to unlock as a child's moneybox. This was either all too simple, he thought, or Helmut was a lawyer with a very trusting nature. The last drawer clicked and slid open displaying about ten files hanging neatly on their rails. As he removed the first folder, Bond tried to use some logic on the situation. Helmut Saal had installed no special alarms or security equipment because Wasserburg, in all probability, had a low crime rate. The people of this unique little town were all descendants of families who had lived and died here over the centuries. Wasserburg was not the kind of place you moved into from somewhere on the other side of the country. This, being a given fact, meant that few would ever want to look at the files concerning Tarn and the estate. True, there had been small legal skirmishes over the years, when consortiums, and even the authorities in Munich, had tried to take over the estate, but even that would not be any cause for concern. Possibly there were very old documents which traced the estate's history back over centuries, but they would be stored in some safe vault. More recent papers could be kept here in the office with impunity. Any legal firm that still clung to archaic laws concerning generations of Saals and Rollens would not give a thought to having its documents behind ultra secure locks and warning devices.

He moved the file over to Helmut's desk and began to examine the papers within, holding the small torch in his teeth. The very first item showed that he had struck pay dirt, for it was a copy of an application for one Maximilian Erwen von Tarn to reclaim his German citizenship. Attached to it were copies of the official correspondence concerning the application, and the final page showed that the whole thing had been granted in March of 1992.

Other papers in this one file alone concerned the issue of a passport to Tarn, while the last section of documents were copies of a court order banning anyone else's claim to ownership of the house called Tarnenwerder and its considerable estates. The whole shooting match had legally belonged to the said Maximilian Erwen von Tarn since January 1992, even though he had not officially reclaimed his German citizenship until March.

There was enough here to satisfy The Committee that Sir Max Tarn, business tycoon and philanthropist, was not quite what he seemed. Certainly, as dual nationality could not apply, he had been sailing and flying under a false flag for some time.

He took out the camera and began adjusting it in order to get clear, well-lit shots of the papers. As he put his hand down on the corner of Helmut's desk he glanced towards the right hand set of drawers that ran down to the floor.

The bottom one was slightly open and he glimpsed a small red pinpoint of light from within.

Opening it further revealed a combination answerfone, set to pick up any incoming messages. He touched the little arrowed button marked *Rewind*, knowing that sometimes people did nothing about rewinding the tape after they had played it back. When it stopped he pressed the *Play Messages* button, heard the beep and then the second shock of the night. 'This is most urgent,' said a disembodied voice on the tape. 'An agent from the British Intelligence Service is on his way to Wasserburg. His mission is to run a check on Max and on the current Tarnenwerder situation. The man will be operating under the name James Boldman and I would advise that Max gives him the disappearing treatment.' Then followed a description of himself, James Bond, together with a few other facts – facts appertaining to MicroGlobe One, and the current situation in England.

It was not so much the message as the voice that rocked Bond on his heels. It was one he recognized immediately. Someone with whom he worked very closely and would never have thought capable of penetrating an organization like Two Zeros or even MicroGlobe One. Reaching down, he removed the tape from the answerfone and slipped it into his pocket. Going back to the job of photographing the documents, he found himself working like an automaton. The identity of the person who had betrayed him was so devastating that he could think of little else, but he completed the work, returned the file to its place in the cabinet and, using his picks again, he relocked the drawer. It was one of the things he had learned very early in his training. If you become involved in a covert burglary it is always best to leave things at least approximately how you find them.

He even did a quick search of the other drawers in Helmut's desk to see if there was an extra tape for the answerfone. Eventually he found a small packet of these tucked away beside the instrument itself and cursed that he had not looked more carefully to start with.

Now all he had to do was get back to the hotel, pay his account and head for Munich. If he managed to get that far, it was possible that, by then, Tarn's men could be watching out for him which would pose a new, and difficult, threat.

There was still no sign of life outside the offices of Saal, Saal u. Rollen, and as he quietly made his way down the stairs, Bond at last began to think that, maybe, he would get away with it.

He reached the bottom of the stairs when the lights came on.

'So, Mr Boldman, or should I call you Mr Bond? Would you like to talk with me for a while.' She looked as tempting as ever, in a military style raincoat. The only thing he did not like about her now was the lethal little automatic she held, in her right hand, very close to her delicious body.

'Heidi? Hi,' he said, allowing a smile to creep over his face. 'So you got my note. I didn't really expect you to come.' He showed no sign of having seen the pistol as he walked forward, his arms outstretched as though to embrace her.

'Your note? I . . . ? What're you talking about, Mr . . . ?' His greeting had thrown Heidi just enough for her to pause before doing anything – like pulling the trigger. Bond kept on going, straight towards her. 'Heidi, I'm so pleased. Now where would you like to have dinner?' By this time he was only two steps away and could clearly see the puzzled expression.

187

He moved in really close, and her right hand brushed his left side so that he could trap the wrist and gun with his left arm, cutting in like a vice. She opened her mouth just before he brought up his right elbow and struck her violently on the side of the jaw.

'I do hate striking women, Heidi, but you should have stayed a good little girl.' The pistol dropped to the floor as he applied more pressure with his left arm, while the next blow was a hard chop to the base of her neck with the heel of his right hand.

She went down completely, sprawled at his feet. Quickly he felt the pulse in her neck to make sure she was still alive, which she was though she would probably remain unconscious for a good ten minutes, maybe even more.

Scooping up her pistol, he headed straight to the rear of the building, letting himself out and quietly closing the door behind him. At a steady jog trot he made for the parking lot, now more conscious of the dog bite in his right forearm. Trying to banish any thought of the pain from his mind, he made the car in three minutes flat, realizing that he did not have the time for such niceties as collecting his luggage or paying the bill at the *Paulaner-stuben*.

He had just started the engine and was pulling out of the space beside the main exit when a black BMW roared in front of him and a similar colored Mercedes Benz blocked off the exit.

Two men leaped from the Merc, and a third hit the ground running as the BMW came to a jolting stop. All three men were armed, and he saw that one of them was the huge Kurt Rollen he had seen that morning.

He let out the brake and pushed hard on the accelerator, pointing the VW straight at the lone man who had jumped from the BMW. He muttered to himself – 'I don't know your name, but I call you the lone idiot' – for the approaching figure obviously considered himself invincible. Bond slewed the car to the right, braking hard and letting the offside door swat the foolhardy man. There was a sickening thud, and he just caught a glimpse of the mouth open in a scream, and eyes wide with sudden terror. He was also almost sure that his target had been thrown several yards, but he would soon find out. He put on more speed and then performed a perfect wheel and brake turn that brought him back facing the two men who had come from the Merc. He saw the BMW idiot lying very still a long way off to his right as the first bullets ripped into the Corrado, punching a hole in the shatter-proof windshield, on the passenger side, ripping into the seat next to him.

The only way to fight armed men when you are trapped in a car is to use the vehicle itself, and he slammed the accelerator hard against the floor so that the car leaped towards Rollen who had fired the two shots.

The giant had seen what had happened to the BMW imbecile and he obviously did not want to share the same fate. He paused, fired again, the bullet passing over the Corrado as Bond tried to spin the VW and catch Rollen off balance.

The car began the spin then hit what must have been a patch of oil in the middle of the parking lot. For what seemed to be minutes, he wrestled with the wheel as the VW went completely out of control, snaking its way towards the little wooden fence that separated the parking lot from the road. At one point he saw Rollen's companion suddenly appear on his left side, hands lifted trying to get a shot in, but the Corrado must have brushed him as it went rocketing past, for he heard another bump and then a yell over the sound of the engine.

The long uncontrolled skid ended with the VW crashing straight through the wooden barrier and out onto the road. He whipped the wheel to the right, straightened up as he saw the Merc attempting to back up and cut him off. But he had control of the car again and went barreling past the rear of the Mercedes, screeching around the corner and away.

No, he thought. No, not away. It would be a gamble but he would take it. The alley with its danger signs was coming up fast on his right, so he braked and swung into the narrow road, then put on speed again. He had not fastened his seatbelt when the attack had begun, so he was able to hang onto the wheel with one hand, his arm rigid, holding the wheel at twelve o'clock to steer with accuracy, while his left hand began to unlatch the door.

In front of him he saw that the white posts which ran along the top of the cliff face had red reflectors on them. It was simply a question of judgment. He hit a rock and the car lost contact with the ground for a second, landing a little to the left as he regained control.

It was only when he was roughly twenty yards from the line of posts, that he gave the car its last burst of speed, then threw open the door and rolled to his left.

He hit the ground hard, winded for a second before he could move towards the nearest piece of cover, a small clump of rocks. Just as he rolled, the Corrado hit the warning poles. He saw it leap forward as though it were trying to grab at air and fly, then the nose dipped and it fell. From his cover he heard the first crunch as the metal hit the rock face, then the sudden boom and whoosh as it hit again, rupturing the petrol tank, sending a sheet of flame up to the top of the drop.

The Mercedes and BMW both crept from the alleyway,

their drivers obviously well briefed in the danger of driving too fast into this dangerous place. Four men, plus the massive Rollen were out of the cars as the final crunching and clatter came from two hundred feet below. As Bond sneaked a peep over the rocks he saw that one of the men was Maurice Goodwin.

'My God,' one of them said. 'He's gone over the edge. Careful, Kurt . . .' as Rollen walked towards the sheer drop and looked down.

'He's burning,' Kurt said in a slow, unbelieving voice. 'We've failed. Oh my God, we've failed.'

'Kurt,' Maurice Goodwin said. 'We haven't failed. He's dead. Nobody could have survived in that wreck.'

'Then, we've not failed.' Slow. 'We've won, eh, Mo. We've won.'

'Please, Kurt, don't call me Mo. My name's Maurice.'

16

Dead or Alive

HE STAYED WHERE he was, lying on the ground hidden by the little mound of rocks. His body was bruised and sore, while the bite on his arm began to throb. Tarn's men left fairly quickly, and the local police and rescue team arrived within minutes of their jubilant departure. Several townspeople, alerted by the crash and explosion of the car, followed, milling around anxious to see what had happened.

He used the sudden influx of people to get to his feet, mingle for a few minutes, trying to ease the aches in his body, and think of ways and means to get out of Wasserburg as quickly as possible.

Finally, he slipped away, walking back to the hotel across a deserted Marienplatz. There was nobody about in the hotel entrance so he was able to get to his room unseen. Once there he took a quick very hot shower, cleaned off the lacerations in his arm which looked slightly red and swollen, and made a more permanent bandage from a couple of handkerchiefs. He dressed in blazer and slacks and then returned downstairs again.

The elderly waiter was nodding off behind the small reception desk.

'You work long hours, my friend.' Bond shook him by the shoulder.

'Ach.' The waiter slowly opened his eyes. 'I don't sleep much these days. You get older you don't need so much sleep. What can I do for you?'

Bond asked if he knew a reliable taxi service. 'I want to get to Munich as quickly as possible.'

'How quickly?'

'Now. Straightaway.'

'My brother. He's stupid enough to go anywhere at any time. Wait.' He dialed a number and proceeded to have an agitated conversation with somebody he called Wolfie. Putting a hand over the mouthpiece, he grinned. 'He'll do it, but you'll have to make it worth his while.'

After a little haggling they settled on a price. Bond paid his hotel bill and went back to finish his packing. Fifteen minutes later he carried the suit bag and the briefcase, repacked with the weapons in the safe compartment, downstairs and found the waiter's brother chatting in the small foyer.

The brother turned out to be older than the waiter, and wore thick lensed glasses, but he grabbed the bags and set off towards his car. Before following him, Bond pushed a handful of notes into the waiter's hand and half whispered, 'You've never seen me, okay?'

'I never see anybody. That's how you get from being a teenager in Hitler's Germany. It always pays never to see or hear anything.'

Wolfie appeared to be under the impression that he was a Formula One driver, but he still took well over an hour and a half to get to Munich airport. There were only four really frightening incidents during the drive, and Bond paid up, hurrying into the almost deserted airport to find that he had a very long wait as there were no flights to London until a British Airways departure at seven-thirty in the morning. There were seats on the flight so he managed to exchange his Lufthansa ticket, to the delight of the young woman at the BA desk.

Speed was essential, he thought, once he arrived in London, so he did not check in any luggage. His next step was to use a telephone carefully enough not to give any prior warnings to the person whose voice he carried on the tape in his pocket.

Using a credit card, he called Bill Tanner at his home number, and very quickly laid the news on him, covering both Max Tarn's bid for a Fourth Reich in Germany, and the name of the person who had betrayed MicroGlobe One and the entire country.

'You're certain?' Tanner was as shaken as Bond had been.

'One hundred per cent proof positive, Bill. Here's what I want you to do.' He outlined the exact steps that needed to be taken in the morning. 'I'll call Flicka just before the flight departure,' he ended. 'You can both meet me; but for heaven's sake have everything else fixed.'

'It'll all be done.' Tanner was about to close the line when Bond asked if they still employed Burke and Hare?

'We certainly do.'

'Better have them on hand as well.'

Burke and Hare were nicknames for Bill Burkeshaw and Tony Hairman, probably the two most experienced inquisitors who worked for the Intelligence Service. They would certainly be needing them if things were to run to a smooth climax.

He found a seat in front of one of the airport television sets where you could watch CNN in English. It was positioned so that he had an uninterrupted view of the whole concourse, and he remained there until the British Airways flight was called. Only then did he use the telephone again to call Fredericka von Grüsse, who answered brightly.

He gave her the flight number and time of arrival at Heathrow, tersely telling her to meet him, closing the line quickly.

The BA Airbus 360 landed at exactly eight-thirty local time – a two hour trip with a time difference of one hour between Munich and London.

Flicka embraced him as though he had been away for a month, not just a couple of days. Bill Tanner stood to one side, then clasped his hand.

'Everything done?' Bond asked, and Tanner nodded without speaking.

'What the hell's going on?' Flicka looked confused.

'You'll see.' He gave her a mischievous smile. 'Hope you didn't do anything rash, like bringing a hire car and driver out, because we're heading straight for the Home Office in Bill's car.'

She gave a resigned sigh. 'Might as well talk to a brick wall.'

Everyone, except M, was gathered in the reading room at the Home Office, and two members of the Security Service loitered in the passageway outside the door.

'Ah, our wanderer returns.' The Minister spoke with a little surprise. 'Tanner, you didn't tell us that Captain Bond was back.'

'He wasn't, sir. Not when I spoke with you early this morning.'

'With your permission, Minister, I'd like to tell you exactly what I've been doing in Germany.'

'Of course. Go ahead. Nobody's going to stop you.'

So, Bond gave what he later called his "recital" particularly stressing the facts concerning Tarn's German citizenship, and the scene he had witnessed on the previous evening. When he came to the end, the Minister asked if he could be excused for a moment. 'I have someone coming over from the Foreign Office.' He made towards the door and had almost reached it when Bond stopped him. 'Minister, I'm afraid I am the bearer of even worse news.'

'Oh?'

'I suggest you stay and hear me out.'

Reluctantly, the Minister returned to his seat, grumbling that he hoped this would not take long.

'I've made no secret of the fact that I've been unhappy with MicroGlobe One from the outset,' Bond began, and Wimsey made an exasperated noise.

'We're not going into all that again, surely.'

'I'm afraid we have to, Commissioner. My feeling is that Tarn has been leading us a merry dance from the beginning. For instance, who actually suggested that Fräulein von Grüsse and myself should tip him off about the impending arrest and search warrants?'

'Not me,' Wimsey proclaimed loudly.

'No,' Bond looked at him, steely-eyed. 'No, Claude, I'm now sure it wasn't you. The whole of that idea was rather cleverly arranged. You voiced the idea, but someone else put it into your mind. Have any of you really thought deeply about how Tarn could have faked his death at such short notice? That business on the way to Duxford wasn't organized at a moment's notice. It had been set up long before Fredericka and I even arrived in Cambridge.' He made a gesture towards Tanner who nodded and left the room.

'There are other matters, which I touched on very briefly when we were last gathered here. How, in blazes could your people, Wimsey – the police – and the Security Service have been so left-footed when Tarn and company came back into England? How did the timing work when Fredericka and I went up to Hall's Manor and found Lady Tarn's body? There are too many coincidences, and Tarn had just too much luck. He, and his partners, knew I would be in Wasserburg well before my arrival. I very nearly lost my life in Germany, and there's a possibility that Tarn actually thinks I am dead.' He turned to Flicka, 'That's why I didn't talk to you very much when I got back this morning, my dear. I'm covered in bruises and my right arm's giving me a little trouble, but I'm sure the dog that bit me wasn't rabid. As the Führer elect, I am certain Tarn would have made certain that his stable of guard dogs is free from any infection.'

'Where are we actually going with this?' asked the Minister.

'Bear with me, Minister.'

Tanner came back into the room carrying the tape recorder they had used on the previous occasion.

'You see, ladies and gentlemen,' Bond indicated that the machine should be put on the table. 'Max Tarn could not have pulled off his various little dodges unless he had a very special kind of help. Help from inside this room.'

'Oh,' Wimsey sighed. 'Who the hell do you think . . . ?'

'I don't think, Claude. I know. I know because our mole – as they say in the spy novels – left his voice behind in Germany.'

'What're you talking about, Bond. How much more of this . . .'

Tanner, who had inserted the tape, pressed the *Play* button—

'This is most urgent,' said the Minister's voice on the tape. 'An agent from the British Intelligence Service is on his way to Wasserburg. His mission is to run a check on Max and on the current Tarnenwerder situation . . .'

There was an audible gasp, even from the Director General of the Security Service, and the Minister tried to make for the door.

'No good, sir.' A pistol had appeared, like some smart conjuring trick, in Tanner's hand. 'There are people waiting for you there.'

'This is . . . That's a fake . . . Someone's . . .' the Minister blustered, stood, sat down and then stood again. His manner now was of defeat.

Tanner suggested that he surrender to the Security Service people outside, and as the door opened, Bond caught a glimpse of the two interrogators nicknamed Burke and Hare, loitering in the background.

'I'm sorry, Ma'am,' Tanner addressed the DG of MI5. 'I'm afraid I've probably overstepped my authority in bringing in a pair of your people . . ?'

'Not at all.' She waved the apology away. 'Well, I suppose I'm the senior member of The Committee for the present, so I'd better take the chair . . .'

'Sorry again, Ma'am. After James – er Captain Bond – telephoned me from Munich almost in the middle of the night, I spoke at length with the Prime Minister. He's appointed a new chairman of MicroGlobe One. A friend of yours, I think. Lord Harvey of Danehill. He's a member of the Joint Intelligence Committee.'

'Yes. A very fine man.' The DG looked a shade put out.

'He'll take the chair very shortly. He didn't want to come in until this whole business had been dealt with. It is a touchy matter so the Prime Minister's office has asked that nobody talks about it to *anyone* outside this room.' He turned to Bond. 'There wasn't much doubt, even without my hearing the tape. I checked as you asked. He's known Tarn for a long time. Same university. Same college at university also. They've been cronies for years.'

'I think,' the DG interrupted them, 'this would be a good opportunity to take some coffee. We've all been up for quite a long time.'

'Want to take a look-see before you face The Committee again?' Tanner asked. 'He went to pieces as soon as they took him out.'

Bond nodded, reaching for Flicka's hand, and Tanner led them to a small room within shouting distance of the reading room.

He knew this pair of interrogators rarely failed to extract whatever information was held by the target – the 'subject' as they called all of their unhappy clients.

The Minister was in his shirt sleeves and seemed to have aged by at least ten years in just over ten minutes.

'Hallo, Minister,' Bond greeted him brightly. 'Treating you well, then?'

The Minister did not reply, so he looked at the interrogators, raising an eyebrow.

'Coughing like a man smoking seventy a day,' Burke smiled.

'Singing arias like Pavarotti,' Hare nodded.

'He's admitted complicity?'

'Friend of Max Tarn's for years, he says. He also says that he didn't realize the extent to which the man went. He just helped oil the wheels from time to time, but we know he did more than that.'

'May I ask him a couple of things?'

'Be our guest.' Hare turned back to the Minister. 'You'll have no objection to this gentleman's questions?'

'Depends what he asks.' The Minister had that look, deep in his eyes, which said he knew his career had ended and his only chance was to be completely candid.

'I can promise you,' Bond began, 'that, if you come clean, I'll personally do my best to see that we keep all this out of the comic papers. Also, I don't expect anyone will want to shout about your activities from the rooftops. Be *really* co-operative and you'll not even see the inside of a courtroom.'

'I've heard all that before.' The Minister did not even look at him.

'I just want information about Tarn's associates. Did you know Lady Tarn's bodyguards? A pair of grotesques called Cuthbert and Archibald?'

'You mean the pair of cross-dressers? Cathy and Anna?'

'Oh, you did know them.'

'Saw them around. His fixer, Maurice Goodwin, told me who they were.'

'Well, who did they really work for – Lady Trish or Sir Max?'

'Max, of course. *Everybody* worked for Max in the long run. All you had to do was send someone really straight down to Sir Max and he'd come back bent as a corkscrew.'

'Anything special about Duxford?'

'I think the original plan was for them to fly out of Duxford airfield, though that would have been a bit tricky.'

'They managed to do it after Lady Trish's murder.' Tanner was standing just behind Flicka. 'On that dark night, a corporate jet landed at Duxford just after midnight. Claimed he had a fuel problem. They let him fill up and the pilot made a telephone call. About an hour later, as I understand it, a pair of Land Rovers turned up and the occupants climbed out and boarded the aircraft. The jet took off, but the radio transmissions were, to say the least, on the sparse side. The general feeling is that money changed hands, but I doubt they'll prove anything.'

'That was exactly how they were going to do it the first time.' The Minister seemed to have gained a small amount of confidence since Bond's promises. 'I think they had a genuine problem with the aircraft that time because, at the last minute, I was told to give them an extra twenty minutes if possible.'

'And you were well recompensed for all this, Minister?'

'I took money, yes. I've already told these people that I took money.' He made the word "people" sound like an obscenity.

'Max only used money?' Flicka asked.

'Meaning?'

'Meaning what I said. Did Max only use money to bribe people?'

The Minister gave a bitter laugh. 'Max used anything available. Money always worked because he paid out beyond people's wildest dreams, but the man has no conscience. Would snuff out his mother if it would do any good, and he'd sleep soundly at night. He was equally at home with blackmail, and providing other little favors – women, even boys.'

'Anyone we know?'

'He pimped Cathy and Anna for friends. I know that for a fact. When you finally get to him, Bond, wish him well from me just before he dies. You'll certainly not take him alive, I'd put money on that. Without doubt, Max Tarn is the most evil man I have ever known. He's moved through the world like a plague, sowing germs of death disguised as arms and military equipment to anyone willing to pay. He sees nothing wrong in that. In fact he believes that, in the end, the world will accept him because he reckons to have some great plan that will do immeasurable good.'

'Didn't I mention that to The Committee?' Bond thought he had told them. 'You've no idea what this great boon to mankind actually is?'

'None. Except a code word. *SeaFire*, he called it. I've heard him laugh and say that when he reveals *SeaFire*, he will have no enemies in the world.'

'Any idea where he's headed next?'

'None. He was in Germany – but, of course, you knew that. You were there.'

'And *you* allowed me to go. You let me talk you into it, and agreed to use that four day recommendation rule. Now why did you do that?'

'What option did I have? You were pressing me. I thought it was safe . . .'

'You also thought it would be the end of me, didn't you?'

The Minister did not reply. He just shook his head, indicating this was not the case. Then—

'He might still be there, as far as I know. He did say he had a great deal to do.'

'Personally,' Bond sounded as though he were detached, speaking words that were simply thoughts in his mind, nothing to do with any of those present. 'Personally, I think he's headed somewhere completely different.' He turned to Tanner. 'A word in private, Bill.'

Flicka followed the two men out of the room.

'Bill, the old Service? Do we still employ Q Branch?'

'Barely, but the divine Ann Reilly still labors in our vineyard.'

'Good, Q'ute's still with us. Can I get to see her?'

'James, I have to be honest about this. Because of all this business, The Committee's going to insist on *everything* going through them.'

'I can live with that. Let's go in and ask them. Oh, and by the way, Bill, I'll need to have a word with M again. How's he doing?'

'Making Nurse Frobisher pretty miserable. You'll be a sight for her sore eyes.'

'So shall I,' said Flicka firmly. 'If he's going to see M, then so am I.'

'Whatever you both wish.' Bill Tanner prided himself on being a diplomat, so he added that he had organized coffee and sandwiches for The Committee. 'Shall we join them?'

As they reached the reading room door, so the new Chairman, Lord Harvey came up the stairs. Tanner introduced Bond and Flicka.

'Ah, the man of the moment.' Harvey was one of the younger peers. In his early forties he was reckoned to be the catch of the year for any young girl who had aspirations to the upper crust. It was said that whoever married him would be forced to share Harvey with politics and government, as he was reputed to be one of the most able men on the Joint Intelligence Committee. 'Glad to see you made it back in one piece. But you've caused me all kinds of problems. I've been reading reports since the crack of dawn. This fellow, Tarn? Is he really as black as he's painted?'

'Blacker, sir. But I think I know how to hook him.'

'Really? Then you can be a great help to me here and now. Let's go on in and I'll give you the floor.'

The members of The Committee rose as they saw their new Chairman come through the door, and he made much of shaking hands with each of them before calling the meeting to order.

'Captain Bond has asked me to allow him to put a proposal to The Committee, so I've promised to let him speak to you first.' He smiled his charming smile and gave a deferential bow to Bond.

'As you say, sir, I'd like to make some propositions to The Committee.' Bond looked around him belligerently. 'More important, I'd like to draw up an order of battle. I think I know where friend Tarn has gone, and I'd like to follow him there and bring him back. Dead or alive, I don't really care which.'

17

Busman's Honeymoon

'YOU'RE ALL AWARE,' he started without preamble, not giving anyone a chance to relax. 'You're all aware that Max Tarn has known our every move since before the start of this business.'

There was a silent nodding of heads, and he noticed Commissioner Wimsey did not look him in the eye, though his face was flushed with anger.

'The police have worked in tandem with the Security Service, while the Minister controlled every action made in the field. Through him, Max Tarn has known the who, why and when regarding law enforcement, security and intelligence since long before we even started to take him seriously. He's literally got away with murder, and what's more he's been playing a game with me, as your authorized agent in the field. In some ways he's been acting as a puppet master. He's led Fräulein von Grüsse and myself on a merry dance, luring us into places where he wanted us to be. In fact we're very lucky to be alive. I believe it's possible that he wants to make an example of Flicka and myself, and show the world that he's not the diabolical agent we would like people to believe. I'm pretty certain, now, that I know exactly where he is, or at least where he will be within a few days. All I need is The Committee's permission to take certain actions.

'Within a short time, Tarn will be on the island of Puerto Rico,' he finally declared. 'Through this entire business, he has dropped hints which have put us exactly where he wanted us. I think it follows that he will be expecting me, at least, to be in Puerto Rico either just before or just after him. I believe he has chosen that island as the site for the final – what can I call it? – final showdown? Also some form of demonstration. Max von Tarn is a man desperate to do the trick of suddenly becoming moderately respectable before he announces his bid for political leadership of a new National Socialist Party in Germany. At the same time the world will be told that he has renounced his British citizenship, and returned to his rightful place as a German. In simple terms, I need your permission for Ms. von Grüsse and myself to be there. I know you'll say, why put ourselves in obvious danger?'

'Yes, why, Captain Bond?' Their new Chairman began to sound very reserved. 'There *is* a technical point here, though. If Tarn has already reclaimed his German citizenship, the ball might well be out of our court.'

'His lawyers, who seem to be mainly concerned in property matters, are the only people who know that – apart from the German authorities and myself.' He had already sifted this one through his mind and knew it was a technicality that the bureaucrats could argue about for months. 'I think, with all respect, sir, that we should ignore the change in citizenship, unless Tarn makes some early announcement.'

'Well, possibly.' Lord Harvey was obviously well versed in the tangled niceties of this kind of thing. 'However, I did ask you why you required permission to hunt for him in Puerto Rico?'

'Sir, what began as a relatively simple operation to

prove that Sir Max Tarn was guilty of certain acts of fraud, and possible illegal arms dealing, has become a personal vendetta between the two of us.'

The Chairman spoke softly, leaving nobody in doubt that he also carried a big stick. 'I thought that went against all the tenets of your Service, Bond. You should never make any operation personal. It's the impersonality of such things that keeps you distanced; allows you to act only for your country, and remain detached from the people involved.'

'Times are changing, sir. Also, there are moments in this business when you have to get close up and personal, as our American cousins would say.'

'Talking of our American cousins,' Bill Tanner spoke quietly. 'If you're sent off to the Caribbean to operate in Puerto Rico, then the Americans will have to sanction this as well as The Committee.'

'Puerto Rico is a Commonwealth of the United States.' There was a trace of irritation in Bond's voice. 'At their last referendum they refused to join the United States with full status.'

'That doesn't mean we can just let the Americans go hang.' Lord Harvey was no fool. 'What you appear to be asking might not be in our power to give. The Yanks've turned us down before. They have the right to ask for complete details of any legal infringements and go after the party, or parties, concerned, using their own agencies on their own turf, so to speak.'

'And you won't consider turning a blind eye?'

'How could we, and where's your solid evidence regarding Tarn and Puerto Rico?'

'You can probably get that in twenty minutes flat. My people are working on the financial and legal aspects of this case, in Bedford Square. They can probably track down evidence that either Tarn himself, or Tarn International, owns property in Puerto Rico. Damn it all, his container ships are in and out of there all the time; his cruise ships call in regularly; he has friends in moderately high places and *they* turn a blind eye to what he's doing. I think it's the least *you* can do.'

'This Committee *cannot* do that, Captain Bond. We're accountable. We're the ones who'll end up with empty rice bowls if things go wrong.' Harvey smiled, as if he were saying, "sorry old boy, but it's out of the question. Nothing personal."

'Again, with respect, sir, I'm the one who could well end up without his life.'

'Add me to that.' So far, Flicka had stayed silent. 'You do realize what's going to happen if someone doesn't go after Tarn from here? If we don't take complete action and run him to earth? He's going to get away with it. *Everyone* will turn a blind eye, including the Americans. Our so-called civilization will be the loser, Tarn will emerge victorious, and we'll all be back in the dark ages. I have respect for our American allies, but even if they did take over, even if Tarn were arrested, we'd still be haggling over him ten years from now while he would be sitting on his own pile of wealth and possibly the power of the Chancellorship of Germany. The fact that several thousand deaths will lie at his door won't even cross his mind. Only Tarn will be the winner.'

'Maybe.' Thickness, of the Security Service, spoke for the first time. 'But the Chairman's right. Puerto Rico is not in The Committee's bailiwick. Before we could even discuss letting you go, the American agencies would have to be brought in.'

'It's going to take months, if you do that.' Bond was truly angry. This is what happened when you allowed a series of committees, and the by-the-book attitude of frightened politicians to take over. 'Next thing, you'll be saying that permission'll also have to be granted by the EEC.'

'Could very well be,' muttered the Chairman.

'So you're all prepared to sit here, hold meetings with the American Intelligence agencies, and their law enforcement people, before you allow us to go and deal with the business?'

'I see no other way.'

'Look, James,' Bill Tanner used his most conciliatory voice. 'There *is* a way. What if we promised to give you an answer in, say, a week's time? You could take seven days' leave and just wait it out. I don't suppose a week's going to make any difference, is it?'

The look that passed between the Chief of Staff and Bond spoke volumes. Bill Tanner knew how, in the old days, at the height of the Cold War, their old Chief, M, had got around red tape by simple and direct means. Tanner was telling Bond to get on and do it, in his own time, without getting tied hand and foot by the same red tape that M snipped through, putting his own position on the line.

Bond opened his mouth, then thought better of it. Finally he said—

'Bill, you're right, of course. Just as The Committee is right. Fredericka and I cannot expect any of you to put yourselves in jeopardy over this, and a week probably won't make any difference. I change my plea. Might we have a week's leave while you sort matters out with the American Services?'

'Granted.' Lord Harvey looked relieved. 'Get a good rest, Captain Bond, and leave us a number where we can contact you – and Ms von Grüsse as well, of course.'

'How?' Flicka asked when they were settled in the car.

'How?' he parroted. 'How d'you think, Flick? We just go and do it.'

'So where do we go first?'

'Get some lunch, then go for a sick visit. We see M, because if we don't there'll be one hell of a stink. I have to let him know where we'll be. I also want his okay to use things over which he still has control.'

They stopped for lunch on the way to the M4 and, eventually, *Quarterdeck*.

Halfway through the meal, she leaned over and took one of his hands in both of hers. 'James, darling,' she spoke in almost a whisper. 'I love you as I've loved no other man. I took your side in there with those idiots who would see the whole of Europe down the drain rather than compromise themselves . . .'

'They don't mean to be like that, Fredericka. I'm sure that in about five days they'll have it all sorted out. Deep down they know I'm right. It's just the whole idea of a Committee being responsible for Intelligence and Security that bothers me, and in five days it will almost certainly be too late.'

'Just let me say one thing, James,' she persisted. 'I feel like you, and I'll do whatever you say. Tarn has got to be brought down, but please don't feel it's necessary to take huge risks simply because you've had to act over a matter of principle. I'll stand by you all the way, but you *can* back down if you feel it's wiser. You certainly won't lose face in my eyes.'

He thought for a few seconds. Then—

'Flick, I truly mean this. I'll be honest with you. We could both quite easily die when we get close to Max Tarn again, but I have to try and topple the man. The world's dangerous enough place without people like him who make it even more hazardous and unhealthy. Neither of us know what he's got going out there in the Caribbean, and it could be something more horrific than either of us could dream about. No, I couldn't sleep peacefully in my bed unless I at least make a final attempt to get him. *You* don't have to risk your life by coming with me. In fact, I'd rather that you stayed here in the comparative safety of London . . .'

'Enough!' She squeezed his hand. 'If you're set on going, you're not leaving here by yourself. Where you go, I go, no matter the risk.'

He knew that any argument he put forward would be useless. When Fredericka von Grüsse made up her mind, there was no way of stopping her.

They pulled off at the first service station on the M4 so that he could call *Quarterdeck* from a public telephone booth and comparative safety. Nurse Frobisher sounded quite excited at the news he was coming to visit the Admiral – until he told her he would be bringing a lady friend.

M, still propped up in his sick bed, seemed delighted to see both of them, and after a little small talk, asked the reason for their visit. 'I don't believe that you would both come down here just to see an old and sick man.'

'I think you already know why we're here, sir. I'd be surprised if The Committee has not already told you, via Bill Tanner most probably.'

M grunted. 'Well, Tanner *did* telephone me. Said The Committee had turned down a request from you, or some such. I didn't truly understand what he was talking about.'

'Then the conversation we're about to have has never taken place, if you follow me, sir.'

'What conversation?' Bond could not be certain that

M's eyelid closed in a wink, or whether he simply imagined it.

Carefully, leaving nothing out, he went through the entire story. Then he outlined what he proposed to do about Tarn.

'And what if the fellow's not in Puerto Rico, eh? You thought about that?'

'He'll be there, sir. I'd bet my job on it.'

'That's what I think you're probably doing. Your job, your future and your marriage plans. I can't say that I blame The Committee for their action, though I *do* understand your own point of view – even though I haven't heard it.'

'There's no alternative really, sir.' Flicka joined in. 'We either do this now or forget about it. Tarn has his own timetable, and he's not going to hang around waiting for someone to show up.'

'So what do you want from me?'

Turning his face away, so that his smile was not visible to the old man, Bond cleared his throat, 'Who said anything about wanting things?'

'My dear chap,' M seemed to blossom with goodwill. 'When people're in a meeting where the walls have no ears, and there's nobody to give evidence, because we can make this little threesome into an event that never happened, somebody wants something, and I don't believe you merely want the blessing of your old boss. So fire away, James. What do you need?'

'A meeting with Ann Reilly for a start, sir.' Be bright and straightforward, he told himself. 'Preferably within a few hours. She should also have your tacit instructions to provide us with anything for which we ask – within reason, of course.'

'Oh, of course, within reason, yes indeed. What else?'

'That's about it, sir. That and your word that, should things get very difficult, you'll inform on us; tell The Committee where we are.'

'So your bodies can be brought home for burial, eh?'

'Something like that, sir.'

'You have it, but on one condition.'

'Sir?'

'They'll be putting me out to grass soon, Bond, and I need to be certain of my successor. I'd like your assurance that you would consider the job when I step down.'

'Consider it, yes, sir. But that's all I can do. Consider it.'

'Understood. Enough said. You can meet Ms Reilly by the bandstand in Green Park at four o'clock sharp. Now, go, James, Fredericka, before an old man gets stupidly sentimental.'

It was Flicka who bought the tickets on their Busby identities. The following morning's Delta flight direct into Atlanta, with a connection to San Juan, Puerto Rico. Bond had explained that he did not want to take a direct flight into San Juan. 'It's a little bit of insurance,' he told Flicka. 'Nobody in their right mind would fly into the States to connect with a flight to Puerto Rico, so it will leave a small, but efficient, paper trail. Also, if the boys and girls on The Committee get on to us, I think we can say that we held the onward tickets in case they gave us the okay. Small point, but worth it.'

The journey was going to be a slog, but going in via Atlanta, Georgia, was less risky than entering the United States via New York, Miami, or Washington – the other possibilities. She paid in cash which Bond drew from his personal account.

After taking care of financial business he took a walk in Green Park, and there, close to the bandstand, bumped into the trim figure of Ann Reilly, Q'ute as they called her in the trade, now the head of Q Branch.

'And what can I do for you, Mr Bond? I've been given instructions to give you anything within my power, but that rules out my body, I'm afraid.'

For years, Bond had made a steady stream of passes at Ms Reilly, with one in three being successful. Now he was able to smile, but could not tell her why.

'Now, what can I do for you?' she asked, briskly.

He went through his list and she checked off items telling him either yes or no.

'The wet suits and diving gear you can buy openly when you're there,' she said. 'I can get the two briefcases in, and delivered to the hotel before you even arrive, there's no problem with that. We've been working on a new design and they'll carry the bulk of what you'll need. As for the other thing, I don't really know. This is a large item, you sure you're going to need it?'

'I'm not certain we'll require any of the stuff, except the weapons, but I'd feel happier if everything was there, on tap.'

'Well, I'll do my best. There'll be a cryptic note in one of the briefcases. If I can get the other thing in, it'll tell you exactly where it's been dropped off. That's all I can promise.'

They talked for another ten minutes, then he gave her a farewell embrace and they went their different ways.

He insisted on travelling light, and in the flat that night there was much argument regarding what could, and even should, be taken. Though she was probably the most efficient field agent he had known, Flicka had a tendency to take far too much luggage.

'If we were going on a camping holiday, you'd take at least three evening gowns,' he chided her.

'Well, one must have something to wear.' With ill grace she removed a couple of designer suits and one evening gown from her case.

'It'll be denims and sneakers most of the way.' He came over, put an arm around her shoulders and held her close. 'Just between the two of us, think of it as a busman's honeymoon.'

She turned, lifting her face, and things developed into much more than a simple act of affection.

They were late getting to sleep that night.

On the following morning, they drove to Gatwick; put the car into the long term park and began the process of getting to the air side of the terminal.

As they reached the passport control desk, the officer took their passports, looked at them, then began asking questions – 'How long are you going to be out of the country?' 'Are you carrying return tickets?'

It was a small delaying tactic which served to give some time to the two burly men who, as if by magic, appeared, one on either side of them.

'Now we don't want to make a fuss,' one of them said quietly. 'Just come with us. There's no way either of you is going to get on that flight. Sorry.'

Bond asked to see their authority, and they both flashed Security Service laminated cards. He had no way of knowing if these were the real things, or part of a ploy by Max Tarn whose influence seemed to reach into the very heart of the establishment.

18

Apocalypse

IT QUICKLY BECAME clear that this was official business. A sleek Jaguar pulled up in front of the terminal and their luggage was stowed away in the boot, while the two escorts helped them into the back of the car. They both seemed to be in good humor, which was more than could be said for Bond or Flicka.

'Cheer up, it could be raining.' One of their custodians climbed into the back of the car with them. The other rode shotgun in the front passenger seat. The driver had given them a pleasant and polite greeting of "Morning sir, ma'am.'

Bond glared at nobody in particular, his face a thundercloud. 'This had better be good,' he muttered angrily to the officer in the back.

'No idea if it's good, bad or indifferent. I'm just obeying orders.'

The one in the front chuckled, 'That's what we do for a living these days. A lot of the fun's gone out of life.'

'Like hell it has.' Bond knew that he should keep his mouth shut. He also knew that the real problem was getting caught, and that the fury he felt was aimed at himself, not his captors. 'We all like to pretend it's over now that the Soviet Union seems to be a dead issue,' he snapped. 'People don't like to think we're still doing the work.'

'Well, you'd know all about that, Captain Bond, wouldn't you?'

It was a short drive back into London, and Bill Tanner stood outside the door which they used at the Home Office.

'Sorry about this.' He also appeared to be in good spirits.

'We were going on a little holiday, Bill.' Flicka did not even try to disguise her anger.

'So we were told.' Tanner ushered them into the building, instructing the Security Service men to make themselves comfortable. 'It might be a long wait,' he told them as though this were the happiest news he had to convey.

The whole Committee was there, except, of course, for M. *They* looked spry and in good humor also. They were certainly very polite, showing Bond and Flicka to their seats at the far end of the table, seeing they had coffee, asking if they wanted anything else. Finally Lord Harvey brought the meeting to order.

'I presume that M's Chief of Staff has offered our apologies.' He smiled. Charm will get you anywhere, Bond thought. 'Really we had no option after we spoke with our cousins in the United States, but I'll let Tanner put you in the picture.'

Bill Tanner opened with information that made Bond curse himself for being so lax. 'I should tell you that Nurse Frobisher, looking after M, is one of us.' He smiled, rather like the Chairman. 'After your meeting with the Chief yesterday she called, so his Lordship went down and had a chat with him. He has great fondness for you, James, and for Fredericka. Hardly told us anything. However, we do have his bedroom taped so we already knew what you were up to.' The smile again as he picked up a sheaf of notes. 'But that's not the real reason you're here. Yesterday, as the Chairman said, we had some lengthy discussions with the Americans. It turns out that we were wrong. In fact they'll happily allow you to work on their turf. They'll also provide a bit of back-up if it's necessary.'

'Couldn't you just have got word to us, instead of hauling us back?'

'Ah.' It was Lord Harvey who replied. 'Would that we could, Captain Bond. Unhappily you were in a technical breach of our instructions, and we also have quite a lot to tell you. The Americans really want Max Tarn as much as we do. It was something they shared with us. In truth, they're pretty happy about the possibility of nabbing him in Puerto Rico. They hadn't actually put the finger on Tarn – that's their expression not mine. What we told them was music to their ears. We gave them some information, practically everything as it happens – except for the Nazi connection of course – and then they recognized him straightaway.'

'How so?'

'Our evidence on Tarn fits the profile of someone they've been searching for. Their code name is apt, so we've taken it upon ourselves to share it.'

'And the code name is?'

'Apocalypse. That's what they've been calling the shadow they've been chasing. Good, Apocalypse?'

'Very original.' He could not keep the satirical edge out of his tone.

'Thought you'd like it.' Harvey raised an eyebrow, indicating that he fully agreed with Bond.

Tanner took over and told them the long story. The United Nations had been looking into the murky business of what they called 'The International Arms Bazaar,' and its Disarmament Commission had already made some progress within the American and British connections.

'So far, the United States have been more concerned with the guns which have found their way onto the streets of their cities, but that's a domestic issue, and a very serious one for them.' Tanner glanced at his notes again. 'They now realize that the trade in weapons, through America, has reached incredible proportions. We have also been able to give them evidence that Max Tarn is behind at least two thirds of the deals, making America, and his base in Puerto Rico, a kind of convenience store for small arms – pistols, assault rifles, semi-automatics, explosives and ammunition.

'These items are being farmed out to a whole slew of organizations and countries. We've talked about that in connection with Tarn already, and the Americans sat up and took notice when we showed them what we've got on him. Already we know that among his clients he has the Colombian drug lords, the Irish gunrunners, the Japanese crime bosses and – no surprise – the embargo-busters of Croatia. The Americans, in turn, have linked him to the off-limits countries in the Middle East.

'Tarn's really been working overtime. Only last month half a million firearms were licensed by the US Federal Government for export to Argentina. Those weapons went nowhere near Argentina, but were neatly diverted by the Tarn organization and split between the Colombians and buyers in Europe.'

Tanner went on to say that Max Tarn's people had gone further than any other illegal arms dealers. They had even managed to infiltrate the government computers in Washington and, with high-tech cunning, had sanctioned hundreds of deals which resulted in the diversion of weapons and military *matériel*.

'The US Defense Trade Controls offices have been seriously undermanned during the past few years,' Tanner continued. 'Recently they've tracked down not only the question of small arms shipped out to Argentina, but also large amounts of artillery shells, fighter aircraft, fuses and missiles licensed by the State Department for Jordan, but ending up in Iraq. The entire business has reached incredible proportions. We were able to supply a lot of information.'

'Which means you're actually going to allow us into the field?' It was all Bond was interested in: getting back into action.

'Among other things, yes.' The Chairman spoke from the far end of the table. 'Yesterday we didn't imagine in our wildest dreams that the US authorities would embrace such a plan. So things have altered dramatically, and while I cannot praise you for trying to override our orders, I now have the authority to change those orders. Netting Max Tarn would be a triumph as far as we're concerned.'

'So we can get on with it and go with your blessing?'

'Not so fast, Bond. Yes, you are going to be allowed into Puerto Rico – possibly along with one or two other people who you aren't likely to see – but I should warn you that, as of this morning, the American agencies have no trace of Tarn being anywhere near the Caribbean. He is, in fact, still in Germany – Tarnenwerder and Wasserburg.'

'I didn't expect him to be in San Juan when we arrived.' Bond raised his voice, almost shouting. 'I told you he would certainly be going there soon.'

'Oh, yes, we have no doubt about that, providing nobody tips him off and tells him to stay clear. We've even got an address for you. He keeps a fair-sized villa on the island. Near the town of Ponce, on the Caribbean side.

His facilities in San Juan are confined to a small flat and, most important, his warehouses in the port area. These are almost certainly stockpiled with enough military equipment to start World War III, and they're used exclusively by his container ships. But for relaxation he has all the trappings of luxury in what our American friends refer to as his compound near Ponce – tennis courts, swimming pools, servants. Tarn does not stint himself when he's off duty.'

'With the money he's making by dealing in death, he can afford to lash out a bit.'

'Yes.' Harvey raised his eyes and gave Bond a withering look. 'Yes, I was told that you preferred luxury to a more suburban way of life.'

He ignored the remark. 'So, what're we waiting for now?'

A short pause was followed by a nod from the Chairman towards the head of the Security Service. 'I'm told, Captain Bond, that you seem to have a way with our own personal penetration agent, the former Junior Minister.'

'I spoke with him yesterday.'

'Yes, to great effect. You made him some very unauthorized promises, though.'

'They were based on the realities of life. You know as well as I do, Ma'am, that nobody in this room wants to see the little rat in court, with every newspaper and television reporter at his heels. Put the ex-Minister in front of a judge and some of you become laughing stocks. A few decades ago he would have probably caught the measles – I think that was the term we used in those days. We'd have a little suicide on our hands, and someone in high places would trot out evidence that he had been under incredible strain. Nowadays we don't do things like that, so we have to offer him a deal. After all, very few people know what's been going on.'

'I, for one, cannot comment on any deals, Captain Bond. We *do* have to consider the law. None of us is above it.'

'Or below it.'

'If you say so. Now, Captain, *we* have a deal to offer you. We feel that, whatever the final outcome and its effect on our former lord and master's life, he does appear to trust you. Nobody in Tarn's camp can have any idea that we've turned him, so we want you to arrange that he passes on a little information to his former master.'

'What kind of information, Ma'am?'

'Oh, simple stuff. The fact that our search continues in the UK and in Germany where he was last spotted, plus anything else that comes from your fertile imagination. I'm sure you'll give him the right words. Incidentally, he's being kept in one of our few remaining safe flats not fifteen minutes' drive from here.'

'You said you had a deal to offer me.'

'Certainly. You get him to say the right words, hold his hand, stay with him while he passes on the information, and we'll let you and Ms von Grüsse leave for Puerto Rico first thing tomorrow morning.'

'Done.' He glanced at Flicka who nodded back. 'I presume Fräulein von Grüsse can be present?'

'We'll all be present, Captain Bond. You won't see us, but we'll be there.' She gave him a knowing look. 'Oh, by the way, they're all on first name terms. Our former Minister is called Christopher.'

The safe flat was known to him, high on the fourth floor of a block of service apartments on the corner of Marylebone High Street and New Cavendish Street. They had made the Minister very comfortable.

'Got everything you want, Christopher,' Bond greeted him. 'Hot and cold running security, good takeaway Chinese and Indian?'

'I hate Chinese food, but the curry's good.' He looked much better than when they had last seen him during the interrogation at the Home Office. 'You come to give me a pardon?'

Bond shook his head, and Flicka said she was sorry but they couldn't do that just yet.

'I've told them that I'll give evidence against Tarn *in camera*. Time we had a good witness protection program over here, like they do in the States.'

'We can't have everything, Christopher.' He turned to the two Security Service officers who were minding the prisoner, asking them if they could leave them alone with him. 'Man talk, you know the kind of thing.'

With a somewhat hammy reluctance – for they already had orders – the two men withdrew.

'So, what's the deal?' Not unnaturally, the man could only think about himself and his future.

'Nothing's been decided yet, Chris. We've talked to a lot of people and, as I told you yesterday, I don't for a minute think you're going to see the inside of a court room. Mind you, it's possible that you'll spend the rest of your life in some godforsaken part of the world with a pair of minders who'll be changed every three months. If you want total freedom you'll have to co-operate.'

'I've already told them I'll . . . !'

'Yes, yes, Christopher, we know what you've promised. Believe me we know, and, as far as that goes, everyone's going to show gratitude. However, there is gratitude and gratitude. It comes in many disguises, and in different packages. Now there is one thing you might be able to do for us that will move you up a few notches.'

'Anything.'

Christopher, Bond considered, was a pushover.

'Tell me, the telephone number in Wasserburg, was that your only method of contact with Max Tarn and his unsavory friends?'

'Took a leaf out of your book, Bond. We used various dead drops, and false telephone codes.'

'Nothing else direct?'

'Only the telephone you managed to spike. Tarn's end has been ultra secure, until that last time. I suspect it's some kind of electronics gadget because sometimes I get through and sometimes I get that piece of rubbish, Maurice Goodwin. We're even on first name terms. I was able to use it when I wanted to set up a proper meeting with one of them.'

'So, you *sometimes* used it when you wanted a meeting with some intermediary who handed you money, right?'

'Well, occasionally.'

'Usually.'

'Not always, no.'

'Would you care to make a call on that line for us?'

'I said I'd do anything.'

'Your end would be scripted.'

'I'm not absolutely stupid. I understand that.'

'We can even do it from here, Christopher. Mind you, any deviation from the script and I'll put a bullet through your head. We can do that kind of thing, you know.'

'I believe you. What's in the script?'

'We'll work on it together.'

Christopher waited for at least fifteen seconds before he asked if they could get on with it.

What they worked out in the end was aimed at putting Tarn into an even higher state of *folie de grandeur*, and it was an hour later that Christopher dialed the number.

They had taken the extra precaution of attaching a speaker to the instrument, linked to headphones so that Bond could hear everything. Flicka passed the time by playing patience, and her future husband noticed that she handled a pack of cards rather like an experienced gambler.

'Yes,' came from the distant end, and he immediately recognized the voice of Tarn's fixer, Maurice Goodwin.

'Maurice, it's Christopher,' the ex-Minister read from the pad on which his script was jotted down in his own clear, and rather schoolboyish, handwriting.

'So what can we do for you, Christopher? Don't expect any money for the time being. We're a shade busy.'

'I'm sorry to trouble you, but I thought I'd better pass on the latest. It is rather important.'

'Shoot.'

'They were pretty angry about your little disappearing act in London. Now Sir Max is wanted for murder, though they're not issuing anything to the Press. As far as *they're* concerned, Lady Tarn died in the car accident, so the authorities are keeping quiet. In fact, there's still a search going on for Sir Max in Germany as well as here. The agent, Bond, went missing as well.'

Goodwin chuckled, 'He ended up dead. Very nasty. Bad business about Lady T, but it *had* to be done. Poor Trish went right off her chump. Threatened the chief, and she wasn't joking. Anyway, good to know that she won't make the funny pages again. Anything else?'

'Yes, the man Bond isn't dead. He pulled a fast one on you and turned up back here yesterday.'

Goodwin cursed violently. 'What about him, then? What's happening?'

'He's been fired – him and his girlfriend. Well, they've been suspended from duty. I think he wanted to go after you mob-handed. I'm supposed to be keeping them under surveillance – that's a laugh. I've got complete control over the whole thing.'

'And?'

'And, guess what? The pair of them have been dashing around London getting money and buying airline tickets.'

'Going anywhere in particular?'

'Right into Sir Max's arms, I should think. They leave tomorrow. Gatwick/Atlanta, Georgia; then on to San Juan. I can pull the police and Security off, and let them out if you'd like another crack at them.'

'What a coincidence.' Goodwin gave a bray of laughter at the distant end. 'When Winter comes, then Spring's not far behind. Thanks, Christopher. Maybe you'll get a bonus for this. Let 'em out.'

'Just earning my keep, Maurice.' The distant line went dead, and Christopher slowly put down the handset. 'How did I do?'

'Best actor of the year. Oscar and our grateful thanks.' Bond even managed to grin at the unpleasant man.

On the following morning, there was no hold up as they went through the routine passport check at Gatwick, and the flight to Atlanta took off on time.

Flicka seemed preoccupied as she looked out of the window next to her seat.

'You okay, Flick?' he asked.

'Sure, my dear. Sure. I think someone just walked over my grave and I got a bit maudlin. Wondered if I'd ever see this view again.'

'Of course you will.' He looked away, for if he had told the truth, he also had a lurking fear, an echo of his own mortality, something he rarely thought about.

19

The Old Texas Cowhand

FROM THE AIR, it looks lush and very beautiful: a green and pleasant land ringed by a shimmering sea. As their aircraft approached the rocky beaches, it seemed that the surf below was unmoving, as though sculpted onto a wonderful model, surrounded by an unreal emerald sea. Puerto Rico – Rich Port – is exactly what this island was for over four centuries: wealthy and powerful, the strategic gateway to the Caribbean, cooled by the gentle trade winds; guarded and nurtured by Spain, but also prey to pirates and acquisitive countries who coveted this staging point to the New World.

In the late twentieth century, it has again become rich, this time through tourism. Hardly a day passes without a major cruise ship lying in the port at San Juan, and the new luxury hotels and casinos, which line the shore of San José Lagoon, entice holiday makers and high rollers.

Yet, side by side with its opulence and natural wonders, this lovely island has a dark side. The problems of drugs, poverty and violence lurk, often unhidden, particularly in the old city of San Juan.

As they made the final approach into Luis Muñoz Marin International, Bond remarked that it looked as though they were landing on the huge strip of bridge which had only recently been completed across the lagoon. They seemed to be so low that they flew below the tops of high-rise buildings and Flicka, usually oblivious to approach and landing dangers on commercial aircraft, closed her eyes and waited for the safe bump as the big jet's wheels touched down on what even Bond considered a slightly narrow runway, a shade close to a long line of trees on their left side.

Nobody asked to see passports or any other documentation, and the porter who took their luggage from the carousel for them seemed quite happy to summon a taxi, and even happier with his tip. The driver of the cab asked if a price of twenty dollars was okay by them. Bond nodded, and the driver immediately switched off the meter.

They drove alongside the lagoon, glimpsing the new hotels where cruise ship passengers often stay in their hordes for one or two nights either before leaving or at the end of the cruise. These smart beehives, complete with large casinos and a multitude of restaurants including fast food joints imported from the United States, were often all visitors saw, except for a quick outing to Old San Juan and the two great forts, Castillo San Felipe del Morro – usually referred to simply as El Morro – and Castillo de San Cristóbal. Fortifications which rank among the greatest still standing.

Their driver skirted the old town and finally deposited them in a small open square facing the San Juan Cathedral. Porters hurried down steps to their left, and as Bond paid off the cab, he turned to see the imposing entrance to the Gran Hotel El Convento, undoubtedly one of the most extraordinary hotels in the world. For two hundred and fifty years, El Convento was home to the island's Carmelite nuns. Now, centuries later, the building has emerged, beautifully refurbished, as a unique caravanserai.

Once up the steps and through the ancient doors, they found themselves greeted like royalty, and, unusually, shown straight to their accommodation. They traversed a high, vaulted area, passed under cloistered arches, getting a quick look at an enclosed garden with a modern swimming pool, and then up to the second floor and a beautiful airy room with a large canopied bed: the modern additions blending expertly with the old.

'You think there's the ghost of a nun here?' Flicka laughed. 'I mean we're probably usurping some old holy woman's cell.'

'I don't think whoever lived here before would even recognize it. The Carmelites are a rather strict order. Wouldn't know how to work the TV anyway.'

They had been told to go through the registration procedure once they had settled in, so Bond went down, completed the paperwork and asked if any forwarded luggage had arrived for them.

The young woman at reception told him that there were two special cases which would be delivered to the room directly.

He was on his way back, when an instantly-recognizable voice spoke from behind him.

'Just in time for a pre-dinner drink, James, old buddy.'

'Felix!' He turned and could hardly believe that his old friend, Felix Leiter, stood behind him, leaning on his walking stick, a broad smile on his leathery Texan face.

'Sure, fancy meeting me here, James. You haven't changed, I see. Noticed you arrived with a gorgeous lady in tow.'

'There's a surprise for you regarding the lady.' He looked affectionately at his old friend who, for many

231

years, had served with the Central Intelligence Agency. That career had been cut short by an argument with a shark while he was working with Bond, though you would hardly know that he had lost both a leg and an arm. True, he walked with the aid of a stick, but the prosthetic leg and arm allowed him to live an almost normal life.

'You here on business?' Bond stepped close to his old friend.

'You never get to leave the business completely, James. You should know that. They just pulled on my leash and brought me back. When they told me it concerned you, I couldn't say no. Anyway, the hotel's good, and the food and drink are more than bearable.'

'How's Cedar?' Cedar Leiter was Felix's daughter who had followed in her father's footsteps. Much to her father's concern, she had even worked with Bond on a case some years ago.

'Cedar's as lovely as ever. Thinking of getting married, but I have my doubts.'

'Why? She's a great girl.'

'Can you see Cedar married to a young man who never had to do a day's work in his life because his Daddy made a killing in oil, way back when the USA produced all the gas you needed and then some?'

'She'd know how to spend his money.'

'Sure she would, but I have a feeling that she'd soon find him dull as dirt. The guy has all this money and he's never been any further than New York City – and he thinks that den of iniquity is 'cool and awesome.' Those were his exact words, and he's over forty years old.'

Bond leaned closer and his lips hardly moved. 'You know everything?'

'About Apocalypse? Sure, I know most of what you know. I've even been across the island to look at the little

232

country place he has here. I'll take you over for a look-see tomorrow.'

'So, we're working together again, eh?'

'I am your guide, philosopher and friend, James. Now, off you go and bring your lady down to the Campana Bar. Still like your martinis shaken not stirred? And with the same ingredients?'

'Yes indeed, even though the author of a book called *Drinkmanship* says that the mix is all wrong.'

Leiter's laugh followed Bond as he took long strides in the direction of the cloistered arches and their room, where a porter was just delivering a pair of heavy aluminum cases.

'What have we got in those?' Flicka had already unpacked and showered. She sat at the elegant little dressing table putting on her warpaint, as she liked to call it. 'They look like camera cases.'

'A shade more lethal.' He dialed in the prearranged codes on the locks of the cases, and found the note in the first one he opened. Ann Reilly had done her best regarding the larger item for which he had asked.

Some of our friends, she had written, *will see to it that you get the thing if you really need it.*

As he went through the weapons, ammunition and the like, held within the cases by eggcrate foam rubber, he told Flicka about Felix Leiter.

'You mean I get to meet him at last?' She had heard much about his old friend.

'You certainly do get to meet him.' He lifted the foam rubber from the bottom of the second case to reveal five boxes, about six inches long and two across. 'She did it,' he muttered. 'Little jewels.' Wondering how on earth Q'ute had managed to smuggle explosives onto the island.

'Where?'

233

'Not your kind of jewels, darling. This kind will blow people to kingdom come. By the way, are you wearing a skirt tonight?'

'Well, I'm not going downstairs in only what I'm wearing now, darling. I don't think I'd be very popular.'

'On the contrary, you'd be exceptionally popular with every man in the place, except me. Skirt or a trouser suit?'

'Skirt.'

'There you go, then. Your favourite Beretta and a thigh holster.'

'Oh, your favourite, James.' She took the holster and strapped it on, reminding him of the first flash of her thighs that he had ever seen – when she had suddenly drawn a pistol from that same type of holster in Switzerland.

While she finished dressing, he took a very quick shower, changed into slacks, comfortable moccasins and a white shirt, over which he put on a lightweight blazer – mainly to hide the bulge made by the ASP.

Finally, after numerous changes in her small items of jewellery – and a lot of, 'What do you think, James? This one, or this?' – they went down to join Felix in the Campana Bar, where he already had a couple of martinis lined up. 'Just so you don't get too far behind.'

He gave Flicka a warm embrace, saying he had a kind of *droit du seigneur* where Bond's girlfriends were concerned.

'I'm afraid not with Flicka, Felix.' He went on and broke the news to the American.

'You're kidding me? You, James?' Then, looking at Flicka, 'Tell me he's kidding me.'

''Fraid not, Felix. It's the real thing this time, but for heaven's sake don't tell anyone. They'd whiz me out of here like a speeding bullet.'

Felix said he was the most trustworthy man this side of George Washington, but this news, of course, called for champagne which he ordered immediately. Under cover of the small ceremony by the waiters, he leaned over and spoke quietly to Bond. 'There's a face over there, I kinda recognize, James. You ever seen him before?'

There were only three other people in the bar. Two men and a woman, sitting together, very relaxed and in deep conversation.

'The one with the beard?'

'That's the guy. I've seen him somewhere, or maybe just his photograph.'

'America's Most Wanted?'

'Don't be a fool. I'm talking big time names here. That guy's famous for something.'

'I vaguely know the face, but can't put a name to him. Nothing for us to worry about.'

In spite of the last remark, Bond quickly gave the trio a thorough once-over. The bearded man was short and stocky, probably in his late forties with a fine weather-beaten face. The woman could be any age between eighteen and thirty-five as she had one of those faces with a scrubbed look, dark hair that hung lank around her shoulders, so that it regularly had to be pushed back with a thin hand. The final member of the party was clean shaven, earnest-looking, with his hair beginning to recede. He had the manner of an academic, the shoulders slightly stooped, his eyes bright behind a pair of wire framed glasses.

Felix was on form and kept the three of them going with a fund of stories, all of which were supposed to be true, most of them having happened to him personally. Bond had forgotten what a good raconteur and companion his old friend could be, and they relaxed over dinner which, as was his way, Felix ordered for them.

Tonight, he obviously realized that they would not want anything heavy after the long journey so they ate simply – smoked salmon and Salad Niçoise, followed by an unforgettable chocolate mousse.

It was Leiter who suggested they return to the bar for coffee and what he called, 'A little firewater to make us sleep.'

The trio were still there, and he caught the bearded man's eye as they walked in. Immediately, Felix being Felix, addressed him. 'I'm only an old Texas cowhand, but I seen you somewhere, sir. You're kinda famous for something and darned if I can put my finger on what exactly.'

The bearded man's face broke into a wide, almost youthful, grin. 'You must have been reading some very rare magazines, sir. I'm only known in my field. The name's Rex Rexinus . . .'

'I'm Felix Leiter, and you're a Marine biologist, right?'

'Absolutely right.'

'See,' Felix turned to his friends, 'I told you this guy was famous. You wrote a book about deep ocean fish.'

'If you've worked your way through that, then you're very well read, and I doubt if you're really an old cowhand.'

'Maybe I stretched the point with that. I been in and out of all kinds of business. But it's been great meeting you, Dr Rexinus.'

'Please, join us.' Rexinus stood and was already pulling up chairs.

'Well, you've got to meet my friends here. This is . . .'

'James Busby, and this is my wife.'

'And my friends.' Rexinus leaned over and shook

hands. 'This is Dr Vesta Motley, and my other friend here is Professor Afton Fritz.'

'Not Professor Fritz, the biochemist?'

'You're a walking encyclopaedia, Mr Leiter. Yes, I'm a biochemist, as, indeed, is Dr Motley – among other things.' Fritz had a slightly high-pitched voice that somehow did not go with his face, while Vesta Motley's 'How do you do?' was very English.

They ordered drinks and there were a few moments of small talk until Felix, still playing the Texan abroad, asked, 'What in heaven's name brings a couple of biochemists and a marine biologist of renown to San Juan? I've never heard of any biochemists in San Juan. So what y'all doin' here?'

'Good question, Felix.' Rexinus put his head back and laughed. 'We thought we were on to something good. About a year ago the three of us had an idea which we felt would benefit the world, but we didn't have the money to carry through our research.'

''Ain't that always the way?'

'Usually, yes. But suddenly we found a benefactor, though now we're at a loss what to do. We have the most magnificent floating laboratory out there in the harbor, and we've found that all three of us were wrong.' He punctuated this with another laugh. 'You see we were only half right in our theory, which is about as good as being completely wrong. Now we're in even deeper water because the very generous and rich man who backed the entire venture has gone and got himself killed in a car accident, and we can't get a peep out of his company offices in London.'

'And who's the filthy rich benefactor?' Bond stirred in his chair.

'Man called Tarn,' Rexinus grunted. 'Sir Max Tarn.

You may have heard of him.'

'Vaguely,' said Flicka a shade too quickly.

'I mean I'm sorry for the fellow, getting killed, but it makes life easier for us in some ways.'

'Why would that be?' Bond asked stiffly, as though just getting over a shot of Novocain.

'Well.' It was Vesta Motley who answered him. 'Sir Max is one of these people who demand results. He gave us a year, and – just before his death – he cabled us to say he would be coming here to San Juan to see a demonstration of the thing we cannot demonstrate.'

'A hard taskmaster,' Leiter muttered.

'Oh, the hardest,' Dr Motley replied, with wise nods from her two colleagues. 'But you'll have to come aboard and see our laboratory, *Mare Nostrum*. It's an incredible ship. Quite the last word.'

Last word is probably right, Bond considered. Aloud, he said, 'We'd love to. How about tomorrow night?'

20

Things Ancient & Modern

'AN OLD TEXAS cowhand,' Bond all but sneered. 'Old Texas cowhand my backside.'

'Don't be horrible to Felix, now, James. He did get us a lot of information,' Flicka chided.

'Thought it sounded better than Old Texas cowpoke. Always considered there was something highly suggestive in that word.'

It was late afternoon, and the day had provided more information, none of it comforting. Now, they stood on the topmost platform of El Morro, looking out across the harbor.

The banter between Bond and his old friend had begun early that morning when they left the hotel to drive across the island to the town of Ponce named after the island's first governor, Juan Ponce de León. Felix, it appeared, had thought of everything, including hiring the car which he could drive with the advanced prosthetics he now used, but Bond took over with both Flicka and Felix as navigators. Not that there was much navigation to do for the roads were straightforward, taking them across the breadth of the island, from the Atlantic to the Caribbean sides, touching the coastal towns of Salinas and Santa Isabel.

'You're quite a well-read little devil for an American,' Bond began.

'It's all the time I've had, lying in hospital beds and hippety hopping around.'

'Yes, but to recognize a couple of obscure scientists was quite a feat.'

'Not really. I already knew who they were.'

'You did?'

'I've been here for a couple of days, and those three are almost permanent fixtures in the hotel bar. A word here and a word there: you know how we glean information, James. At least you used to know.'

'Fraud,' Bond muttered.

'No, just checking out the opposition. Those three are in some danger, but I don't need to tell you that; you've been up against their boss in person. Don't you think we should warn them?'

'They're innocents as far as Tarn's concerned. Won't know what hit them when he does arrive. Yes, I had thought of giving them most of the information tonight. I'll suggest that they whiz their floating lab off to one of the other islands, or set a course for Florida.'

'That's where old Ponce de León got himself killed,' Flicka contributed from the back of the little Japanese car.

'How do you know *that*, Flick?'

'Says so here, in this guidebook. Juan Ponce de León was originally lured here by the promise of gold. Then he went off with his army to conquer Florida. Got himself mortally wounded.'

'Mine of information, that guide book. Does it mention our haunted bedroom in the convent?'

'You've got a haunted bedroom?' Felix asked.

'Every hour on the hour. The walking nun. Comes in and goes out straight through the wall. Got everything, including a wimple.'

'How would you know, James? I swear, Felix, that he

240

was asleep last night before he even got into bed.'

'Intuition.' Bond took a hand off the wheel and laid it alongside his nose. 'I sense when ghosts walk, it's my speciality.'

'Don't listen to him, Flicka. I've known him for a darned sight longer than you. If you take my advice, you'll slip out of his clutches and run for cover. The man's dangerous to be around.'

'I know.' She gave a throaty little laugh. 'That's part of his charm.'

'Pray you don't lose an arm and a leg like I did.' It was part of Felix Leiter's strength of character that he could joke openly about his handicap.

'You've spent your time checking up on the trio of scientists, Felix. What are they up to on Max Tarn's behalf?' Bond changed the subject quickly. He could never forgive himself for what had happened to Leiter, even though it was not his fault.

'What are they doing? Well, as just a plain old Texas cowboy, it's difficult to explain. In fact, even if they do explain the scientific bits to us, we'll probably be none the wiser. I gather it's something to do with an anti-pollution device. That's the talk in the local bars and bistros. They're trying to produce a substance that will nullify the effects of oil spills.'

'That would be handy.'

'It's only talk, but I've seen *Mare Nostrum* from a distance. She has these pipes, like mortars, set at angles all around her outer deck. The locals say that they would spray a kind of foam on oil spills – rather like dowsing a fire. The difference is that this foam would suck up the oil and purify the water at the same time, but you heard what they said last night. The thing doesn't work.'

'Tarn's not going to like that. When he puts money into

something, he always counts on a return. Like as not, he'll expect the thing to work.'

Flicka stirred in the back. 'Like as not, he'll demand it to work. The man's a loony.'

'A loony and his money are not easily parted, either,' Bond said without any humor in his tone. 'But we all know he's damned dangerous and, I suspect, is getting more dangerous by the day.'

Presently, Flicka asked Leiter if he had visited any of the caves. 'This says Puerto Rico has the third largest underground river in the world, and there is a network of caves and caverns along the Atlantic side.'

'Haven't had the time, but I gather the entire coastline – Atlantic and Caribbean – has caves, though the largest ones are on the San Juan side.'

'What're you thinking about, Flick?' Bond asked.

'Nothing in particular, only it struck me that if there really is a submarine out here, one of these caves would make a good pen for it.'

'Submarine!' Leiter's jaw dropped. 'What submarine?'

'We know Tarn has one – an old Russian boat. I think World War II vintage, or just after, but he could've been feeding us a line, so I suppose the real thing might even be a modern boat.' Bond's thoughts were already way ahead of Flicka's. 'He gave us some cock and bull story that it was for a military museum he was going to set up on one of the deserted islands he owns. Planned to have his cruise ships visit the place. None of it rang true.'

'That's all we need, a rogue submarine prowling around these waters.'

Flicka launched into the story of their cruise and the damage done to *Caribbean Prince*. 'The US Navy square searched the whole area after that. Found nothing, so he must've squirreled it away somewhere. If we were, in fact, torpedoed.'

They stopped for coffee in the little town of Santa Isabel with its view of the Caribbean and the long, broken reefs of rocks. Before going on their way, Bond and Flicka bought the wet suits they might need, considering they would pay probably twice the price in San Juan.

The sun shone, sparkling off the emerald sea, and the sky was clear but for a few high cirrus clouds as they drove on. Felix made a remark about Tarn certainly picking a nice spot. 'It's only a few miles up here to Ponce, and his place is a couple of miles up the coast. Those rocks down there look like a lunar landscape.'

'It all looks volcanic to me.' Bond glanced down towards the beach.

'It says here,' Flicka was still working on the guide book, 'that if you go down to the beach near the Condado Plaza hotel, right on the Condado Lagoon, you can see a rock formation that looks like a dog. There's a local story that it was a fisherman's dog which waited for his master to return every night. One night he didn't return, and the dog eventually turned to stone.'

'You're making that up, Flick.'

They skirted the town of Ponce, and Leiter told Bond to slow down. 'We can turn off along here, and take a very narrow road that'll bring us out above the Casa del Tarno.'

'He doesn't actually . . . ?' Bond began, then glanced at Felix and caught his flickering smile.

Minutes later they reached the turn, and traveled on a bumpy track, leading uphill in a series of sharp bends. Ahead there was a small wooded area. 'You can just get into the trees,' Felix told him. 'Then we have to walk.'

It was some kind of picnic area, deserted at the

moment, and Felix soon led them from the car, along a winding footpath that took them to the edge of the trees.

Below them, was a long, low oblong building, the four sides enclosing a garden with a swimming pool, similar to the architecture of El Convento. The house, with its many arches, was painted in a light blue, the whole surrounded by a wall. On the outer perimeter they could see tennis courts and a parking area for cars.

'Nice little place for week-ends.' Felix had conjured up a pair of binoculars from somewhere and he handed them to Bond, who scanned the house which was perched above a rocky incline leading to the sea. There were two cars in the park, and several people worked in the central garden, or could be seen moving along the cloisters. Of Tarn and his closest colleagues there was no sign.

'Doesn't look as though the master's arrived yet, does it?' Leiter asked.

'No, but there are several men down there who look as though they're guests.' He had picked out a group of eleven or twelve men, sitting under one of the cloister-like arches, drinking. He sharpened the focus of the binoculars, trying to make out faces, but he recognized none of them.

He was just going to hand the glasses back to Felix when one of the group, a tall and greying, bearded man dressed in jeans and a sweater, pushed back his chair and spoke to the others who began readying themselves to leave.

'Watch this.' He realized that the illusion of the group's proximity made him whisper. 'They're off to do something.'

'I hope it's not a little stroll up here,' murmured Flicka. 'Some of those people look like cutthroats.'

'I'd forgotten your exceptional eyesight.'

'It's my youth, darling. Seriously, from here they look like hoodlums.'

'Or sailors,' added Felix.

The group straggled through the cloister and disappeared into the house, emerging seconds later outside, walking down the metalled driveway which ended at a pair of stout iron gates opening onto the road.

'Wait!' Bond had the binoculars focused on one figure – an unusually tall man, with a slow and lumbering gait. 'I know one of them. He damned nearly killed me in Wasserburg. He's a half-witted man mountain, disguised as one of Tarn's lawyers. Name of Kurt Rollen.'

As they watched, the gates swung open and the men crossed the road: two of them waiting while a tourist bus went by. At the edge of the cliff, each man seemed to disappear, as though there were some route down to the rocks and sea below. Within a few minutes they had all passed out of sight.

'I'm going to take a look down there.' Bond's hand moved to his jacket, as though reassuring himself that he was armed.

'Take care, James. You want me . . . ?'

'No. Stay here with Flicka. If I'm not back in an hour, you can come looking.' He stood up, stepping from the treeline to start walking, zig-zagging his way down the steep slope, keeping well to the left of the house and its perimeter walls. It took almost fifteen minutes to reach the road with the house and walls still on his right.

Crossing the road, he glanced up to the trees above Tarn's house, and could just make out the two figures of Felix and Flicka. He then headed directly towards the point where the men had disappeared.

As he had guessed, there was a way down, a series of steps cut into the rock, dropping at a steep angle. There was also a large red notice which carried a warning sign of skull and crossbones, below which were the words *Private and Dangerous. Only authorized personnel beyond this point. Danger of Death* in four different languages.

Slowly, Bond made his way down the first few steps, then stopped to listen. There was no sound of voices, only the crashing of the surf against the rocks below, though he could see, even from here, that a wide channel ran from the cliffs between two reefs: enough room for a ship to get through.

The steps became slick with water as he neared the bottom which ended in a wide concrete platform fashioned around rocks. Once on the platform, his sneakers were soaked with the spray which burst regularly over the platform. Inching his way along the concrete with his back to the natural rock, Bond could clearly see the beginning of an opening in the cliff – a great arched entrance to a cavern. The noise of the sea abated as the surf was sucked back and for the first time he heard voices, and a Scottish accent speaking loudly enough for him to hear the words, 'Come on . . . Only about twenty-four hours . . . Hell to pay if we're not ready for him . . .'

He leaned out, to take a quick look inside the cave, only to find that the entire entrance was screened by a thick mesh curtain, camouflaged in the colors of the surrounding rock. Gently, he caught hold of the edge of the netting and pulled it back. Though he allowed himself only a few seconds, it was enough to take in the long concrete walkways and the sinister bow and conning tower of a black, rust encrusted submarine, nestling within the cave while a dozen or so men climbed over her. He had seen much bigger, nuclear boats being prepared for the sea, and he had no doubt that they were going through the preliminaries.

The ascent back up the rockface took much longer than the descent, while the climb up the grassy incline to the wood almost winded him.

'You want to inform your people, or the local authorities?' he asked Felix Leiter after he had apprised them of what lay at the bottom of the cliff.

Leiter frowned. Then – 'I don't think so. It would be much better if we caught them in the act, don't you think?'

'Certainly, Felix. Certainly much better, but I think the prudent way would be to get the US Navy here as quickly as we can.'

'Plenty of time for that when we see what the timetable's like. Let's talk to the scientific trio and give them the option.'

After returning to San Juan, they had walked through the narrow, gaudy streets of the old town, the shops dispensing souvenirs, mainly garish pottery frogs – Coqui, the tiny tree frogs that are indigenous only to Puerto Rico, their chirping from branches and leaves often mistaken for birdsongs. Intermingled with the shops crammed with tourist junk were other stores containing more expensive items of jewelry and local art.

The shops and streets were crowded with locals and tourists alike, but they did have a certain charm, particularly if you looked up at the long balconies and the bracketed wall lights, a mixture of Spanish and Moorish influences.

Now, at the end of their long day out, they stood on the top gun platform of El Morro, having seen everything else within the massive thick stone walls. The fortress still had about it an atmosphere of unreality, for it was built at the far promontory entrance to the harbour: rising up several levels, and sweeping down to the sea itself.

Its strategic position, coupled with the amazing ingenuity of its building, had made this place impregnable.
Even Drake had been unable to conquer it, and others
who tried had always been beaten back.

The secret was, of course, in its layered construction,
coupled with the masterly design which had enabled
great cannons to be let down, or winched up steep
cobbled ramps, so that the lowest emplacements – only
feet away from the rocks and sea – could cut down any
men who happened to get a toehold on land. Above
this, the gun positions were set in higher, serrated walls
which allowed them to fire with accuracy on the old big
men-of-war, cutting the masts and crippling the ships
with ease.

Here, at the highest elevation, the large cannon, still in
position, would fire heated cannonballs down into the
ships. When Drake had tried to take the place in the
1590s, he had finally been dissuaded when one of the
heavy red hot balls had crashed into the stern of his ship,
through his personal cabin window.

They made their way down to the so-called patio, really
the parade ground, living quarters and store houses. It
also contained a big water cistern, the chapel of Santa
Bárbara, and the old centre of all social life within the
castle.

'Now this place *is* haunted.' Flicka was at the guide
book again. 'A lady walks around at night searching for
her lost love, and sometimes soldiers appear, sitting
around and talking.'

'It all depends on what you've been drinking,' Bond
replied. 'Isn't there some story about one of those sentry
boxes?' The sentry boxes were in fact little stone turrets
that stood out away from the walls: stone tubes with
ornate lids and one observation slit. The old design was

beautiful, and had been taken on as the general logo for the island.

'No, the sentry box story concerns the other fortress, San Cristóbal. A sentry on duty was visited by his true love. In the morning they had disappeared. They're supposed to make regular appearances.'

'I'll bet. Every hour on the hour. More likely the sentry went AWOL with his love and they both lived happily ever after selling those nasty little tree frogs.'

Felix sniffed the air. 'You know, I wouldn't be surprised if this place *is* haunted. Nobody stays here at night, you know. These Historic Park Rangers all pack up and go home when they close.'

'You mean the Park Rangers are Historic, or . . . ?'

'You know exactly what I mean, James.'

They walked back to El Convento to change for dinner, then set off to the harbour. Rexinus had given them explicit directions as to where *Mare Nostrum* was tied up. 'You can't miss her,' he had said, rightly, because nobody could possibly have missed the exotic-looking ship.

That she had been purpose-built was obvious. This sleek 250 foot, sea-going motorized yacht still had the patina of newness on her. She also looked like the kind of craft you saw only on classified documents. The mortar-like tubes, about which Felix had told them, poked into the air at forty-five degree angles, but it was the super-structure that immediately caught the eye. Aft of the wheelhouse was a long square Plexiglas framework which looked like a modern greenhouse. It climbed higher than the wheelhouse, and the edges along the top were curved, giving it the look of something from science fiction.

Rex Rexinus stood by the gangway, his infectious laugh splitting the air.

'You found us, then.'

'How could we miss you, Dr Rexinus?' Flicka had already said that she would handle Rexinus should he get difficult when they laid the news on him.

The marine biologist welcomed them on board, saying that he would take them on a tour of the ship after dinner. 'Poor Vesta doesn't get to entertain very often. She's provided only a cold supper, but it seems to have taken her all day.' He turned and laughed again as though this were a great joke.

Bond was finding his laughter a little hard to bear.

Below decks the quarters were more palatial than they expected: a wide and high oblong, oak paneled, living area had been arranged as a dining room, complete with a long adjustable table which was laid out with plates of cold meats and salads of every possible variety. There were crystal glasses and bottles of both a good claret and a somewhat fine Chablis.

'What's through there?' Bond asked immediately, nodding to the closed door at the far end. He always liked to know the quickest exit when he arrived in a new environment.

'Our modest sleeping quarters.' Fritz had the distinct trace of a squashed Mid-European accent.

'Modest indeed.' Vesta Motley came forward to greet them. 'I have the best bedroom I've ever had in the whole of my life. I *do* hope you don't mind this buffet thing I've prepared. It's so difficult to know what one should do.' The cut glass British accent clashed heavily with Rexinus's American.

'Just what we'd have chosen for ourselves,' Bond said gallantly. In the depth of his heart he could have done with a really good dinner tonight, but he figured that beggars could not be choosers.

Vesta Motley did not appear to have any of the social

graces. They had hardly entered the living quarters when she started to pour wine and asked them to 'Dig in, chaps,' which made Bond wince and Flicka stifle a snort of laughter.

While they moved around, eating and drinking, they tried to chip away at the job the trio of scientists were doing for Max Tarn. To give credit, Rexinus himself tried to explain the theory behind what he referred to as 'An automatic anti-oil pollution system AAOPS for short,' but the concept was daunting, and they really were none the wiser by the time he had finished.

Eventually, Bond nodded to Felix who, they had agreed, would set things in motion. 'Well, folks,' he began, using the same old Texas cowboy manner that he had kept up all evening. 'I fear we've brought you some disturbing, and almost certainly dangerous news.'

The three scientists looked at him as though he were quite mad.

'What kind of news?' Rexinus did not laugh.

'You haven't yet been able to get any instructions from Tarn International in London?'

'We told you that last night. Since Sir Max's death we aren't getting *any* answers at all. It's like the whole organization has died with him.'

'Max Tarn isn't dead.' It was Bond who exploded the bombshell.

'Isn't . . . But . . . ?'

'Worse still to come,' Flicka said softly.

'The man is wanted for a number of quite heinous crimes, I fear.' Back to Felix. 'Murder is probably the least important. He's wanted for weapons running on a huge scale. I don't think we need to go into the complete story now, but you have to believe us, he's very danger-ous, has firepower of his own – they travel with him usually – and we expect him in Puerto Rico any day.'

Flicka finished it off – 'The really amusing thing about him is that he thinks he's the Nazi Messiah, and it appears that a zillion or so German far right groups believe him.'

'Oh, my God!' from Vesta.

'Who the hell are you, with these idiotic stories?' Rexinus had possibly given up laughing for a long time, and his face became even more grave as Felix showed them his own credentials, and introduced Bond and Flicka in their true identities.

'We're going to suggest that you pull out of Puerto Rico tonight,' Bond told them. 'You can always make for Miami or somewhere, and Felix can organize protection for you. Really you are in the gravest danger. Max Tarn will brook no explanations. I doubt if he'll even listen when you tell him the AAOPS won't work. The man thinks he's above any laws, natural, manmade, or scientific. Tell him your original concept doesn't work and he'll tell you that's nonsense. Also, we believe that he's all set to show your invention off to the world, and we think his planned display will cause many problems – including death on a fairly grand scale.'

'I don't believe it.' Rexinus seemed to be standing his ground. 'This is some kind of trick.'

'Wish it were, friend,' from Felix.

'Rex,' Flicka dropped her voice slightly, an old artifice used to gain everyone's attention. 'Rex, please, listen to us. Max Tarn *is* very dangerous, and when he gets here he'll bring some of his playmates. They're an ugly bunch and include a couple of psychopathic girls. I'm pleading with you. Get out while there's time. Let us deal with him. Us and the local authorities.'

'You mean this, don't you?' Vesta looked quite bewildered.

'I've never been so certain of anything in my life. These are truly perilous people.'

Suddenly, Bond quietly called for silence.

'What . . . ?' Rexinus began, then they heard the call from above.

'Ahoy there. Ahoy, Dr Rexinus. Permission to come aboard. It's your admiral. Where the devil are you?'

They all recognized the voice. Max Tarn called again, 'I'm coming on board. Rexinus! Fritz! Dr Motley! I've brought a few friends to see how you're getting on.'

'Out,' Bond whispered. 'Grab your plates and get through into the sleeping quarters.' He was talking to Felix and Flicka. 'Keep him out of the for'ard part of the ship, and don't commit yourselves to anything.' He opened the door, and Flicka was close behind him. Felix stayed where he was.

'Felix. Quickly, man.'

'Thought I'd stay on and see if I can talk any sense into the man.' His eyes were hard, and Bond knew there was no way he could even begin to argue with the American.

'Permission to come aboard, damn you, Rexinus.' Tarn was at the top of the companionway. As he began to descend, Flicka closed the door behind her and slipped the lock.

21

Briefing

THEY LEANED AGAINST the door, hardly daring to breathe, listening intently to the conversation from the main cabin.

'Ah, so there you are, Dr Rex, I've been calling for what seems like hours, but no harm done. Brought some friends to meet you.'

'Sir Max, what a . . . But, how . . . ? I mean . . . ?'

'As someone else once said, reports of my death have been greatly exaggerated. Maurice Goodwin you know, I think. But you certainly haven't met my heavenly twins, Cathy and Anna. There, say hallo to the nice Dr Rexinus, and Anton Fritz, and we mustn't forget the lovely Dr Motley.' Then he raised his voice, 'Connie, stay up there and don't let anyone else come aboard.'

There was the faint sound of Connie Spicer's voice, then the shuffle of movement as Tarn and his three companions began settling themselves.

'Sir Max, it's . . .' Rexinus began.

'I shall do the talking for the time being, Doctor. First, you seem to be having a nice little party. Are you not going to introduce me to your guest? A glass of wine wouldn't come amiss either.'

'Certainly. I'm sorry. Mr Felix Leiter, from Texas. Sir Max Tarn.'

'From London, I guess.' Felix raised his voice slightly, trying, Bond thought, to push up the levels of everyone's speech.

'You guess correctly, Mr Leiter, though I'm not simply confined to London. I regard myself as an international citizen. I've heard that name before, somewhere. Leiter. No, Felix Leiter, I've seen it in print.'

'I doubt it, Sir Max, I'm just an old Texas cowboy.'

'And I doubt that, Mr Leiter.'

'Well, I owned the cows and there were quite a lot of them.'

'Really? Well I fear that you've accepted an invitation to come aboard *Mare Nostrum* at a very inconvenient time.'

'Oh, gee, well, I can make myself scarce. I'll leave now. Y'all get on with your party.' There was a shifting sound as Felix got to his feet.

'No!' Max Tarn barked. 'You have a limp, and a prosthetic arm. A leg *and* an arm.'

'Sounds like you're a kinda Sherlock Holmes, Sir Max.'

'Hardly. Now I think I recall where I read about you. You're a friend of a friend of mine. A Mr James Bond. You were also once a member of the American Intelligence Service. Oh, Mr Leiter, I fear you've fallen among thieves and I think you'd better stick around – as you people would say.'

'Whatever you fancy, Sir Max. But I guess you've been reading the wrong books. I don't recall anyone by the name of Bond. Knew a fella from Houston called Bind, and another one who hailed from Dallas, name of Band. Big Jim Band, but no Bonds – except on the stock market, of course.'

Tarn laughed unpleasantly and told Cathy to watch Felix. 'This is a live one, Cath. We're going to have to take him into custody and keep him safe until *SeaFire*'s over.'

'Sir Max, if I could . . . ?' from Rexinus.

'Dr Rex, please shut your mouth. I've spent a fortune on you and your friends. You said it would take a year. You've had your year and now it's payback time. The demonstration we promised ourselves will happen tomorrow night, and it's going to be quite something . . .'

'But, Sir Max, I *have* to tell you . . .'

'You don't have to tell me anything, Rex. It's time for *me* to tell you. I'm here to give you a briefing. *Operation SeaFire*. Has a nice ring to it, eh?'

Rexinus seemed to have given up, but Anton Fritz's voice came piping with, 'I don't think you quite understand, sir. What Rex is trying to say is that the AAOPS isn't quite . . .'

'Please, no excuses and no explanations. We run a public demonstration of the AAOPS tomorrow night. If you have final touches to perfect then you'll just have to work at them in the next twenty-four hours.' Pause. 'Actually a shade less than twenty-four hours.'

Through the door, Max Tarn's voice sounded even silkier than it had when Bond last heard him; silkier and, somewhere mixed in with the silk, a rough undertow as though the smoothness was slowly being ripped apart. Sir Max Tarn had reached some terrible pinnacle from which he could only fall. It was the voice of a person utterly unbalanced. A man who believed himself invincible, safe from anything, even death.

Vesta Motley also tried, 'Sir Max, there *is* a problem. We . . .'

'There is *no* problem as far as I'm concerned, Dr Motley. It's taken a long while to set this up. We go ahead tomorrow night. Now, if you'll all cease talking and be quiet, I'll give you the briefing.'

Barking mad, Bond thought. Just as he had predicted. Tarn probably already knew what they were trying to tell him, but was going ahead whatever the outcome.

He was speaking again. 'The oil company, MetroTex, has one of their supertankers coming into this harbor at precisely eight o'clock tomorrow night. It is a huge affair and will be fully loaded. Thousand upon thousand gallons of oil and gasoline. The name of that enormous ship is *Golden Bough* and she's a regular visitor to these shores, so her timing is like clockwork.

'What *Golden Bough* contains will make this rich harbor golden alright. Golden with fire and flames. The amusing thing is that there's already a precedent for what will happen, because in the late sixteenth century no less a sailor than Sir Francis Drake set fire to every ship in this harbor.'

'Which lit the way to his defeat,' said Leiter.

Tarn did not even pause. 'Your job, Dr Rexinus, will be to dash in and let the world see that an oil spill of this magnitude can be contained. It will be your triumph. More importantly, it will be my triumph. The demonstration *has* to be big. It *has* to be impressive, for if it is not contained then this entire island will be surrounded by an oil slick which will make any other disaster of this kind look insignificant. Every other major oil spill the world has seen will be as small as scum on bathwater.'

There came the noise of what would normally be a slow handclap, only this sounded like a hand being slapped onto leather. Felix was pushing his luck.

'What the devil does that mean, *Mr* Leiter?'

'Simply applauding. I'm all in favor of spectacles, and if *Golden Bough* is as big as I think she is, you'll do more than light up the harbor here, and run oil around the coastline. It could drift a long way. We're talking about almost total pollution of the Caribbean.'

'You're not taking Dr Rexinus into account, Mr Leiter. He and his companions are wonder workers. With the flick of a switch they can pour trouble on oiled waters. I've put several million into a brilliant idea, so tomorrow night we see if I've wasted my money or not.'

'How're you going to set *Golden Bough* ablaze? You got some special kindling to do that?'

Tarn gave a small bark of a laugh. 'Yes. Yes, good. Kindling. Yes, I *do* have special kindling in the form of a somewhat ancient Russian submarine. She's old, rusty, noisy, I think a little leaky also, but I've put money into her as well.'

'A submarine?' Rexinus' voice quavered.

'And torpedoes – two of them. Should have been three, but one was wasted. At least we know it works. I had a slight problem with the captain. He's a Scottish gentleman and I fear he bends his elbow a shade too much. On a trial run earlier this year he actually targeted one of my own cruise liners. He tells me that he didn't know the torpedo tubes were loaded, or whatever the expression is. My ship escaped with a little damage and no loss of life. In other circumstances I might have fired the man – preferably from one of his own torpedo tubes – but I think we can trust him to do the job thoroughly this time, can't we, Maurice?'

Goodwin grunted, and Tarn repeated, 'Maurice?'

'Yes, Max, we can trust him now. I don't relish the job, but I'll be with him to make certain he doesn't go astray.'

Tarn sighed. 'It's a terrible thing when a man has to put his own watchdogs onto people he pays to do specialist jobs – pays handsomely as well. I really wonder what the world's coming to.'

'You're going to watch the display from here, then?' Felix was feeding him questions that might help Flicka and Bond.

'Not quite from here, Mr Leiter. I prefer a grandstand view. I shall watch it all from the top of that grand old fortress they call El Morro. If you behave yourself, I might even let you come with me. No. No, I don't think that's a good idea. I'll leave you to the interesting charms of one of my other girls. You think Beth would like to play with this one, Anna?'

Anna gave a sound which lay somewhere between a cough and a laugh. 'Beth would love to play with him. Probably remove his false arm and leg first. She likes pulling the wings off flies.' There was something disgustingly sinister in the way she said it, and Bond reached for his weapon, turning as though to put his shoulder to the door, but Flicka caught his arm and shook her head silently.

He knew she was right. It was his old trouble, guilt from the past about Felix. Now he had put his friend in danger again. He looked down at Flicka, gave a sad little smile, nodded and relaxed.

There was rustling from the main cabin. 'This chart,' Tarn said. 'Heed me, Dr Rexinus, you're going to have to follow my instructions to the letter. You will leave this berth at seven o'clock tomorrow night. On the dot of seven, so that you will reach here.' He was obviously showing Rexinus a point on the chart, and aloud he gave a latitude and longitude. 'This will bring you to within one nautical mile of the initial explosion. As soon as the fire begins to spread, you will take *Mare Nostrum* straight towards the outer edges of the flames and begin to operate the AAOPS. If I recall our previous conversations correctly, you will be able to move quite close to the centre of

260

both fire and oil spill. Did you not explain that to me when we finalized our agreement?'

'Yes, that's what I said.' Rexinus sounded resigned. 'I think we'll take her for a run out tomorrow morning, just to go through the drill.'

Good, Bond considered, he's going to make a dash for it.

'Why not do that, Rex? I didn't tell you that there'll be an extra hand on board. Well, he's one man, but he carries a great deal of weight. He's up on the deck at the moment. My man Connie Spicer. Martial Arts expert, crack shot, carries all kinds of lethal things with him.'

'We can always do with another pair of hands.' Rexinus' voice betrayed his disappointment, and Bond mouthed a "Damn." With Connie left on board, there was little chance of the three gullible scientists overpowering him. Come to that, if Connie stayed on the craft now, there might be difficulties in getting ashore themselves. He looked back along the passageway. There were cabin doors to left and right, and, at the far end, the passage seemed to connect with another, running across the breadth of the laboratory ship. A third door was visible. Three night cabins. If the craft had been properly designed, there had to be a way up to the main deck somewhere for'ard.

Felix had started to speak again. 'Sir Max, what if something goes wrong with your firework display? What if Dr Rexinus and his friends fail to contain the oil and gasoline?'

'I hate to even contemplate that, but I suppose one must face the possibility. First, *Mare Nostrum* will probably be consumed in the flames and, second, I shall have to start all over again. But I have faith in these good people, Mr Leiter. They'll not fail me. Now, back to the operation.' More rustling. 'This is where my submarine will be at eight o'clock. She will turn bow on to *Golden Bough*. The two tin fish, as I think they used to call them, will be fired. Heaven knows, I don't think even my captain, Jock Anderson, can possibly miss. The target is so large and he'll be quite close. After he's fired the torpedoes, he turns tail and runs for it. I have no doubts that part will go like clockwork. Maurice here will want to get out as quickly as he can.'

'Too damned right,' murmured Maurice Goodwin.

'Any further questions?' Tarn had become all business-like. 'I haven't got all night. No, Mr Leiter, please, no questions from you. Cathy, take Mr Leiter topside and put him in the car, it's time we were getting back if we're to have any sleep tonight.'

More movement, then Tarn again – 'Tell Connie to come down here, would you? I want to make sure that the gallant crew of *Mare Nostrum* understands that his orders are my orders, and they have to see what will happen should they disobey him.'

More sounds of movement, then Connie's voice from the main cabin. 'You wanted me, chief?'

'I would like you to impress upon these good people how important it is to stick to the timetable and jump when you tell them to jump.' He paused, then addressed the others, 'Connie is an amazing man. You should know that he can go without sleep for days at a time. In fact, he has promised me that he will not sleep until *SeaFire* is safely over. You understand?'

Bond signaled to Flicka, indicating that they should move back along the passage. She nodded and followed him, drawing her Beretta from under her skirt.

The door in the cross passage was flanked by two narrow companionways leading up to the deck. They took the one on the starboard side, Flicka behind him, covering the rear. At the top, he peered out, then whispered, 'We're right by the wheelhouse. With luck we can slip off after Tarn leaves.'

He could see Tarn's car – a low, sleek black Jaguar – pulled up near the gangway, and Cathy with Felix. She held a pistol and stood well back while he leaned against the car. For a second time, the thought of rescuing his friend flashed in and out of Bond's mind. No. There was no point in trying foolhardy heroics which could well put them out of action and ruin any further chance he had of stopping the madness of what Max Tarn called *SeaFire*.

They waited for what seemed to be a very long time, but, finally, Tarn came up on deck with Anna and Maurice Goodwin in tow. Bond smiled when he saw Sir Max, for he had entered into what he saw as the spirit of the affair, dressed in white ducks and a blazer, a yachting cap set jauntily on his head.

He stopped by the car, staying behind Cathy's right shoulder and talking to Felix for the best part of a minute, then Goodwin moved forward and opened the rear passenger door, roughly helping Felix into the car.

It was Tarn himself who took the wheel, and seconds later the Jaguar pulled away from the gangway.

He waited until the sound of the engine was far away, then motioned to Flicka, moving silently and slowly along the deck. From below voices were raised. He even heard Rexinus almost shouting at Connie Spicer, 'But it won't work. We'll all be sailing out to certain death.'

Connie's reply chilled Bond's spine. 'You heard the chief's orders. You do as I say. I do as I'm told. Sir Max knows exactly what he's doing, always has done and always will.'

Bond thought of all he had read about Hitler in the

Berlin bunker during his final days: issuing orders to military forces which had long ceased to exist. Fighting with ghosts, and then joining those armies with the assistance of poison and a bullet.

Seconds later, they were on the quayside and walking quickly back in the direction of the Old Town.

22

U-Boat

'NO, FREDERICKA, CAN'T you see the folly of you coming with me?'

'If you're going to be back here by dawn, it makes no difference. I can cover you, and it'll be safer. We've always worked together – well, ever since . . .'

'Flick, what if I'm *not* back by the morning?'

'Then I'll be with you. I don't think I want it any other way. If I'm to hang around here, I'll go crazy.'

He sighed in irritation. They had been arguing for the best part of twenty minutes in their room at the hotel. 'Flick, listen. If I don't get back by early morning, it'll mean one of three things. One, I'm dead meat . . .'

'James, don't. Don't talk like that.'

'Face it, Flicka, we've got ourselves in a damned dangerous situation. Now, one, I shall be dead; two, I shall have done it, spiked the sub and gone in to rescue Felix – he can't be anywhere else but in Tarn's compound, and I didn't like the sound of the girl, Beth. We've only been near her once – at Hall's Manor – and she doesn't seem exactly the kind of playmate you'd take on a picnic. So, if they aren't putting the crew on board the sub until they sail, I'll probably have time to get rid of the damned boat *and* get Felix out.'

'What's the third possibility?'

'That they've caught me in the sub. There's one more that I've just thought about. It is quite possible that I'll not even get into the submarine.'

'And what happens then?'

'I probably come high-tailing it back here, and we do something else. As it is, there's plenty for you to get on with. Just think about it. If you'd come to Germany with me, we'd both be dead by now. Like Germany, the sub's a one person job.' He was dressed in the black jeans, rollneck and sneakers. The two aluminum cases lay open on the bed, with his wet suit lying between them, and beside it the other item which had been in the case: a wide leather belt, with fixed pouches into which he could place everything he needed. The belt also had clips for a holster, a long, vicious-looking knife, and a torch. 'There is *no* other way, Flicka. In fact, you'll have to do several things. A call to the Harbormaster and the local police to begin with.'

'You said that was last resort stuff. You were adamant about it.'

He knew she was right. Someone calling or going to the authorities here in San Juan, would probably be shipped into the nearest mental hospital. Tales about prowling submarines bent on torpedoing a supertanker would almost certainly be regarded as the ravings of a lunatic. He re-locked the two cases and stowed them away in the fitted wardrobe.

'Then call the States. Call Langley, or even London. They'll see things are dealt with.'

'Why can't we just do that now, and quietly bow out? Leave it to the authorities.'

'You know why we can't do that. It's a question of time.'

'Balls, James, it's a question of your pride. *You* have a

personal vendetta with Tarn and *you* want to finish it by yourself.'

Deep down he knew she was perfectly correct, but he *was* concerned about the time factor. He knew exactly how things might go if they called London. The Committee could sit around for most of the day deciding if it were wise to give the whole story to the American service. Anyway, his own motivation had taken over. There was no turning back from the way he had planned.

'James, we got the all clear to do this because the Americans wanted to get Tarn – Apocalypse as they called him. Nobody'll hold up any signals we send. Not now, that we've eliminated Tarn's man, Christopher, and are operating here with the okay from the Americans.'

He sighed. 'I'm not even convinced that we *do* have the okay from them.'

'What do you mean, James? You're getting paranoid about this.'

'Give me a little time. If I'm not back by noon, make all the telephone calls you want. At least let me have a shot at the submarine. Perhaps you're right. Perhaps we *should* report to everyone and pray for the marines to arrive to put an end to this madness. But will you just give me a little time to set them up?'

She was very unhappy, but, in the short time they had been together, Flicka von Grüsse had discovered that James Bond could be more than stubborn.

'Okay,' she glared at him. 'You have your moment of glory, James. Go and deal with the submarine, but, if you're not back by nine, I'm going to alert London. Not a minute too soon either. You've got until nine in the morning. Right?'

He gave her a bleak smile, signaling agreement to the compromise. Glancing at his watch he saw it was just after nine now. 'I've got less than twelve hours.'

'Well, you'd better get cracking, James, because I'm not going to be responsible for any cock-up that leaves this harbor in flames, and half the Caribbean polluted for all time. So get going.'

He distributed the items he needed around the belt. Pistol, knife, the small high-powered torch, compact tool kit and the five oblong boxes from the bottom of the second case. The boxes he had called his "little jewels". He slung the wet suit over one arm and went over to Flicka who still looked angry. 'Don't worry, Flick. I'll be back. This is just a safeguard. The minute I'm back we'll both call London and Washington. You're basically right, but I want to cover all the bases.'

She clung to him as though saying goodbye for the last time. 'Be careful, darling James. I want you around for the wedding, remember?'

'I'll be there, with a smile on my face and everything intact.'

'I'm not so worried about the smile. Just make sure *everything's* in working order. I'd hate you to be encumbered with prosthetic body parts like Felix.'

Minutes later he retrieved the car from El Convento's parking place and was heading out of San Juan taking the most direct road, across the island to Ponce.

Flicka pulled herself together once he had left the hotel. She even cursed herself. During the years she had spent with the Swiss Intelligence and Security services she had been known for her cool and decisive courage. Now that Bond was in her life she seemed to have lost some of that calm reserve, and she was not overjoyed by the lapse. She presumed that it had something to do with her body chemistry, for Fredericka von Grüsse had to admit she had never, in her entire life, loved a man with this kind of intensity.

Well, she thought as she began to undress, he really only has until nine in the morning. Then I'll make such a fuss that London and the Americans will have to send an entire battle group if necessary.

She went into the bathroom and surrendered to the soothing warm shower. When she eventually turned off the shower, she reached from behind the curtain and grabbed a towel before stepping out.

She screamed when she saw them, Maurice Goodwin and the black girl called Beth. They stood just inside the bathroom door and Beth held the Beretta which Flicka had left with her clothes on the bed.

'Honey, you're all alone here. Thought we'd keep you company.' Beth was eyeing her unpleasantly. 'It's okay,' she continued. 'Maurice has to go, but I can keep you company until your friend comes back.'

Flicka took in a lungful of air. 'He isn't coming back.' She kept her voice level.

'A likely tale. If I was a man there's no way I'd leave a sweet piece like you on your own.'

'Please yourself. But he's not coming back and there's an end to it.'

'So where's he gone?' Goodwin eyed her lecherously. 'I need to know, Ms von Grüsse, and I need to know fast. Beth here is clever at inflicting pain. She's made a kind of art form of it. So tell me now. Where's he gone?'

'Off the island. If you want to know, we've had what you might call a falling out. He stormed out of the hotel and said he wouldn't be back.'

'You tellin' the truth, honey?' Beth came towards her. Close up she was a little older than Flicka had thought. Late thirties. Her fingers were heavy with rings and her eyes looked red and sore, like someone with conjunctivitis, but they did not stop moving, flicking from side to side, as though she had the extraordinary vision of a chameleon.

'You tellin' the truth, honey?' she repeated, and before Flicka had a chance to reply, Beth's right hand whipped back and slapped her full and hard on the cheek, the heavy rings scraping at her flesh and knocking her head sideways.

She fell against the wall, steadied herself and tried not to show how much the blow had hurt her. 'Talk to me, bitch.' Beth's voice had a slightly slurred note, and it crossed Flicka's mind that the woman was on some kind of drugs.

'I've told you . . .' Her words were cut off by another stinging, pain drenched slap. This time harder, and followed by an even heavier back-hander to her other cheek.

Taken by surprise, and stark naked from the shower, there was little she could do, but she had to fight back. Turning her body to present a smaller target she launched herself towards the woman, one hand chopping at her assailant's neck. It was like hitting a solid punch bag and only seemed to enrage Beth even more, for, out of nowhere a ringed hand caught her hard with two heavy blows to the breasts.

'Talk to me, bitch. Where's he gone?'

'I don't . . . Truly, I don't know.'

'The truth, honey. The truth shall set you free, that's what's in the Good Book. Now, set yourself free.' The hand rose again and this time Flicka could hardly see from the pain that saturated her face. The back-hander which followed almost made her black out, but she could still hear the voice: intimidating and relentless. 'The truth, honey, just tell me the truth, then we can all have some real fun.'

She heard her own voice, from what seemed to be a long way off. 'I've told you the truth. I don't . . .'

The pain again. Now it was as if she were living in her own private world of agony, though the voice of her conscience repeated to her again and again – 'Don't tell them anything. Keep James safe.'

She felt for the corner of the wall with her feet, and tried to push herself towards Beth, hands bunched into fists, striking out for the woman's throat. Before her hands got anywhere near their target, another blow sent her sprawling back onto the floor.

'Talk to me, bitch.'

'I really don't know. Stop. I don't . . .'

She prayed for the darkness of unconsciousness or even death, and knew that at least one of her cheek bones was almost certainly broken. The hands of this black horror, reinforced by the heavy rings, were like pieces of steel. The hurt filling her life.

Again. 'The truth shall set you free, honey. Where's he gone?'

Then one more time, to the left cheek and then the right. She felt blood wet on her cheek and running down her nose, while Beth's voice sounded distorted. 'Tell me the truth, bitch.' Crack. A whole avalanche of torment. A numbness as she cannoned off the wall, and voices coming from miles away; from the end of a long dark tunnel.

'You've done it again, Beth. She's out.'

Flicka could hardly make out the words.

'Then I guess she tellin' the truth. You've seen this before, Mo . . .'

'Don't call me Mo. The name's Maurice.'

'She don' know where he is, that's for sure.'

'Then we'd better get her out of here. Take her to Max's place. You can work on her quietly there, just in case you're wrong.'

'I'm seldom wrong, baby. You know that. She tellin' the truth, so why don' I just set her free, here and now?'

'No. Let's get her across the island. You've got the white coats in the car. Let's do it. Let's . . .'

The voices faded as Flicka slipped deeper into the comfort of oblivion. She could feel nothing, nor could she understand anything.

Bond drove fast, but with great concentration. His conscience was already pricking him, because, of course, he knew Flicka had been right. They should have called in. Passed the whole business over to their superiors and got out, knowing that Tarn and his mad, obsessive plan would come to nothing with the deployment of the right forces.

Yet a part of him wanted to see it through. Was it a question of glory? A reluctance to give up the life of danger for a desk and the boredom of assigning other people to this kind of work?

Then he switched his mind away from those questions. He glanced at the dashboard digital clock. Ten p.m., he had eleven hours and if nobody was guarding the submarine he could set his little jewels. For a couple of seconds he wondered what intuition had made him ask Ann Reilly for these particular items. Each consisted of two pounds of plastique explosive, a recently developed substance with three times the effect of Semtex. Two pounds of this stuff would do a lot of damage, especially if it were placed in the right spots. The heat it generated, for one thing, had the power of a thermal lance and it could blow through steel as though it were butter.

Pushed into the two pound blocks of plastique was a

fuse with the latest in electronic timing devices. Small, with tiny powerful batteries, the fuse could be set in a similar manner to a miniature alarm clock. The dial on each was no bigger than an American 25 cent piece, and could be activated using a tiny screwdriver, over a twenty-four hour period. Now, he had plans for these deadly devices, and, once they were set, the military would not have to waste time trying to find the submarine. All he could do was hope and pray that the sub had been left unguarded that night.

He turned his thoughts to Q'ute's ingenuity. Not only had she got the explosive devices to him, but her note had been very specific concerning the other item – large and cumbersome. It would have to be somewhere out in the open, and just where he needed it. She had been very definite about that, and, considering the lack of hiding places, and the number of people who – during the day – would be passing near anywhere in San Juan, the task of dumping it for him really would have to be left until the last moment. How would Q'ute *know* when the last moment had arrived? He had missed something all the way, and now logic told him one new significant truth. The drop-off for this equipment led to the indisputable fact that there were other active service people on the island, ready to move in should he need them.

What was it Q'ute had written? *Some of our friends will see to it that you get the thing if you really need it.*

With a sudden feeling of elation, he knew what this meant, and felt a fool for not envisaging it until now. Only one kind of operative was up to hiding and waiting for the right moment to leave the piece of equipment he had in mind. He cursed himself. Of course; and of course they should have called London. He would put money on there being members of both the SAS, and the American élite

Delta Force waiting it out, watching him, ready to move in as soon as they received signals. Flicka was right, he told himself. They could have left it to London and Washington. Everything was already in place, and if the élite forces had done their job properly, they would know by now that something was about to go down.

It flashed through his mind that perhaps he should drive into Ponce and make a call from some public telephone booth, but he stubbornly dismissed the idea. He would try and set the explosives, get away and call Flicka to put things in motion.

He turned off at Ponce, taking the road along the coast, eventually finding the narrow trail that led to the clump of trees from which they had observed the Tarn mansion.

Before leaving the car, he pulled on the wet suit, and snapped the belt into place, checking the equipment in the pouches and clips. He then walked up into the trees and looked down on the Tarn compound. There was no sign of life below, save for one lighted window. The submarine crew were either sleeping until dawn, or already down in the cave, readying the boat for sea.

Finally, he turned to set off back down the track and narrow road up which he had come. He paused on reaching the main road, his eyes fully adjusted to the night blackness. There was no sign of life, and no noise coming up from the rockface across the road but for the sound of the sea. He ran, crouching low, towards the warning notice, and began to descend the steps, his ears hearing only the hush and crush of the surf. No voices, and still no human sounds as he reached the bottom of the steps.

As on the previous day, he inched along the rocks towards the netting which covered the entrance to the cave. Silence, and no lights from within the makeshift submarine pen. He lifted the edge of the netting and stepped inside, standing perfectly still, all his senses attuned like radar to pick up any hint of another human being.

Nothing.

Smiling to himself, he unclipped the torch and switched it on, allowing the beam to play along the whale-like metal structure as he moved forward. His first suspicion was that this was no Victor Class Russian sub, as he had been led to believe. Its size and shape suggested something much older. Even a World War II German U-boat. As he got closer, and was able to reveal more of the submarine in the light from the torch, the more certain he became of what this really was: a Type VII C U-boat.

He crossed the small makeshift gangway and climbed up the ladder to the top of the sail, realizing that, when this boat first entered the water, it was not called the sail but the Conning Tower – the *Kommandoturm*. The hatch was up, and he played the beam of his torch down into the bowels of the boat. Silence. Nothing there but the narrow space of the tube which ran straight down into the control room. The interior smelled of a mixture of oil, polish and human bodies. The crew of this boat had been working down here until quite recently. They would be back, at the latest, for a dawn departure but he did not allow this to worry him. If he were to do the job properly, he had to take his time and make certain of the layout of the submarine.

He stayed for some time in the control room, looking at the periscope, the steering and dive controls and the dials that went with them. Part of the mystery was now explained. All the controls and instruments were labeled with neat stick-on metal tags, stating their use in English, though these same essentials had been originally marked up in German. The German had been either partly scraped off, or covered with notices in Russian, even inside the dials relating to pressure and depth. The glass fronts had been removed so that Russian labels could be stuck onto the clock-like instruments before the glass was replaced.

It was a former German U-boat, probably captured by the Russians and converted for their own use until they began building their giant nuclear, missile-carrying fleet which, throughout the Cold War, had been the USSR's most potent weapons.

Bond moved aft, along the narrow catwalks and corridors, wondering what it must have been like to serve in these extraordinary cramped conditions for months at a time. He spotted several improvements which he presumed had been made by the Russians, including more modern escape equipment – a state-of-the-art escape trunk, with a hatch hidden from the companionway below. He pulled himself up into the boxlike hatch and saw that a number of the latest Steinke Hoods were lined up in a container that ran around three sides of the hatch. Above was the cylinder of the escape trunk with its wheels to open and close the trunk.

Easing himself down onto the companionway, he traversed right to the stern of the boat, then back, moving forward, through the control room again, and so for'ard towards the bows. He brushed the small curtained off sections which served as crew and officers' Mess decks, and on towards the torpedo tubes in the bow, noting as he went that the Russians – or its present owner – had provided an escape trunk almost identical to the one aft.

There were red tags wired to the wheels of the torpedo tubes with the words *Tube Full. Loaded* scrawled on them. Behind, to both port and starboard, were the racks which would normally hold other torpedoes. They were empty, and he remembered Tarn, aboard *Mare Nostrum* saying they had only two torpedoes with which to do the job.

Bond began to take out the deadly little jewels of plastique from the pouches on his belt. He placed them in a neat row, and removed the small screwdriver with which he would arm the fuses. Holding his torch under his chin, he picked up each device in turn and worked with the screwdriver until all five fuses were set for nineteen-fifty – ten minutes to eight on the following evening. He left the final arming, the moving of a small button in the center of each dial until last, then moved to the port torpedo tube, spinning the wheel which allowed the breech door to swing back.

Years ago he had spent some time being spirited onto the shore of another country in an old British submarine, and recalled the hours spent waiting. Some of that time had been passed with an old submariner who had showed him the comparatively simple mechanism they had used on these World War II boats. In memory, the German U-boat was not much different. A lever on one side of the tube lifted a curved metal stretcher on which the torpedo could be slid into, or out of, the tube. The mechanism here was very similar, and had been well oiled and maintained. The long and deadly fish came sliding back on the stretcher until the tube was empty.

Carefully, he took the first of the plastique devices and unwrapped the actual explosive which he molded, like a big lump of plasticine, as far forward as he could on the top side of the torpedo. The second bomb he stuck firmly around the center of the weapon, then he reversed the steps with the levers and stretcher, feeling an enormous pleasure as the torpedo went back into its tube and he turned the wheel which would make the whole thing watertight.

Then he went through the whole business again on the starboard side. In all, the process took him the best part of two hours, and there was one plastique bomb left. He had kept this for another vulnerable spot, and began to make his way aft again, knowing that at ten minutes to eight on the following evening the plastique would explode, probably also igniting the two torpedoes. This alone, almost certainly, would blow off the entire bow section of the boat.

He reached the far end of the sub and searched for the main pipe which carried diesel fuel to the engines when the boat was on the surface. While submerged the craft ran wholly on the huge batteries which had to be recharged by running on the surface under the diesel. But submerged or not, there was always fuel in the pipeline, and he molded the last bomb around the pipe, so that it was completely hidden from view – high up and out of sight among the other pipes and cables which traversed almost the entire length of the boat. When the time came, the bow would be blown away and, with any luck, a secondary explosion would ignite the diesel fuel and rip through the rest of the old craft.

He sighed with some relief as he finished the job and, making certain he had left no traces of his visit, Bond began to move forward. He had gone half way towards the control room when he stopped, stock still, listening. There was a clanking sound from above him and then the unmistakable noise of men climbing the ladder up the outside of the conning tower. He heard the first one come down into the control room and then a broad Scottish accent shouting, 'Wall, there'll be nay turnin' back now, lads, so let's be having you down here.'

He was trapped inside the old U-boat.

23

Between the Devil and the Deep

FOR A SECOND he seemed to be frozen to the deck below his feet. He was so close to the control room that he could smell the men coming down through the tower. Then he moved, softly backing up until he stood just under the aft escape trunk. As the men's voices became louder, he swung himself up into the hatch close to the trunk, pressing his body into the small space which would hide him from men moving about below.

Something crackled from just beneath him and the Scottish voice came clear through the PA system. 'D'ye hear there! D'ye hear there! All hands close up for leaving harbor. All water tight doors closed.' The captain, he knew from the mode of address, must be a former member of the Royal Navy. His blood boiled with anger at the thought of an officer of his own former service being in charge of Tarn's submarine: bent on causing death, destruction and a possible ecological disaster the like of which the world had never yet seen. Bond was truly between the Devil and the Deep Blue Sea.

He was crammed into a foetal position within the hatch and moved an arm to get a glimpse of his wrist watch. It was almost two-thirty in the morning. Had he really been that long in setting the plastique explosives? Well, he certainly had not hurried. Now the thought of being confined to this tiny space for at the least seventeen hours was distinctly unappealing. Why were they leaving at this time, in the dead of night? He brushed the question aside, for the answer was obvious.

The submarine would have to work its way quietly around the island from the Caribbean to the Atlantic side, then manoeuvre itself into position in order to catch *Golden Bough* as she came past the promontory on which El Morro stood, and cripple the super tanker just within the harbor basin. They dared not allow the submarine to be seen from mainland, cruising quietly along the coast, which meant that as soon as the sun began to rise it would be necessary to dive and continue on the journey submerged.

What about radar detection? It was unlikely, unless the search was still active for a submarine, that the signature of this relatively small boat would show as anything more than a small blip which could be read as a school of large fish.

Someone hurried past, below him, feet thumping on the deck, and, for a second, his hand moved towards the pistol on his belt in case the crew member was there to check the tube of the escape trunk above him to make certain the locking wheel was tight and closed up.

The footsteps passed directly below him, bent on some job aft. He relaxed again as he felt a quivering in the metal around and below him. The diesel engines were running and he caught a faint whiff of air being drawn into the hull. Then – 'D'ye hear there! D'ye hear there! Engines slow ahead. Cast off for'ard. Cast off aft.'

Then he heard another voice, and his stomach turned over. 'This is good. Very exciting,' the voice said in slow and careful German. Kurt Rollen, the retarded partner of Saal, Saal u. Rollen, was aboard.

He flinched, as the voice seemed to come from very close to him and he heard the thud of feet above him: presumably the two crew members up on the rounded exterior, releasing the boat from its restraining lines.

Seconds later there was movement. A wallowing motion as the submarine edged slowly forward out into the sea, and the distinct tremor that passed through the metal hull, so that the entire boat seemed alive.

Again the voice of the captain. 'D'ye hear there! D'ye hear there, all hands at dive stations, close up main hatch.'

He thought he could hear the scramble of the two men who had been topside as they came down into the control room, and the squeal of the wheel lock which would seal everyone within the metal coffin, for it would be the final casket for the entire crew when the clock ticked around to seven-fifty that night.

Above him was his own means of escape, the trunk. He had no worries on that score, for only a few years ago he had been through the usual refresher courses that M had made him take regularly. Those courses brushed up his seamanship, allowed him to put a few more hours in his pilot's log, and examine the most modern weapons and procedures – including submerged escape. As long as the submarine stayed within about one hundred and twenty meters – roughly four hundred feet – of the surface he would have no problem getting out. If she went deep, there would be severe difficulties.

To operate the escape trunk he would first have to put on the Steinke Hood, which goes over the head and is attached firmly around the upper part of the body. The top section is similar to the breathing apparatus worn by firemen to guard against smoke inhalation, while the lower part acts as a life jacket. This combination allows a crew member to leave the submarine by climbing up onto the trunk, securing the watertight hatch below and then flooding the entire cylinder apart from a small air space. The escapee then charges the breathing apparatus from an air port set beside the space. After the upper part of the hood is charged, the hatch above opens and the crew member is drawn up into the water, climbing rapidly to the surface. Flooding the trunk and making a successful escape takes only a minute. Any longer and there is a risk of being attacked by 'the bends' – small bubbles of nitrogen gas can form in the blood causing excruciating pain and the inability to operate properly as you shoot up to the surface.

The real danger only comes if this method is used at a depth lower than four hundred feet, as the pressure at these depths can be deadly.

He tried to think his escape through. Flicka had been serious about passing on the information if he did not get back by nine in the morning, and he had no doubts that she would do exactly that. Would it be feasible to operate the trunk at around ten in the morning? At first he considered this as a definite possibility, even though the crew of the submarine would be immediately alerted to the fact that someone had used the escape trunk. Yet, after more thought, he concluded that this was not the best option.

They were bound to be several nautical miles from shore, and he might have great difficulty swimming that kind of distance, particularly as the captain – and Tarn's lieutenant, Maurice Goodwin – could well order an experienced diver to the surface to pursue him and hunt him down in the sea.

No, there was only one course of action that he could take. Sit tight, endure the discomfort of the cramped hatch and make his escape at around seven forty-five, as the U-boat was preparing to maneuver itself into position for the torpedo attack on *Golden Bough*. It would be a long haul, with plenty of risks which he factored into the situation.

It was still quite possible that his presence would be detected by a crew member. If that happened, he would at least have some warning. There would be time to disable the man, kill him if necessary, then climb into the trunk and make his egress no matter where they happened to be.

Leaving things to the last moment was equally dangerous. Once Flicka had alerted London and Washington, there was no knowing what action would be taken. He realized, with some horror, that after nine in the morning there was the distinct possibility that helicopters would be quickly prowling around the coastline, dipping their sonars into the water, pinpointing the submarine, which they would promptly blow to pieces with depth charges.

The more he thought about his situation, the more Bond came to the conclusion that he was in a 'no win' state. He even considered the possibility of climbing down from his hiding place, roaming the boat, killing off the crew one at a time, though this would seem just about impossible. There must be at least twenty men in the submarine, and some would certainly be armed. His chances of taking out the entire crew were minimal to say the least. Sit tight and wait, he decided. Act only if anything dramatic occurred.

The captain's voice came crackling through the PA again. 'D'ye hear there! We are making maximum speed on the surface, and will remain in this status until dawn, unless another ship appears. As soon as the sky changes we shall dive. In four minutes we will pass close to the Caja de Muertos lighthouse. This means we will be well into good diving water in around fifteen minutes. Once we go down we shall, as planned, run silent and deep until we approach San Juan harbor tonight.'

So that put paid completely to any chance of making an escape while they were en route to San Juan. He rested his head against the metal side of his hiding place, tried to stretch and ease his already aching muscles, and closed his eyes.

The throb of the engine and the wallowing rocking motion of the submarine began to have an hypnotic effect. Slowly, Bond slid away into the depths of sleep.

He was wakened by the captain's voice seeming to shout, 'Dive! Dive! Dive!' The angle of his small metal prison tipped alarmingly and he could feel the pressure in his ears as they began the descent. Looking at his watch, he saw that it was almost five-thirty. He had bad cramp in both legs and his back and arms ached as though he were recovering from long and sustained physical exercise. He sighed quietly. At least another fourteen hours of this. He genuinely wondered if he would be able to stand it.

The motion of the boat changed to the feeling he had experienced before, the dipping and rolling forward movement as they swam far below the sea's surface. Even from where he lay, the regular ping-ping of the radar was audible. For a few minutes Bond again thought about taking on the entire crew. Once more he dismissed it as being impracticable, so he turned his thoughts back to the entire operation so far.

As often in these circumstances, he had requested items from Q Branch that he really did need. It was almost like second sight, he considered, knowing that the truth really lay in his long experience. What had told him to ask for the plastique explosives? The fact that he knew, long before leaving, that Tarn was planning something concerning the sea. Also, he had nearly always asked for some form of plastique while on a difficult operation. Once more, it was experience. Then he reflected about the other main item which he was now certain was being held for him by élite forces who had probably been watching his every move.

Would he really need the Powerchute? He wondered, for that was what he had asked for, and Q'ute had gone to great pains to get it onto the island. The Powerchute, which had been in sporting use for a few years, was being adapted and worked on by people like the SAS. In essence it consisted of a triangular structure made from a very light alloy. There was a padded seat for the pilot – no licence was required to fly this machine – and behind him the small lawnmower engine which drove a propeller, encased in a wide wire mesh drum like those put around household fans as protection. The entire framework was attached to an almost oblong, airfoil parachute. The pilot opened the throttle, the propeller caused the machine to move forward, inflating the parachute and driving it into the air.

Once airborne, the craft was controlled in much the same way as a hang glider: movements of the body, with increases and decreases in power, caused the parachute to climb, turn and descend.

The SAS had been experimenting with this popular flying machine over the past year. Bond had even flown one on a couple of occasions. The Special Air Service, who are the world's most experienced trained HALO (High Altitude Low Opening) parachutists, had made changes in the Powerchute so that it could carry one or two people over longer distances and at greater speeds. Their favorite practice use was to travel over difficult terrain, climb to a height of around ten thousand feet, cut the engine and glide down silently, maneuvering themselves onto a specific target.

His request for a Powerchute, he felt, had been made on the basis of the terrain around Puerto Rico, and Ann Reilly had told him that the craft would be set down and waiting for him below the outer walls of El Morro – on the Atlantic side looking out to sea – where grass sweeps up from the sea and rocks below.

Intuition had made him ask for a Powerchute. Before setting out, he had no means of knowing that Tarn would, at the moment his operation was going down, be up on the top level around the highest gun emplacements of the fortress.

Now he had put the pieces together and knew, without the shadow of a doubt, that élite troops *must* be nearby, probably under joint British and American command. He began to think of what action he could take to get himself to the churning water which foamed dangerously against the rocks on the outside of El Morro. It was as good a way as any to pass the time, for he was now also sure in his mind that by nine o'clock Flicka would have made her telephone calls. In that case there was no way they would even get as far as the harbor. His preparation had to be the speed with which he could escape through the trunk before the sub was shattered by depth charges.

He dozed for a while, never far from the surface of consciousness, and woke with a start to the sound of voices. Shifting in the confined space, he leaned out, surprised to discover that with only a slight dropping of his head below the level of the hatch he could hear anything said in the control room.

'If we keep this up, we're going to be in gey good time.' The voice of the Scottish captain.

'Better to be early than having to dash in at the last

minute.' Maurice Goodwin sounded pompous.

'Aye, well, I can probably move out to sea a little. Maybe even put the pair of torps into *Golden Bough* before she reaches the harbor.'

'You'll do no such thing,' Goodwin snapped. 'You're going to play this one by the book, Jock. Understand me. By the book, page, paragraph and line. That damned ship has to be hit inside the harbor. In fact, just as it passes in.'

'I was only pullin' yer leg, mon.'

'Well, kindly leave my leg alone, Jock. This is a bloody dangerous business.'

'Dinna worry, mon. We'll put the fish into the tanker and be away from the area in minutes flat.'

'Well, be certain you're in the right place at the right time. I want to be able to see *Mare Nostrum* close up on our port side before you get the torpedoes away, and you do that on the dot of eight.'

'I said, dinna worry, Maurice. I'm enjoying this. Takes me back to my young days when I was chasing Nazis in the Atlantic.'

He withdrew his head, flexed his shoulders, again stretched his limbs as far as possible, then leaned back. The Scottish captain was obviously a man who did not take people like Maurice Goodwin seriously. Tarn must be paying the old sailor a great deal of money, though knowing him as he did, Bond wondered if the plan had actually included the captain and crew ever getting off the submarine. The thought crossed his mind that he should have made a more thorough search. It was always possible that Tarn had already sabotaged the boat so that she would be lost on the way back around the island. That would be his way, and maybe he also wanted to get rid of other weak links like Maurice Goodwin. That would fit.

He dozed again, waking at just after eight. Less than

twelve hours to go and the fatigue was creeping into every sinew of his body. He slid quietly back into another doze and quickly fell down the long dark tunnel of sleep. He dreamed of diving for pearls, feeling the water wash him as he swam to the bottom of a clear sea and picked oysters from between rocks, scooping them up from the sand.

On a long beach Flicka waited for him, and there was a smile of pleasure on her face as she took the oysters from him, cutting them open to reveal the pearls neat in the center of the flesh.

Then the dream went and he half woke, feeling too tired to even try to move, allowing himself to sleep on.

When he woke again it was with another start, and the sensation that he had been unconscious for a very long time. He could hardly move for the cramp and ache in his limbs, but he did manage to glance at his watch. It was impossible, for the hands on the stainless steel Rolex showed ten past three.

The submarine was still making way, rolling and pitching at speed under the surface. There was the mutter of talk coming from the control room, the hum of the engines, ping-ping of the radar and nothing to break the smooth rhythm of their progress. For the first time he had a waking nightmare about Flicka. She was going to alert people at nine that morning, over six hours ago. If she had done so, this boat should now be either lying silent and deep, or trying to escape from sonar dragging helicopters.

He shook his head and heard Flicka, only a short time ago, speaking to him, saying that someone had just walked over her grave. He felt a cold chill of horror envelop his body, while there seemed to be hammer blows crashing down on the inside of his skull.

If anything had happened to Flicka, it was his fault and his alone. If he had listened to her, they would have been together now, bringing things to a conclusion without either of them being in any immediate physical danger.

His mind was numb, and he realized that his hands were shaking. Three o'clock in the afternoon. He looked again to make certain that he had not dreamed the time on his watch. No, it was correct, and something deep in his subconscious told him that Fredericka von Grüsse was in great peril.

24

SeaFire

THE MINUTES BECAME hours; hours became days. There was no question of sleep for Bond now. Every nerve and sinew had become alert, nervously jumpy with anxiety. It was not often that he allowed problems to so besiege his mind, but this was Fredericka, the woman he loved. The woman he intended to marry. In his mind a terrible ghost from the past appeared: a blurred picture of his first wife of only a few hours, Tracy di Vicenzo, lying dead, her face buried in the ruins of the steering-wheel of his Lancia which had been raked with bullets fired by his old enemy Ernst Stavro Blofeld.

The picture was overlapped in his head, Tracy's features going through a metamorphosis, changing to Flicka's own sweet face. If anything has happened to her, he thought, then pushed even the idea away. He had already made up his mind to bring Sir Max Tarn to justice, dead or alive. If anything has happened . . . Death would not be enough for Tarn.

The picture returned, and with it a kind of certainty that there was something wrong. With that certainty came a new sense of hatred towards Max Tarn. In his long career, Bond had rarely allowed any true emotion to exist between himself and any target he had followed, or dealt with. Now, there was true anger, a fury which seemed to rend him apart. If he had the fortune to come out of this alive and face Tarn, it would be really close-up and personal.

At around six o'clock, his worst fears were confirmed. They had stopped engines and were simply running silent, hove to under the sea. He had heard the captain say that it would only take them a half-hour to get into position. 'No sense in pushing our way in too early,' he had told Goodwin.

Now, the captain and Goodwin had walked back towards the stern, pacing along the deck as though taking a little exercise. They traversed the deck twice, and finally stopped, almost underneath the hatch where Bond was curled, not moving a muscle.

'So what happens when Sir Max proves his point with this AAOPS thing?' the captain asked.

'God knows.' Maurice Goodwin's voice was flat, with no hint of how he really felt. 'I suspect that I shall quietly disappear. I've saved enough money to keep myself comfortable for the rest of my natural, in Rio or some other place. I just don't want to be around if he gets his Party really organized in Germany. The way things are in Europe, the mood of the people, leaves the way open for him. If that happens, true hell's going to return and this time the madman could win.'

'Ye'd leave the Man then?'

'I suggest, Jock, that you grab *your* money and get the hell out as quickly as you can. I'm pretty sure that this AAOPS thing is unworkable. There's going to be disaster up there when you slam the fish into that tanker, and I've no doubt that the authorities will do their best to hunt him down. The man's mad, Jock. Mad as a hatter, but he's bloody clever. I wouldn't count on him getting caught, and if he is . . .'

'You think he'll *let* himself be caught?'

'You mean he'd rather be a suicide? Oh, no. Max will always think he's in the right, just as he has no true conception of right or wrong. Men like me – and you for that matter – know where we stand. We know the things we've done and we can differentiate between good and evil. Not so with Max. He *has* to be in the right. If he murdered his mother and was caught standing over her with the axe in his hand, he would have some argument, however spurious, to show that he was really doing the right thing. He's also a bad enemy to have. If you'd seen the things I've seen, Jock, you'd know.'

After a few seconds pause, the captain asked, 'Wasn't there some talk of people actually after him, here in Puerto Rico?'

'Indeed, yes. One of them's still out there somewhere. British and American intelligence people. We've got the Yank and the Brit woman at the house. They're there with Beth. You've met Beth, haven't you?'

'Aye, and I'd rather not spend too much time with her. In fact, it wouldn't worry me if I never laid eyes on her again.'

'She's Max's secret weapon, and a very nasty weapon at that. He provides the drugs and she gets her rocks off providing the pain and even death.'

'She's no killed the Yank and the Brit?'

'Not yet, but give her time, with Max not around to control her, Beth could get homicidal. Strange woman. I've seen her kind and tender, but when she's on the drugs and Max suggests things to her, it's a different matter. Mind you, those two girls, Cathy and Anna, they can be deadly. They'll fight like trained soldiers.'

'I thought as much. They like teasing the men as well.'

'Either of them would sleep with a goat if they thought it'd give them pleasure.'

Bond, stretching and trying to get his circulation going, had listened to the exchange with the kind of horror most people had when they faced a cobra, or even something less deadly, like a scorpion.

At least he knew Flicka was still alive, or had been when Goodwin last saw her. For the umpteenth time during that long day, his hand moved towards his pistol. Part of his senses told him to go now, try to take out the crew and to blazes with anyone else: just get to Flicka and make sure she was out of danger. The more sensible part of his emotions held him back. After all, it wouldn't be so long now.

It seemed even longer than the earlier part of the day. His watch ticked on, and he began to glance at it automatically about once a minute. Finally, at around seven in the evening, they began to move again.

Half-an-hour later he heard the captain call, 'Up periscope.' The mechanism whined and shortly after – 'Five degrees to port.' At seven-thirty exactly the captain gave the final order. 'Stop engines. We're there and *Golden Bough* is coming in. I can see her heading straight towards the headland. She's on time and I reckon we'll have her bang in the sights at twenty hundred. On the button.'

Another wait and Bond's watch showed seven thirty-five. Fifteen minutes before his plastique would blow the boat to hell. Time to start getting ready. He slowly rose, his legs, arms and back protesting after the hunched position they had been forced into all day.

From the control room he heard, '*Mare Nostrum*'s up on our port side ready to go in. Fifty yards to port and holding steady. Stand by.'

He took down one of the Steinke Hoods, then reached

up, pulling himself towards the trunk. As he moved, so the Hood slipped from his fingers and went clattering onto the deck.

He froze, then quietly began stretching back for another Hood. As he moved, his right ankle was caught in what seemed like a steel trap. There was an immense tug and he fell, down onto the metal deck. Leaning over him was the huge shape of Kurt Rollen who hissed, 'Engländer!' For a fraction of a second, Bond found the word both amusing and apt, then two ham-like hands grabbed him by the shoulders, lifted him high in the air and dropped him on the deck again. He drew up his knees into a fetal position, then shot his legs forward with all the strength he could muster, his heels catching Rollen just below the knees.

The German gave out a gruff cry, half anguish and half rage as he staggered back against a stanchion. Big he might be, but he was far from being agile. Rollen hit the metal hard, his arms waving about like branches in a whirlwind.

It gave Bond just enough time to draw his knife, and he moved in very fast, the knife held in the classic position – thumb down and fingers curling over the haft, blade forward. He threw himself onto Rollen who was flailing around trying to get up. The blade of the knife slid home, like pushing a spade into soft ground.

Rollen managed one terrifying cry before he weakened and fell back with blood fountaining from his stomach.

The clatter and cry would certainly bring someone from the control room, so Bond slid the knife back into its scabbard and leaped upwards, towards the hatch, grabbing another Steinke Hood, then scrambling into the trunk. He heard shouts and the clank of feet on the deck just before dropping the circular bottom hatch into place, rotating the wheel to lock it and so make the trunk not only completely watertight, but also impenetrable.

Adjusting the belt to ensure his automatic and the knife were both well strapped on, Bond turned the two palm-sized wheel taps, glancing at his watch to see that he now had very little time left. Water began to flood the compartment, much more quickly than he recalled from his last practice in one of these escapes. He put on the Steinke Hood, securing it and screwing the valve onto the air port, making sure that his head remained in the bubble at the top of the hatch.

By now the water was up to his shoulders and rising rapidly. He saw the pinpoint of light come on to show that his air reservoir was full, twisted so that he was free of the air port. As he did so, he caught a glimpse of his watch. It was seven forty-six.

The water came rushing up over his head and the upper hatch popped open, catapulting him upwards.

Though he rocketed to the surface in a matter of seconds, the journey seemed to take endless minutes, and when he burst through into the night above, he was completely disoriented. Just darkness, then the lights from San Juan. Tearing at the headpiece he pulled it off, sucking in great gulps of air and kicking with his arms and legs to get moving again. He looked around, a full 360 degrees, and saw *Mare Nostrum*, with only her riding lights on, less than thirty feet away.

He began to swim, circling so that he would come in astern of *Mare Nostrum*, and was also aware of the sound of other engines nearby. There, coming through the channel, directly past the headland from which El Morro rose like a long stone battleship, was *Golden Bough*,

He reached the stern of *Mare Nostrum* just as he felt the shock wave. For a second he did not associate it with what he had done, taking it as some freak undertow. The sea seemed to lift around him, swirling like a whirlpool, catching him with dozens of hands bent on pulling him down. Then the explosion came from under the sea, a great whooming sound followed by a plume of white water which was the precursor of an even larger, long bubble. It was as though three or four depth charges had exploded just under the surface.

He reached out, grabbing at a rope dangling from *Mare Nostrum*'s stern and hung on, the sea still grappling with him as if it were a human thing, a primeval being turning him around and then throwing him upwards. *Mare Nostrum* was pitching and rolling with the boiling sea and he finally got both hands on the rope, dragging himself up and over the stern.

There were shouts and noises coming from for'ard around the wheelhouse, and he had no guilt about what he was about to do. Unholstering the pistol he slipped off the safety and yelled at the top of his lungs – 'Connie? Connie Spicer?'

'What the hell . . . ?' Connie lumbered from the wheelhouse, peering back towards him, clinging on to keep his balance on the still pitching deck.

Bond fired four shots, two and then another two, grouped nicely around the chest area. Spicer did not cry out, or even look surprised, but went in the blink of an eye from alive to dead. His body, lifted by the bullets as they slammed home, seemed to rise slowly and levitate parallel to the deck as though hanging there before it was flung against the guard rail, over which it pitched.

Vesta Motley was screaming, and he could see Fritz on the deck where Connie had stood, holding out his hands in supplication.

'It's me.' Bond ran forward, the deck still moving under

his feet. Over the bows he could see the sea bubbling white, with pieces of debris beginning to be thrown up. As he ran, he wondered how he could see all this in the darkness of the night, then saw that the big tanker, even half-a-mile away, had two searchlights playing on the water.

'Mr Bond!' Anton Fritz's mouth hung open as he saw the tall figure trying to run towards him.

'Yes! Now, start those bloody engines for me, I've a previous appointment to keep!'

'What happened?' from Rexinus within the wheelhouse.

'Never mind what happened. I just saved you from death by fire. Get those throttles wide open and head out of the harbor. Fast as you can.'

'Was that the submarine?' Rexinus had gone from panic to sudden cool, pushing the throttles forward so that Bond had to grab at the wheelhouse doorway. The bows lifted, turned to circle the huge looming supertanker as Rexinus swung the wheel to take them out of the harbor.

'I want you to take her around the headland. I've got to make some kind of landing on the ocean side, as near to the rocks below El Morro as you can.'

'Aye-Aye,' Rexinus shouted back. Then repeated, 'The submarine? What happened to the submarine?'

'I think the crew must have been eating too much Indian food.' Bond did not even smile. He was bracing himself against the wheelhouse and sliding a new magazine into the butt of the ASP 9mm converted Browning.

They were rounding the headland now, where the walls of the lowest part of El Morro reach down towards the rocks. 'How near do you want to get?' Rexinus shouted.

'As near as you can manage. I've got to make it to those grassy slopes on the other side of the rocks.'

'Don't think I'll quite be able to get you right in.'

'I'll get over the rocks myself, just bring her in as close as you can.'

Fritz and Vesta Motley were speechless, soaking wet and white with fear. Then the bullets came, smashing into the woodwork on the deck as an automatic weapon opened up from the lower wall of El Morro.

'Far enough!' Bond yelled. 'Get down. I'm going over the side.' He saw the surf and the rocks coming up to meet them, climbed over the guard rail and, as the boat dipped on the turn, he dropped into the white foam.

It was luck rather than skill that got him over the jagged rocks. As he went into the water the tide was pulling back, gathering itself for another journey inland to slap into the shore. He was able to put his arms around one of the larger, slippery boulders and ride out the crashing waves until the sea drew back again, allowing him to move in over the old sea-worn stones. Halfway and he found another point between two rocks, where he hung on as the sea vented its force on him. The tide sucked back again, and, on the third attempt, he made it over the final barrier and onto the rough grass above.

As he lay, on all fours, winded and gasping for breath, a figure rose from the ground in front of him and snapped, 'Who goes?'

25

Ride of the Valkyrie

HE STAYED EXACTLY where he was, but absolutely still. 'Bond,' he said. 'Captain James Bond, Royal Navy.'

'Thank heaven it's you, boss. Dodd. Jim Dodd. Captain 22nd SAS. We've been waiting half the night for you.' He put one arm under Bond's right armpit and helped him up. 'The other lads are just up here. The bad boys've got automatic weapons in the fort, but I think we can deal with them without too much bother. You up to a little flight, boss?'

'Yes, Jim. Just let me get my breath back. You brought the Powerchute?'

'Five of them, chief. Four for us and one for you. Got some other surprises as well. Decent chaps those Delta Force lads. Letting us have first crack. Old Tarn and his people – there's three of them altogether – were up there, on the lowest emplacement of this amazing fortress, but I think they've moved up to the top now. Delta Force said they'd keep an eye on the other two sides. If we don't finish them, they will. Very decent.' He spoke in a whisper and Bond was breathing more normally now as they reached the towering old walls, from which another figure seemed to detach itself.

'That you, boss?'

301

'Yes, and I've found Captain Bond for us, so we're all set.'

'Good, they were shooting at that boat.'

'I know,' Bond grunted. 'I was aboard.'

'The explosion?' Dodd asked. 'That you as well? Submarine bought it?'

'Yes.'

'Too much curry again?'

'I've already done that joke.' He stopped as the remaining three SAS men crowded around. 'Actually a little too much plastique. I sort of over-indulged.'

Dodd motioned for silence. 'Easy mistake to make, sir. Let's show you what we've got,' he said brightly.

They moved in close to the wall. There, hardly visible, were the five Powerchutes, the actual parachutes made of matt black material. 'You *have* flown one of these, boss?'

'Yes. At the same place you learned, Jim.'

'Only wanted to make certain because we've added a couple of little refinements.' He shone a torch, which gave out diffused light, onto the framework. 'Landing light for starters. Usual halogen job, mounted up front under the forward strut.' He lifted the tubing to show a wide light aircraft landing light. 'Operated from this little panel over on the right, just behind the throttle; there's a compass up there as well, and a panel on the left for goodies. Flash-bangs here, three of them. Abreast of the flash-bangs we have smoke – you're familiar, yes?'

'Very familiar.' He leaned down and touched the little smoke bombs.

Dodd hardly paused. 'Then in the forward section we have flares.' He lifted out one of the seven inch long silver cylinders. 'Nice flares because they double as incendiary rounds, if you follow. Just point and pull the little ring. Like opening a can of beer.'

'I'm glad to say I've never opened a can of beer, but I follow very well, old boy. How many of those do we carry?'

'Only four, I fear. Particularly if you need somewhere to mount the old Heckler & Koch.'

'I'll sit that one out, if you don't mind. Stick to the pistol. Done me quite well over the years, though they aren't making this model anymore.'

'A man's favorite weapon is the one he'll do most damage with. Ginger here's got a 12 gauge shotgun.' He indicated one of the SAS Troopers. 'Wonderful with it. Bring down a budgerigar at twenty paces and a man at twenty yards, on the wing – I mean Ginger would be on the wing.

'Now, communications. Headset with a throat mike. The whole thing's self-contained: radio in the right side of the headphones. Just talk and listen. Okay?'

They went quickly through a series of signals and the general order of battle. 'Best if we start at the top and work down, I think?' Dodd queried.

'There's a damned great wide smooth ramp that goes from the top to the second level, then you can just hop over the walls to the Atlantic side, or out on the headland. Even down into that parade ground – patio they call it. You've been around the place, I presume?'

'Lord, yes. We went round on the same day you did – with the nice young lady and the fellow with the game leg.'

'Really? You should have introduced yourselves.'

'Didn't like to intrude, boss. Bad form, you know. Incidentally, what's happened to the nice young lady and the American gentleman with the limp?'

'I was going to tell you about them after we deal with friend Tarn, but as you ask . . .' He proceeded to give a quick rundown of the situation regarding Flicka and Felix, ending with, 'How far can your modified Powerchutes go?'

'How far away is the Tarn house?'

'Thirty-five miles as the crow flies.'

'No problem. Let's get this over first. Swoop down on them like the Ride of the Valkyrie. Pity we haven't got room for sound, like in that Vietnam film.'

'We could always whistle. You do know how to whistle, Captain Dodd.'

'Only after we've surprised them, Captain Bond.'

Together, they examined the map by torchlight and worked out a course that would take them on a straight line for Tarn's villa.

'Let's go then.' Dodd clapped Bond on the shoulder. 'Let's get the bastards, eh?'

They started engines and took off, each with a small torch blinking in order to line up, with Bond leading and the others fanning out behind him. First they circled away from El Morro, then turned, gaining height, then beginning their descent towards the upper gun platforms, sweeping in, watching for movement which Dodd spotted first, on the wide ramp which led down from the San Juan side of the topmost emplacements. Someone to Bond's right fired off a burst from an automatic weapon, which brought some wild shooting from the three people they could see scurrying for cover.

Their shots went wide and Bond considered that they must have thought the attack was coming via a horde of bees. The snarl of five little engines had to be a psychological advantage.

As he pulled up, he glimpsed two of the figures running out into the middle of the parade ground, their hands held high and waving handkerchiefs. He recognized Cathy and Anna. Cathy and Anna coming to the end of the road.

He turned sharply to get a closer look, and saw Dodd on his right, following him down. As he began the run across the parade ground, fire suddenly erupted from one of the arches – he thought the one leading to the chapel. One of the girls spun around, clutching at the air, while the other was lifted off her feet and flung to one side, like an old toy which Tarn had finished with.

'That's how you repay loyalty, is it, Max?' he yelled, knowing that Tarn would not hear a word he was shouting, He piled on the power, making a very steep climbing turn which would eventually bring him back over the area where the two girls lay. As he straightened out, he saw one of the SAS Powerchutes approaching the girls from the opposite direction when a long ratchet of automatic fire came hurtling out from the archway in which he thought Tarn was hiding. He saw the soldier fall back from the framework and the engine disintegrate under the hail of fire. The whole machine just fell apart to crash burning near the great water cistern.

'Right, you bastard,' Bond muttered. 'This is for the SAS.' His hand felt for one of the small flares. He took the Powerchute down as far as he dared and aimed directly into the archway.

The flare exploded in a bright white flash, and he could see Tarn, struggling with a weapon, hugging the side of the wall. Then he broke cover, and began to run, helter skelter back up the ramp. Bond would have put money on Max Tarn having left another weapon up on the top emplacement.

Glancing to left and right, he saw the other three 'Chutes were close on his heels so he spoke clearly, 'Lights, Valkyries. Lights!' All four landing lights came on at once, as they dropped behind the running man who had just reached the top of the ramp and was beginning to

305

stumble towards the center of the large platform.

As he closed up behind Tarn, Bond saw that two of his companions had put on speed and were overtaking him. They hovered in front of Tarn who had got to his feet and was moving to left and right, trying to dodge the snarling Powerchutes. Then he wheeled right around and Bond realized what was going on.

The other three SAS men had begun to circle Tarn, but they had left Bond inside the circle, turning and lighting the way, enclosing Tarn who was like a trapped animal. He put his machine into a tighter turn, holding it and leaning far to his left to keep turning. As he did so, he reached down for another flare. There was no particular feeling of guilt or elation. This man had killed thousands by ferrying and smuggling weapons, placing them into the hands of unprincipled people. His future plans were horrific, so he deserved to die the worst possible of deaths.

He waited, letting his quarry dodge this way and that, trying to escape the relentless lights on the other Powerchutes. Only when he was ready, calm and cool did Bond take aim and pull the ring.

The flare arced from his hand, catching Tarn in the chest, spraying out a blossom of phosphorus as it did so. He wheeled around again, taking aim with another flare. By now, Tarn was rolling on the hard ground trying to put out the flames which would not go out. The second flare caught him just below the neck, spreading its chemical down the already burned front of his clothes. As he pulled away, Bond thought he could hear the screaming which sounded like a plea for someone to put him out of his misery. He seemed to be blundering around – a walking, moving ball of fire heading for the edge of the gun platform with its sheer drop below.

One of the SAS men finished it. The shotgun blast tore away the back of Max Tarn's head. For a moment he seemed to keep moving in a red mist which was eaten by the flame. Then he fell across the battlements and, headless, disappeared over the edge.

As they turned and took up formation on Dodd, heading out across the island, setting course for the house near Ponce, Bond heard the sound of singing in his ears. His companions had their heads back and were giving a somewhat tuneless rendering of Wagner's Ride of the Valkyrie.

26

Tears on his Cheeks

THEY FLEW AT around fifteen hundred feet, straining their eyes to make sure they could see one another. It was not the easiest of flights as the gentle trade winds which cool the island seemed far from gentle from their position in the open on what was a very basic cockpit.

About half-way across, the moon came up and gave them more visibility. Bond would have found the flight exhilarating if it had not been for his concern for Flicka. He had done all he had sworn to do. Tarn was dead, along with some of his closest henchmen and women. There would be no return to Tarnenwerder: no chants of "Heil Tarn" from a hypnotized mob bent on setting the clock back to the days of insanity.

He accepted this as part of his vocation. Danger had lurked beside him for as long as he could remember, and he wondered how he could possibly carry on if anything had happened to Flicka.

'The hill's coming up,' he told the other three through the throat mike, the moment he saw the area where he had stood among the trees with Flicka and Felix only a short time before.

Dodd had already seen the treeline, and responded. 'Roger. Cut engines.'

Suddenly they were floating, silent but for the air and

breeze around them as they crested the rise and saw Tarn's villa lit up below them.

Maneuvering the parachutes, they formed a line astern. Dodd in front, with Bond and the others close behind. The shots came just as the fourth man was putting down to the left of the swimming pool, well inside the rectangle of the villa.

It was an automatic weapon being used from the far right hand corner. One sudden and noisy burst which went wide, some of the bullets slapping into the swimming pool, only feet away from the last man who had landed.

A rip of fire from Dodd silenced the shooter who died without even shouting. Bond followed the SAS officer to the right hand cloister, while the other two troopers took the left side. He had worked in pairs with the SAS before, during training exercises, so knew what was expected.

There were four sets of double windows, each pair with a door between them on the ground floor. As they moved along the cloister so flash-bangs – the so-called stun grenades – went through the windows. On the far side, the grenades brought out only two men who died as they came into view at the end of the cloister.

Nobody was flushed out from Dodd's and Bond's side. 'Let's do a pincer on the next floor up,' Dodd said, as though this was a simple Sunday afternoon stroll. He turned back and jogged to the stairwell, while Bond went ahead, taking the stairs in front of him, two at a time. He reached the top to see a similar cloistered area with four more doors and pairs of windows, but this time, just as he reached the first door, a figure stepped from one of the doorways ahead yelling—

'You broke my jaw, you bastard.' It was Heidi, though he had to interpret the words as they were squashed and came from the back of her throat. For a split second he was back in the offices of Saal, Saal u. Rollen where he had last seen her sprawled on the floor.

Then her arms came up and he caught the glint of the weapon in her hand. He dodged to the right, in through the door, as the pistol rapped out twice and he heard the bullets whip past him. Two more shots followed from further away. There was a sound like a sack of potatoes being dropped on the stone under the cloister. Dodd had taken out Heidi.

For less than a minute, there was the sound of a brisk firefight from the opposite side of the villa. Bond was about to move out from the doorway when an arm slid, like a snake, around his throat. He felt a hand on the back of his head and the pressure on his windpipe. Whoever had him was using a well-tried method – the right forearm across the throat, the hand grasping the left biceps while the left hand held the back of the victim's head. It usually took only seconds to either strangle or render a victim unconscious. There was only one possible response and he knew this must be taken very quickly, before the gray-out as the blood supply to the brain was slowed by the pressure.

He gave a violent kick with his feet, leaning and putting all his weight into falling backwards, at the same time attempting to stamp on his assailant's shins and feet.

The two of them went toppling over. He felt the softness of the body under him, the gasp and oath, then the crack as Beth's head hit hard against the stone floor. The arms immediately relaxed and Bond rolled away, back onto his feet, reaching for the pistol on his belt.

'So you want your pretty lady back, huh?' Beth gasped. 'You want . . .'

He did not even have to pull the trigger. The heavy fall had cracked her skull. Her eyes turned up, as though in horror, and a stream of blood flooded from her nose and ears as she flopped, like some terrible beached animal, her body unnaturally spread out on the floor.

Then he heard Dodd calling to him.

Two doors along, Dodd had found Felix Leiter attempting to crawl across a room to get at his prosthetic arm and leg. He looked dog tired and frantic, but he smiled as Bond entered, then pointed to the far corner of the room, where Flicka lay, covered with a sheet, her face broken and bleeding.

'It's me, Flick,' he whispered softly. 'Me. You'll be okay now.'

She tried to smile through the pain, then with great effort, 'Will you still love me tomorrow, James?'

'Tomorrow and for all time, my darling girl,' he said.

Later, in the SAS Officers' Mess, at Bradbury Lines in Herefordshire, when Captain Dodd related his version of the business in Puerto Rico, he used to say, 'You know, I could have sworn that chap Bond was crying . . . Couldn't have been. Not that kind of officer. But I could have sworn . . . Even thought I saw tears on his cheeks. Couldn't have been though, could it?'